Beyond Forever

Jackie Gould

Published by Acacia Publishing, Inc.
1366 East Thomas Road, Suite 305
Phoenix, Arizona 85014

Library of Congress Cataloging-in-Publication Data

Gould, Jackie.
  Beyond forever/Jackie Gould.
      p. cm.
ISBN 0-9788283-0-5 (alk. paper)
1. Parents--Fiction. 2. United States--History--Colonial period,
ca. 1600-1775--Fiction. I. Title.

PS3607.O885B49 2006
813'.6--dc22

                          2006027937

Printed and bound in Canada.

Also by Jackie Gould

Letters to Allie

Of Angels and Rolling Pins
(coming in 2007)

Dedication

This novel is dedicated to:

Tanner, Zachary, Kaleb, Makenzie, and
Reese. The legend continues...

J.G.

Preface

How It All Began

In tracing back the Herrington Family Tree, all that was known about John Herrington, our patriarch, is that as an eighteen month old infant, his parents ran with him to the safety of a fort, only able to utter the baby's name before expiring from sheer exhaustion and fright. Their flight from marauding Indians is a story that has persisted in the family archives, and is the basis of several versions of family history.

The story of Elizabeth Wood and the twin Herrington men came alive as a result of an urge to unravel the mystery of John Herrington's unknown parents, and is a fictional account of what could have happened. One could guess the trials and tribulations those brave parents endured prior to bringing them to their untimely end. Who were they? What were they like? What was their story? It is the author's hope that *Beyond Forever* will shed a bit of light, fictitious though it is, upon the old family mystery.

Chapter One

F or the first time in five days, Elizabeth was able to go above deck, for the vicious storm had finally blown itself out. She had scarcely been able to breathe the last few days in the dank, dark, putrid hold of the ship that had virtually been the prison of all the passengers on the "Morning Glory" as the vessel bobbed and tossed its way through rough seas in that late summer of 1754. It had sailed from England and was bound for Baltimore Town in the New World.

As she stepped onto the deck, a cool, fresh burst of air rippled Elizabeth's golden hair, sending wisps like spun gold across her lips. She tilted her head back and drew in a huge breath of fresh air... and another... and another, trying to rid her body of the unfortunate stench of the hold. The young girl shivered, thinking of the misery she had left below deck. The rank, stale air had smelled of vomit and human waste; of rotting food and perspiring bodies in the cramped, crowded quarters. For five days the passengers had resorted to tying themselves to their bunks, so they would not be tossed about like so many rag dolls, as they rode out the fury of the storm. They had already been long weeks on the water, and were now within days of reaching their destination. Anxiety, frustration, and dejection had grown among the passengers as the days droned on in endless progression.

Elizabeth joined her mother and father at the rail as the other passengers emerged from below, and soon they were chatting with each other in an animated way, expressing relief and thankfulness that the ordeal of the storm was now behind them. Captain James Wood, Elizabeth's father and an Officer in the British Army, put a protective arm around his wife, Martha, and gazed at the horizon, contemplating what lay ahead.

On the opposite side of the ship, another passenger relaxed, casually leaning an elbow onto the rail. But his gaze, instead of looking off across the water, was intent on the three who were at the other rail. The man was tall and lanky and had a gracefulness in his repose that few men of his stature possessed. Nathan Herrington had watched when Elizabeth came onto the deck and was relieved to note that she seemed no worse for the events of the last few days. He watched the girl tilt her head back, and a warmth stirred in him as he admired her long golden tresses swirling in the breeze.

Nathan had noticed the young lass several times during their journey, but had never had the opportunity to do more than admire her from afar. He had kept close to the many single immigrants in their own area of the ship. Yet, as the weeks had gone by, he seemed drawn to her, and found that he was constantly looking for a glimpse of her. An occasion had not yet presented itself for them to meet on this journey, for all the women had kept to their own quarters.

Elizabeth turned her face in his direction, and his heart gave a lurch, waiting for their eyes to meet. Instead, a group of sailors jostling the rigging at mid-deck blocked his view. When Nathan again could see her, she had turned and was strolling away, and all he saw was her straight back. He sighed deeply, and turned his attention to the activity of the crew as they repaired the damage that the storm had wrought.

Nathan stretched his cramped limbs and gulped the fresh air, thankful that he no longer was subject to the confines below deck. As he surveyed his fellow travelers, he admired their plucky fortitude, knowing that many had left family and friends in England, most likely never to see them again, as they started their new lives in the Colonies with new hopes and dreams.

The tall young man smiled to himself as he realized he was filled with just as many hopes and dreams as anyone on the ship. Reaching his hand into one of his pockets, he pulled out a tattered letter. Unfolding the paper carefully, as he had done countless times before, he scanned the familiar script of his brother's hand. Nathan thrilled again as he read the words that had prompted him to leave everything behind and seek passage on the "Morning Glory" when she sailed to the New World. His brother's breathless description of the wonders of this newfound land certainly held Nathan spellbound.

As excited as he was about the adventure upon which he had embarked, his heart ached at what he had left behind. Memories of the last parting with his dear mother and sister stirred deep visions of all that Nathan had ever known. But the deepest hurt was the tragedy of having lost his betrothed months before.

Nathan thought he had overcome the paralyzing numbness that haunted him these past many months, but it returned again and again to overwhelm him. What seemed like an icy knife ripped at his insides as he once again allowed the memory of his beloved to invade his senses.

"Sarah... Sarah!" he moaned, squeezing his eyes tightly shut while his fingernails dug half circles into the palms of his hands. A dark, foreboding feeling engulfed him as Sarah's face floated before the window of his mind. Nathan tried to recapture her every feature, but the image was becoming clouded... foggy... a misty shadow at once almost clear, and again fading to nothingness. Sarah's pale face, with those great green eyes, surrounded by tumbling auburn hair, was not as clear to him now as it once had been. He longed to remember every detail, yet he desperately wanted to forget. Nathan was torn with grief and guilt because he could no longer bring her image into sharp focus in his memory. How could her loveliness fade so soon? She was all his future had once held. She had been his everything... all his tomorrows.

Now, once again the awful picture exploded into his mind... of the crashing sound of a runaway horse carriage clattering on the cobblestone street, skidding wildly to and fro... of screams... a dull thud... the limp body lying in a pathetic heap on the roadway.

"My God! My God! Sarah!" The words rang in his head now, though Nathan did not even realize that it was he who had screamed them at the time, as he had rushed to the girl's side. The young man remembered, as if in a dream, falling to his knees and lifting Sarah's lifeless form to his breast. Now he could see her face, white as moonlight, a dark, horrible bruise on the side of her head. Sarah's beautiful long hair cascaded over his arms as he held her, and he rocked back and forth, clutching her to him until finally a kindly bystander had pried his arms away, and gently took her body from him. The rest he could not remember.

How long Nathan had stood at the rail, he had no idea, but suddenly he was aware of the present, of the ship slicing through water, sending a frothy path in its wake. He glanced up to see the sails full and straining against an azure sky. Sunlight reflected brilliant silver-white flashes of light as it danced across the waters, causing him to squint.

Nathan licked his lips, tasting the salt from the sea air and turned, looking westward. He wondered if they would ever end the journey. He was tired and restless, growing impatient with the endless blank horizon; seeing nothing but choppy waves everywhere. The young man longed to see land again, and vowed that when he landed on shore, he would never in his life set foot on a ship to sail across the ocean again. No, once he landed in the Colonies, he would never turn back. And so his course was set.

Chapter Two

Three days later, the cry "Land Ho!" brought the excited passengers surging to the rails to try to catch a glimpse of land. They strained their eyes to see through the hazy air, and low on the distant horizon a faint, darker line began to appear. Shouts of joy and laughter erupted, and the happy people began hugging each other, clasping hands, great broad grins on their faces. Children scampered between the members of the celebrating crowd.

Elizabeth and her mother stood with their arms locked and gazed at the horizon, which was still an agonizingly long distance away. A great weight seemed to be lifted from their shoulders, and a feeling of exhilaration filled them. Martha Wood stole a glance at her daughter, and at once felt happy, yet somewhat apprehensive, as she pondered the future that faced them all. What would life hold for them in the new land just ahead? Her husband, James, was being assigned a new post in the Colonies. Martha had heard stories of the savages and the merciless horrors that had befallen some of the Colonists. The woman closed her eyes and a shudder swept over her. Elizabeth felt the quiver and turned to her mother.

"Oh! Isn't it exciting?" the girl exclaimed. "I can't wait until we can walk on good firm earth once more." She was breathless. "What do you think the fort will look like, Mother? Do you think they will have dances? Do you think the other women will give teas? What about the children, will there be lots of little ones there? Oh, I would love to tutor some of them. Wouldn't that be wonderful, to be able to school them and help them read and write?"

Martha smiled at the exuberance flowing from her daughter and got caught up in the daydreams herself.

"We'll see, my love, we'll see," she murmured. "Fort Mount Pleasant is newly built, so I hear. I surely hope they have all the latest conveniences. Your father says he understands it is very sturdy, and will withstand the most vigorous of attacks. He hears there is water inside because the fort is built around a spring, and there are large storerooms filled with food and ammunition. They say our quarters are very comfortable, and I look forward to seeing it all."

The older woman did not mention the subject that was uppermost in her mind, however, that of the Indian problems, and the atrocities she had heard about. All that would come soon enough.

❧

The next day, the ship glided closer to land and turned north. They could see the shoreline on either side, and knew they were making their way up the bay to their landing in Baltimore Town. It was not long before they were docked and the eager passengers were soon disembarking, their arms filled with large bundles of belongings.

A cacophony of sight and sound now surrounded the vessel. Men were shouting, sweating and groaning under loads of boxes, trunks, and barrels that had been disgorged upon the wharf. Nathan, loaded with his tools and clothing wrapped in a blanket, accidentally found himself directly behind the girl with the golden hair as they made their way down the gangplank. When she came to the last step, Elizabeth stumbled, but Nathan quickly reached out a strong hand to grasp her arm, and prevented her from falling.

The young girl turned, surprised, to gaze into her benefactor's face, and smiled a thank-you. She was startled to look into such warm dark brown eyes, set in a most handsome rugged face. His hair was thick and dark, and an unruly lock fell over his brow. She blushed slightly, and murmured, "Thank you, Sir."

The pressure of Nathan's hand on her arm did not go unnoticed, and Elizabeth felt a great strength from this tall, muscular young man. Flustered, she regained her footing, and once more thanked him with the flash of a smile.

"I shall be all right now, Sir."

"Please allow me to introduce myself," Nathan said, surprised at his sudden boldness. "My name is Nathan Herrington, at your service, Ma'am."

He doffed his hat and gave a half-bow.

Shyly, she offered her hand and said, "I am Elizabeth Wood, and this is my mother, Martha Wood."

He took her small hand in his large palm, looking boldly into her hazel eyes, as he felt the softness of her fingers.

"I am most honored to make your acquaintance... both of you." He directed his greeting toward the older woman, but his eyes, now sparkling, never left Elizabeth's.

The young girl gave a little curtsey, withdrew her hand from his, and looked back over her shoulder quickly as she turned away, giving him one more glance. Nathan could detect a slight rosy color rising to her cheeks as she left. Then, shouldering his pack, with a light step, and his heart singing, the tall young man made his way up the dirt road to the clustered buildings ahead.

Inquiring at the Inn on Charles Street, Nathan found lodging behind the tavern for the night. He shared the small quarters with two rough seamen who smelled of rum, the salt sea, and fish. Nathan was sure they had not seen bath water for months. After stowing his gear, Nathan ventured out onto the crowded street, dodging hand carts loaded with goods coming from the wharves. Cattle, goats and sheep were being herded from the ships, and crates of live chickens stacked on some hand carts were being transported by the immigrants. They had brought tools and seed for starting their new lives, having divested themselves of all except what they could carry. Wooden rakes, plows, and crude shovels were piled at the doorstep of the newly opened mercantile shop on Charles Street. Inside, bolts of fabric, ropes, twine, barrels of flour, salt pork, dried meat, tins of crackers, and biscuits lined the shelves, waiting to separate the new arrivals from their money.

Nathan was amazed that there was so much activity. Somehow, he had imagined that it would be desolate right from the start. The young man was sure that going a few miles back into the wilderness would be a whole different story.

Nathan was eager and anxious to find his brother so they could expand the land that Jonathan was free-holding. According to his letter, Jonathan instructed Nathan to wait in Baltimore Town until he, Jonathan, could join the newcomer. In the meantime, Nathan made himself aware of the whereabouts of the British Officer Wood and his family, hoping to see the girl again, even if it were merely a chance glance.

However, three days after their arrival in the New World, Elizabeth, her father and mother, and a compliment of British soldiers left the port city, heading west. Nathan felt a tug at his chest as he watched the party disappear down the trail behind the trees. Then an unexpected emptiness filled him, and a great loneliness set in. What was it about that golden haired girl that so fascinated him? Nathan was troubled, suffering pangs of guilt, for Sarah's memory was still fresh. Yet he could not shake the thought of Elizabeth Wood's flashing smile, those deep hazel eyes, so big and beautiful. And so he fell into a dark mood.

Chapter Three

A week went by and every day the newcomer watched in vain for the arrival of his brother. On Nathan's tenth day of being in the cramped quarters behind the tavern, Jonathan finally arrived. At first, Nathan did not recognize his twin, for Jonathan had put on muscle and was deeply tanned. He wore his hair long, and the dark tresses were confined within a leather strip that was wrapped around the raven locks at the nape of his neck. The borderman wore a soft doeskin fringed shirt over doeskin leggings, and high topped moccasins. One had to look twice to realize that indeed, he was not an Indian, for his long, black hair and dark skin greatly resembled some of the Natives that Nathan had seen trading in town.

The brothers grasped each other by the shoulders and pounded each other's arms in greeting, ending in a long, massive bear hug. They were identical twins except that Jonathan had developed greater strength from his seasons in the outdoors, and was tanned to a rugged bronze. The two shared the same dark hair and warm brown eyes. Their chins were square, and they had high cheekbones on rather handsome faces. Deep dimple lines appeared on each plane of their cheeks when they smiled, which was often. Nathan was impressed as he grasped Jonathan's forearm and found great muscles rippling beneath his fingers.

"My! You look splendid! The frontier must certainly agree with you!"

Jonathan smiled, dimples lining both sides of his mouth, and nodded in agreement at Nathan's compliment. "It won't take you long to harden up, Brother, for the wilderness will surely make you like iron... or kill you!" he grinned.

A chill ran down Nathan's back at that remark.

The following day, after gathering a few supplies, the two set out on a narrow trail, heading northwest. At first the trail was easy and the going fairly swift. The forest grew thicker as they made their way farther from the water of the big bay. Soon underbrush choked the area and the trail became harder to determine. The September heat was stifling, and Nathan found himself breathing hard and perspiring profusely. Insects were bothersome, and he swatted at his face and neck continuously.

The two had not traveled long before Nathan realized that the gear he was carrying was much heavier than he had first thought. He had to admit that it was difficult to match the pace that Jonathan had set for them. Jonathan's long strides became impossible for Nathan to keep up with, and reluctantly he gasped, his chest heaving, and begged for a short rest.

They found a lovely spot near a brook in a little clearing which was covered with moss and ferns. Nathan followed Jonathan's lead by lying flat on his stomach at the edge of the gurgling stream and gulped his fill of the sweet, fresh liquid. The water in the stream glided smoothly between round rocks, rippling here and there, as it wound its sing-song way seaward, many miles off.

They had been steadily climbing, though ever so gently. The land was rolling in long imperceptible undulations, and with not a clearing from which to see any distance, it was hard to tell they had gained any altitude at all from the harbor. Yet Nathan surmised they must have traveled some miles already.

"How far do we have to go?" he panted.

Jonathan smiled his beguiling smile and glanced at this brother, noting that the morning exertion was already telling on the newcomer.

"Three, maybe four days. Think you can keep up?"

Nathan, determined not to let his brother realize how taxing this was on him, replied in an enthusiastic way, "Oh, yes. I am just not used to so much walking after being so confined on the ship for two-and-one-half months. This will be great for me!"

And so they traveled through the forest, pausing only for short periods of rest, when they would chew on dried meat and biscuits, and quench their thirst at bubbling streams when they came across them. Once, Jonathan shot a rabbit that they roasted to a turn over their evening fire. The two spent the long twilight hours puffing on their long-stemmed pipes and catching up on each other's lives. Nathan related the circumstances surrounding Sarah's death, and the resulting devastation he experienced from the tragedy, which prompted his decision to join his twin.

Jonathan drew a long pull on his pipe, reflecting on the events as told by Nathan. He was quiet for a long time, gazing in deep reverie into the fire. The tongues of flame leaped and sputtered, first yellow-white and orange, sometimes with licks of blue. Red embers glowed in the bottom recesses of the flickering fire, fading at the whim of the breeze. This was the best part of the day for a woodsman, when the quiet time had come, and darkness had fallen. Yes, the very best time... to be able to sit by the fire and reflect upon events long past... to puff on a pipe and dream his dreams of the tomorrows to come.

Jonathan opened his mouth to speak, but found his companion had succumbed to the rigors of the trail and was already deep in slumber. *Another time*, Jonathan thought. *Another time I shall tell you the story that is imprisoned within my heart.* And the borderman listened to the night sounds of crickets and the soft who-who of an owl. Far in the distance the chilling howl of a wolf could be heard. Above the trees in the inky blackness, stars were flickering like a thousand fireflies glittering in the softness of space. He drew in a deep breath of night air and was at peace.

Chapter Four

J onathan had been right. In just a few short weeks, Nathan began to feel his body gaining strength and suppleness. The outdoor life was invigorating and hard, but Nathan relished it all as he toughened his muscles and endurance. Together, with their axes, the two felled trees and cleared land enough to build a small log cabin. Jonathan had been living in a tiny lean-to built of limbs and brush on the land he was free-holding. Nathan hauled rocks from the creek and helped build a fireplace and chimney on one wall of the cabin opposite the low doorway. Inside they fashioned a table and used wood stumps for seats. The dirt floor became rock hard within a short time as they moved back and forth at their tasks.

The two also fashioned a loft above the rafters for sleeping. Jonathan showed Nathan how to mix mud, moss, and grass, which they used to seal the chinks between the logs to keep out the drafts. He assured his brother that they would be very thankful once winter came that the cabin would be snug and warm. They assembled a door from thick planks of wood held together by cross pieces, and suspended it from leather hinges. A strong bar held it closed at night. Two small windows allowed light in the room.

A shelf in one corner near the fireplace served as storage for the few utensils they had, which consisted of some bowls and plates carved from wood, and a castiron pot that was hanging in the fireplace. A wooden bucket held water from the spring, and strips of meat and herbs hung drying from pegs on the rafters. Overall, the two brothers made a very snug, practical, cozy place to live.

One day in late October, Jonathan announced that they needed to make a trip to the fort for supplies. Nathan was surprised to learn that they were less than five miles from Fort Mount Pleasant. His heart quickened at the news, for he was sure that the fort was the very one that Captain Wood and his daughter had been destined for when the party left Baltimore Town. Could he be so lucky, perhaps, as to see Elizabeth Wood again?

The morning dawned with a damp mist hanging low as the two were about to set out, left over from a rain the night before. The first of a fall chill was in the air, and Nathan was glad for his wool jacket and tri-corner hat, though both were showing signs of wear. He pulled the hat down upon his head and was about to set out when Jonathan stopped him.

"Here," Jonathan said, as he rummaged through a bundle in the far corner of the cabin. "Put this on, for it will suit you much better in the woods."

With that, he handed Nathan a deerskin hunting shirt and leggings, and high topped moccasins, similar to what he was wearing. Nathan, once again grateful to his twin, was soon decked out in true frontiersman garb. He marveled at the softness of the tanned deer hide next to his skin, and how comfortable the moccasins and leggings were. It gave him much more freedom of movement, and warded off the morning chill.

"Thanks, Jonathan. I really feel part of the Frontier now!"

Jonathan grinned, clapped his brother on the shoulder, and, picking up his rifle and powder horn, started down the trail. Nathan hefted the flintlock musket that Jonathan had given him and joined his brother, wondering just how much the long-barreled instrument weighed. The gun had an octagonal barrel and was finely crafted, having a hardwood stock and steel and brass fittings. The ramrod was fastened to the barrel, and though the gun was heavy, Nathan found it balanced nicely in his hand. He fingered the bullets that they had molded earlier, as they lay in a secure pouch at his belt, and he felt safe.

The mists slowly lifted in areas, and a grand sight began to unfold before Nathan's eyes. Patches of crimson and gold were everywhere, as the sun peeked here and there between the clouds of mist. The young man had forgotten that fall was indeed upon them, and the trees were cloaked in their annual colorful glory. Dew drops glistened and shimmered in the morning sun, gracing each leaf in a moist cascade, as droplets slowly formed at the leaf-points, to slide silently to earth. An exciting freshness permeated the forest, and a pungent, musty odor tantalized Nathan's nostrils. He breathed in the wonderful scent of hefty wet pine trees, beginning to understand why Jonathan loved the forest so much. Birds were twittering in shrill joyous abandon, and Nathan heard the "caw-caw" of a crow in the distance. A sudden thrashing of the leaves caused him to smile in amusement as he watched two squirrels, their tails bushed out like great flags, chasing each other across the ground. Up into a tree they scampered, chattering and scolding at each other all the way, even though their cheeks were full of acorns. Nathan glanced down at the trail before him and saw that many acorns had dropped, some where just the caps were left, a silent signal of forest life in its everlasting cycle.

As they walked, Jonathan pointed out many trees and plants, giving Nathan a quick botany lesson of the native foliage. He also pointed out deer tracks and traces of other wildlife.

"The 'Second Summer' will soon be here, after the first killing frost. We call it 'Indian Summer.' It will be the last of our warmth. Then winter will come, and we will not be able to hunt or fish very much, for the snows will be deep and long. We must hunt now, soon, to take in lots of meat for the long days ahead," Jonathan explained. "When we return from the fort, we will go hunting and store up for the winter."

"How do we keep the meat?" Nathan asked.

"We cut it in strips and dry it, and with some of it, we will cure it with salt to preserve it. Which reminds me, we will have to go to the salt lick to gather the salt we will need. It is about ten miles in that direction." He pointed north. "Animals go there from miles around to lick the rocks and get the salt that they need. It is a good place to hunt, for game is plentiful there."

They walked on in silence for a time, when Jonathan suddenly halted, looking at the ground closely as he knelt down to study the earth before him.

"There was a party of Indians that crossed our trail not many hours ago. See the tracks of their horses? See how small and round the hoof prints are? There were several of them. About twenty, I would guess. That spells trouble. They usually do not travel more than five or six at a time. Something must be up. Better keep our eyes open!"

Nathan shivered, and glanced furtively into the surrounding trees.

"I thought you told me that the Indians were friendly with the settlers?"

"Well, mostly the last couple of years or so they have been, but there have been rumors that some of the chiefs feel we settlers are now encroaching upon their hunting grounds. The more of us that come out this way, the more upset they get. The settlers are clearing land for crops and some of the deer and other game are being pushed farther into the wilderness."

"What happens if they get hostile?"

"Well, we'll make a run for it to the fort. You'll see it is well built. The redskins could never conquer it. Don't worry, the British soldiers are there, and we'll be safe."

Chapter Five

From the day of her arrival at Fort Mount Pleasant, Elizabeth was the center of attention, especially from the young, single officers. They seemed to trip over each other in their eagerness to please her. Elizabeth was amused and sometimes flustered by the attention they heaped upon her. Every evening a group of the unwed Colonists and young officers would appear at the doorstep of Captain Wood's quarters, with their caps grasped tightly in their hands. It was indeed amusing, and Martha Wood tried to hide her smiles as she bent over her needlework, all the while keeping an ear tuned in to the chatter going on at the doorway. Out of the corner of her eye, Martha watched as first one and then another would jostle for a closer place beside

Elizabeth, who sat on the stoop, basking in the adoration being heaped upon her.

In the beginning, Elizabeth was shy, but soon overcame her embarrassment, and joined in the gaiety and laughter. She tried to include the few other young women of the fort, and was always gracious, seeing to it that they were involved in the evening activities as well. There was little doubt, however, that Elizabeth was the beauty of them all. The youthful girl was almost regal in her bearing, with her head held high, her golden tresses flowing to her waist. Her large hazel eyes changed from gray-green to a shade of violet, at the whim of her mood, and were the most striking feature of her delicate face. Light brows arched over her deep set eyes, framed by long lashes, which she coyly lowered at just the proper moment, driving the young men crazy in their attempts to gaze into those delightful orbs.

A few weeks after their arrival at the fort, Colonel James Innes, the commanding officer, arranged to have a reception for his newest officer and his family. It was a gala affair, and everyone was invited to the festivities. Ladies donned their finest dresses, which they had carefully packed, having brought the clothes with them from England for just such occasions.

Candles flickered in the great hall, illuminating a long table laden with platters of roast venison, wild turkey and quail, and bowls filled with the fresh bounty of countless settlers' gardens. A huge silver punch bowl, flanked by silver candelabra, amply surrounded by delicate cakes and deserts, graced another table. Musicians with fiddles, flutes and drums were at one end of the long hall. Soon the floor was filled with couples whirling in time to the music of minuets and waltzes.

At one point, Colonel Innes took Captain Wood aside by the elbow, and said in a lowered voice, "Captain, that daughter of yours is a dazzler! I fear there will be trouble amongst the men until she is safely wed!" The two stately officers observed a crowd of young men around Elizabeth.

"She has turned some heads, that is certain, Sir," Captain Wood replied. "Though we can hardly clamp a barrel over her head and hide her! She has always been impetuous and head-strong, but she has a heart of gold, that one."

"I am sure of that, James; nonetheless, out here on the frontier, we do not have the genteel ways that you and your family are used to back in England. Here, there is more of an urgency to grab life quickly and surely, because of the dangers that lie behind every bush and greet us every day. Men never know when they take a breath if it could be their last. I'm afraid they lose some of the common courtesies that in another time and place they would not dream of abandoning.

Out here, life is short, death swift, and pleasures few. Need I say more?"

The Captain quietly shook his head. "Indeed, not, Sir! I shall not be at ease until I know Elizabeth is married and has given me and my wife grandchildren."

"Until then, James, there will be hell to pay on the border! I will do my best to keep my men in line; however, I must ask that you caution your daughter not to play romantic games with these wild young men's hearts, for I fear the consequences!"

"Good advice, Sir, and well taken. We have much to learn about life in the Colonies, and especially out here on the wild border. You have my word, Sir. I shall try to keep Elizabeth in hand."

The Captain was watching his daughter as she whirled around the dance floor, obviously enjoying every attention, and knew in his heart that the task of controlling her would be next to impossible. He prayed that a proper suitor would come forward and quickly claim this golden haired beauty so he could devote all his thoughts and energies to his new post at the fort.

Meanwhile, Elizabeth, her cheeks rosy, begged her dance partner for a short rest. The young Lieutenant escorted her to a seat where she was immediately surrounded by several admirers offering cups of punch and plates of sweet goodies.

"Please, gentlemen, let me catch my breath," Elizabeth panted, putting a kerchief to her moist temple. "You are all dancing me out of my shoes!"

She smiled her dazzling smile as she spoke, and the men fairly melted at her gaze.

There were murmurs of apology, and shy sideways glances from her bevy of devotees. Elizabeth's gaze happened then to wander to a tall, broad shouldered young officer lounging a short distance away. He seemed aloof, yet mildly amused at the antics of those around her, and she gave a faint smile as she sipped a cool punch. Chatting idly with those men closest to her, Elizabeth implored them to dance with some of the other young girls.

For a moment, but only a moment, she was alone. Without knowing how he got there, Elizabeth suddenly found the tall officer at her elbow, guiding her onto the dance floor where he swept her in his sure arms into the waltz rhythm being played. The rest of the evening, she danced with no one else, and they whirled and swayed the night away.

Chapter Six

Lieutenant George Stillwell was his name, as Elizabeth soon found out. He became a constant visitor to Captain Wood's quarters, much to the frustration of the other young admirers. Elizabeth had to admit that he cut a most dashing figure, with his fine blond hair, which showed glints of copper in the sunlight. He possessed finely chiseled facial features, having a long, straight nose and piercing blue eyes, which Elizabeth felt almost went to her very soul at times, it seemed.

As the days went by, Elizabeth fell under the hypnotic spell of Lt. Stillwell's captivating smile, and was mesmerized by his smooth demeanor. He was by far more fascinating than any of the others, and the girl found she was waiting impatiently for his visits.

Stillwell spent long hours relating stories of his adventures and wide travels, as Elizabeth sat in rapt silence as he told of far-off lands and exciting adventures she had never even dreamed of. She was so trusting, it did not occur to her that the stories he related might not be true. Sometimes, the young girl would walk with him along the paths outside the fort. They would stroll amongst the trees which were now decked out in the golden glory of fall, and she would loop her arm in his.

Elizabeth questioned new feelings that were stirring within her breast as she walked beside him, feeling the overpowering sense of his nearness. She was drawn to him, and certainly was attracted to him, yet there was a part of her that felt uneasy. She could not put her finger on what made her feel such a sense of foreboding, but there was a cunning about him that made her cautious.

One evening, a week after the dance, several of the young men again gathered around the front stoop of Elizabeth's quarters, as was their nightly ritual. This particular evening, they were a little more rowdy than usual, and became a bit quarrelsome. The presence of Lt. Stillwell did not sit well with the men, as they felt intimidated by his higher rank, and could see that Elizabeth's attention was being drawn more and more to the blond officer. Jealous feelings of hopelessness crept over the men, and at one point, a fight broke out.

Fists and arms began flailing about in a rising cloud of dust, as first two, then three and four scuffled in a writhing mass. Shouts and cursing rose to a high pitch, causing Elizabeth to cringe and put her fingers anxiously up to her mouth as she watched the men wrestle each other. She could clearly hear sounds of their fists hitting flesh in sickening thuds. Shocked and bewildered, the girl looked imploringly toward Lt. Stillwell, her eyes begging him to step in and stop the fray. But it was her father who came out of the quarters and broke up the melee.

"Here, here! That will do!" the Captain bellowed, pulling the men apart. "Return to your quarters at once. And do not come back until you can behave yourselves, or I will ban you from this area, and will bring charges against you!"

The men dispersed sheepishly, and soon it was calm again. But Elizabeth was shaken, and a dark feeling of disappointment crept over her.

"Why did you not try to stop them, Lt. Stillwell?" Her voice trembled.

"Oh, those young bucks needed to get some steam blown off. They have been mooning around here for weeks, all trying to gain your favor." *Like they were after a bitch in heat,* he thought. "They just had to thrash it out."

George Stillwell seemed unmoved and little affected by the display. His indifference sent a stabbing chill through Elizabeth.

"Oh, it is all my fault that those poor men were fighting! I never wanted anything like that to happen. I was only trying to be friendly to them all."

"My dear Mistress Wood, out here on the Border, where men scarcely see a white woman, say nothing of such a shining beauty as you, there is no such thing as being friendly. They all wish and hope they will get more from you than just a sweet smile!" *And so do I,* he thought, and his lips curled into a crooked smile.

Elizabeth's eyes opened wide and a blush came over her cheeks as she realized the deeper meaning of his words. She caught a hint of sarcasm in his voice, and again the uneasy feeling overtook her.

"Oh, I had no idea...."

"Elizabeth, you cannot toy with men's hearts. Sooner or later, someone is going to get killed."

Elizabeth's face was burning now. Tears glistened in her eyes, and she moaned softly, rocking back and forth, wringing her hands.

Stillwell continued: "There is only one way to stop the jealousy and bad feelings. You should be married, and that would settle things once and for all!"

This time, Elizabeth clapped her hands over her ears, shaking her head, her eyes wide with fear, not wanting to hear more.

"Elizabeth, marry me!" Stillwell grasped both her hands, pulling the girl roughly up to him, trying to wrap his arms about her. He bruised her wrists and hurt her arms as he bear-hugged her, and his hot face closed in on hers, his mouth reaching to meet those trembling lips. Then his lips crushed down on hers, and he savagely kissed her, forcing her mouth to open, his tongue searching.

Twisting violently, with strength that came from nowhere, Elizabeth pulled away, and with all her might, slapped George Stillwell on the side of his face, leaving him with his jaw set firmly, fire in his eyes.

"You little shit!" he seethed through his teeth.

Elizabeth fled to her room where she threw herself onto the bed. Embarrassment and guilt washed over her in waves, and she sank deeply into dark despair, trembling uncontrollably, and tears stung her eyes. Had she really been leading all the young men on? If so, the young girl had blissfully not been aware that her coy, shy friendliness had so affected the love-starved men.

Over and over, she berated herself for being too friendly, and longed to turn back the clock... to be back in England... wishing she had never come to this strange wilderness... never had met any of the soldiers... certainly never had met Lt. Stillwell!

Rage surged through her at the thought of him. How dare he be so bold as to grab her and force himself upon her? How cruel he had seemed not to have stepped in and stopped the fighting. After all, he had been the ranking officer, and should have taken control of the situation as soon as the disturbance had broken out.

It was true, she had been attracted to him, but now she had serious doubts. Elizabeth agonized over the vague emotions tugging at her heart. For the first time in her life, she felt she might have been falling in love. Now, she felt betrayed.

Elizabeth had little sleep that night, as she struggled to sort out her feelings. Over and over again, she relived last evening, and alternate surges of guilt and rage swept through her time and again. She was too embarrassed to go to her mother for any consoling, so she suffered in silence. The fresh smell of the moist forest night air came through her small window, and as the first light of dawn crept in, she finally fell into a fitful sleep.

Chapter Seven

For several days, George Stillwell tried to call on Elizabeth, but she refused every inquiry, preferring to remain in her quarters. Each time he approached the door, Martha Wood met him and relayed to him that her daughter was indisposed. Meanwhile, Elizabeth kept to her room. Days passed and finally the girl could relax her guard, to resume a more normal life when it was discovered that Lt. Stillwell had departed on an extended mission away from the fort.

However, it was indeed a more subdued Elizabeth who resumed holding court each evening. She was much more demure, and certainly more careful of her actions and responses to the men. The girl made more of an effort to become good friends with the other young ladies of the fort, often visiting their homes, and helping with whatever project was at hand at the moment.

On a certain misty morning, as the fog broke up and the sun played hide and seek behind vanishing clouds, with a basket on her arm, Elizabeth headed off to the trading post just outside the fort. There was a nip in the air, causing her to draw her shawl a little closer about her shoulders. Rounding the corner of the fort, she ran smack-dab into two tall Indians in buckskins.

Alarmed, Elizabeth stepped back and looked directly into their bronze faces. Uttering a little cry, she turned to flee but one of the Indians reached and grabbed her by the arm.

"Mistress Wood? Mistress Elizabeth Wood?"

Elizabeth stared in disbelief, looking first at one and then the other, not believing her eyes, for these men were identical! Long, dark hair tumbled around their shoulders and large, mellow brown eyes peered down at her from beneath their black brows. Their faces were smooth, with square, strong jaws sloping up to high cheekbones.

"I beg your pardon, Mistress, are you not Elizabeth Wood, lately from England?" one of them said.

Looking intently at the figure, but still puzzled, Elizabeth wondered how an Indian would know her name, and why he was speaking in perfect English? Her mouth dropped open, as if to speak.

"I am afraid you do not remember me. My name is Nathan Herrington. We sailed together on the 'Morning Glory,' and met as we disembarked."

She slowly recalled the incident, yet she still looked from one to the other, hardly recognizing the man standing before her. He was heavier and tanned, and of course in frontiersman garb.

"Oh, forgive me, Sir, I never would have recognized you. Yes, I am Mistress Elizabeth Wood," she said, her voice still a bit shaken from the sudden unexpected encounter, as she emerged from her momentary stupor. A nervous giggle covered her embarrassment. "And, oh my, there are two of you! How incredible. I took you for Indians. I beg you, forgive me for staring, but I have never seen two people who look so incredibly alike in my life! I was fearing I had lost my mind, seeing double!"

"Please allow me to introduce my twin brother, Jonathan." Nathan grinned, offering his hand, after which Jonathan also shook hands with Elizabeth.

"We are identical twins, although I am the older. I can understand your confusion," Jonathan ventured.

"Is the fort your home, now, Mistress Wood?" Nathan asked, hoping to prolong the encounter.

Nodding, the flustered girl tried to regain her composure, yet still looked from one face to the other, as she tried to hide a silly smile.

"Jonathan and I are here for supplies. We have a cabin about five miles from here." Nathan gestured to the northeast. "I had no idea we were so close to the fort," he said in a breathless sort of way.

Nathan's eyes searched her face, hoping to find a glimmer of welcome and friendliness. He desperately wanted to establish a link to this girl somehow.

"I was telling Jonathan about our perilous journey aboard ship... about the storm and what misery it wrought." Now, Nathan was reaching for anything that might extend this chance meeting.

Elizabeth brightened, at ease now. "Oh, my! Yes, it was an experience I shall never want to repeat. I would hope never to have to cross the ocean again, although this country is so strange, and rather frightening." There was a pause. "How are you finding the Colonies, Mr. Herrington?" addressing the one she thought was Nathan.

"Well, the wilderness is certainly a far cry from England. However, Jonathan, here, is teaching me well the lessons of life in this new land." He gazed fondly at his brother as he spoke.

Elizabeth flashed a smile, and excusing herself, moved to continue on to the trading post. Nathan put out a hand, touching her arm, and said wistfully, "I hope we may meet again soon, Mistress Wood."

There was a determined look in his warm brown eyes, causing their depths to glow a color Elizabeth had never seen before. A feeling of warmth stirred within her as she gazed back into his face.

"That indeed would be a great pleasure to me, Sir," she said as she extended her hand in parting.

Nathan took her small hand in his and squeezed it just right, he hoped, attempting to convey more than just a casual good-bye. His fingers lingered for a long moment on hers before she withdrew her hand. She smiled and tilted her head to the men.

The two watched her walk away toward the trading post, her skirt swaying just so, and her long blond hair bouncing softly. Jonathan noted that a certain electricity had passed between Nathan and Elizabeth, and contemplated the idea as he leaned on his long rifle.

"She sure is a looker," he said, noting that Nathan neither heard him, nor was aware that he was standing beside him.

"We best get to the fort and report our seeing Indian signs," Jonathan muttered. Again, Jonathan tried to shake Nathan from his reverie. "We need to report in," he said more forcefully, taking Nathan by the elbow.

Jolted from his daydream, Nathan followed his brother to the fort, where they reported their sightings of Indian activity to the authorities.

"We thank you gentlemen for your information about the activities of the savages," Captain Wood was saying. "We have had some reports of increased activity, including harassment of some of the settlers. The

Delawares and Wyandots are on the move, it would appear. We shall keep a sharp eye out."

He dismissed them both. Captain Wood was also learning of frontier life. But when he reported the incident to the Commander, it was dismissed with a shrug, and the Captain soon forgot and little heeded the warning.

Chapter Eight

‘Indian Summer with its warmth and color was fully upon the land as Jonathan and Nathan made their way to the salt lick area for the hunt. They had paddled a canoe far upstream where they stashed it in the underbrush before continuing the remainder of the way by foot.

It was midafternoon as the sun slanted through yellow leaves, and a soft breeze gently fluttered through the trees. Tall ferns swayed in rhythm with the wind, and crimson sumac dotted the underbrush, in brilliant splotches of color. The two made their way up and over the ridge, down a swale and back up another ridge, and when they reached a clearing, the brothers set up their meager camp under an overhanging rock ledge. There, Nathan sat with his back resting against a granite rock and surveyed the cathedral-like area, while Jonathan arranged their blankets, and built a fire, roasting strips of meat for their supper.

"Tomorrow, early in the morning, we will be at the salt lick to wait for the deer to come," Jonathan informed his companion. "We will take only the game we need, for we have a long way to pack it out, as you can tell."

Nathan nodded, chewing on his meal. "I hope I will be able to bag a deer with this rifle. Practicing shooting at pieces of cloth attached to a tree is a lot different than shooting at a moving target," Nathan said between bites of food.

"You'll get used to it soon enough," Jonathan assured his brother. "The main thing is to practice re-loading quickly. Never know when you might need to shoot fast."

"You mean because of Indians?"

"Well, no, I really had in mind an angry elk, or that a bear might charge you. But I guess it would be wise to be on the lookout for any kind of danger."

The air grew cool as twilight descended. The two sat puffing on their pipes, each lost in his own thoughts, gazing at the embers of the fire. Jonathan rose and placed another piece of wood on the fire, watching the glowing embers ignite the branch into dancing yellow flames. He took a long pull on his pipe and let the smoke drift lazily away.

"Can't get the girl off your mind, can you?" It was more of a statement than a question.

Nathan gave a little start, arousing from his daydream.

"What are you talking about?"

"You know, the girl at the fort... the one with the long, golden hair."

Nathan's face flushed slightly, and he was glad that Jonathan could not see the color as it rose in the darkness. "You mean Elizabeth Wood?"

"Nathan, Nathan... we are not twin brothers for nothing! You know I always can tell what you are feeling and what you are thinking. Remember the time when you fell and broke your arm when you were a little lad, and my arm ached without even knowing you had been hurt? Well, I can tell without a single doubt that you have lost your heart to the hazel-eyed lass."

Nathan suddenly was embarrassed. "Nonsense!" he said, as thoughts of his dead fiancee returned, and a silent surge of guilt once more crept over him. "It is too soon after Sarah's death to be thinking of another." He said the words, yet knew the churning in his heart came from his delightful thoughts of Elizabeth, and was aware that perhaps Jonathan was right.

"Nathan... Sarah was of another time, in another world. You are here now, in this new wild country. You need to think of the future. Think about settling down with a wife of your own, to carve out your own spot here in the New World."

Nathan was quiet for a long time. "And what about you, Jonathan? The same goes for you! What about a wife for you? Have you any sweethearts?"

Jonathan sat silent for a long time, his jaw working, before he answered. "I had a sweetheart once," he began, "but that is lost... gone." He stared at the flames while a peculiar look came over his face, and Nathan noticed the difference immediately.

"You never mentioned anything about that, Jonathan! How come you are keeping it a secret?"

"It doesn't matter any more now," Jonathan said in a low, soft voice. His eyes remained fixed on the fire.

"Come, come! Tell me. Out with it!" Nathan urged.

Jonathan remained silent.

"Was it a girl in England? Was that why you left the English shores and came to the Colonies, to forget a lost love? Oh, I see the picture... you ran away from a situation that must have been a heartache."

Jonathan shook his head, and with a great sigh, reluctantly began to relate his tale.

"It is not what you are picturing. It happened three years ago, about a year after I arrived from England. I had befriended a man named Alfred Murdock... a frontiersman extraordinaire... a real borderman. Alf was wise to all the ways of the woods. He taught me everything I know about hunting and trapping, and following signs... about survival in the wilderness.

"We hunted together, went through trials and tribulations together, and became good friends. Alf was on good terms with the Delaware Indians, and was a friend of their chief. Well, one time, some renegade Delawares made a raid on some of the settlers and made off with a young girl and her little brother. Alf and I set out to try to get them back." Jonathan paused, knocking the ashes from his pipe, and then continued.

"We tracked them for three days, and finally caught up with them. We sneaked up on them and watched for our chance to try to snatch the hostages. Our plan was for each of us to grab one of the youngsters, kill as many of the renegades as we could, and high-tail it out of there." Again, Jonathan paused.

"Well, something went wrong with our plan. We jumped them all right, but I took an arrow to my shoulder, and as I fought with the redskins, Alf made off with the two youngsters, leaving me behind, as we had agreed should anything happen to either of us. I fought as hard as I could, and with my rifle, I swung and bashed in a couple of heads, but my wound kept me from being strong enough to escape. Pretty soon I was overpowered by three braves and knocked unconscious. I woke up two days later to find myself at the Delaware Village, a prisoner, and a wounded one at that."

Nathan was astonished. "Jonathan! You never told me you had been captured by the Indians! How did you get away? Were you badly hurt?"

"I was laid up a good while with a shoulder wound. Got infected, and I was delirious with fever for awhile. But an Indian maiden saved my life."

He paused again, and appeared to be in deep thought.

"Her name was Blue Water. She was the daughter of the chief. Well, Blue Water dressed my wound with leaves and mud, and fed me a special brew of herbs. Finally my fever broke, and I recovered. But I was still a prisoner. Was not allowed to leave the village. Blue Water became my constant companion and ultimately my captor.

"She was young and beautiful... very beautiful. She had long shining black hair... soulful big brown eyes. She was kind to me, and protected me from the other tribesmen." Another pause, and then with his voice trembling in a hoarse whisper, "Well, we fell in love."

Then Jonathan once more grew silent, and Nathan sat spellbound, his mouth dropping open.

Jonathan cleared his throat. "Sometime, Brother, I shall tell you the rest of the tale."

With that, Jonathan rolled into his blanket and went to sleep. Nathan, his head in a whirl from the startling information as related by his twin, could not sleep, but stared at the starry sky long into the night.

Chapter Nine

Winter of 1754-1755 hit the area hard and long. Nathan soon learned what Jonathan had meant when he had warned him about the severity of the cold and snow. The chilling white stuff blanketed the region in early December, and drifted to the tops of the cabin windows. Jonathan's land was a parcel high upon a ridgetop, well above Fort Mount Pleasant. The cabin proved to be weather tight, and the two men were comfortable for the most part.

Days were spent replenishing firewood and tending to the daily tasks of preparing soups and stews. Nathan got good at making biscuits and bread, and surprised himself that he could prepare substantial meals under Jonathan's experienced hand. Jonathan also taught him how to tan deer hides and crudely sew moccasins and hunting shirts from the soft leather.

They made candles and molded bullets until they had quite a full storehouse of ammunition. Evenings were spent quietly reading or writing. Nathan was keeping a journal of sorts, and carefully wrote instructions and drew illustrations about all that he had learned so far in this wild new country. It became more difficult for him all the time to remember what life had been like in England. His days in the colonies filled his mind to overflowing with adventures different than he had ever known, and the comfortable life he once knew in his native land was soon just a distant memory.

Nathan practiced all his new skills, even throwing a big hunting knife and hatchet at targets. He became very proficient at knife throwing, and would often emerge the winner from contests that Jonathan instigated. Soon, Nathan could pierce a splinter from across the room with either knife or hatchet.

When weather permitted, the two brothers trapped fox and beaver, drying the pelts to take to the trading post in the spring. Jonathan hoped to have enough pelts to trade for a horse, come summer. All in all, their days were filled with activity, and the time did seem to go quickly.

Meanwhile, at Fort Mount Pleasant, Elizabeth's winter was quite different. She had three small children whom she tutored every day. Snows came and went in the narrow valley, and she was very comfortable in the Captain's quarters. Elizabeth delighted in the progress of her young charges as she patiently went over the lessons every day. Nightfall came early, and the young girl enjoyed spending the evenings close to the fireplace, reading or doing needlework. Occasionally, the other young ladies would gather for girlish chatter, and while away the long hours. One by one, the men of the fort had given up on Elizabeth, and she had few visitors that long winter. It was just as well, she thought, for she could not get her thoughts cleared, and seemed to have a jumble of emotions mixed up in her head. Even though she tried to forget Lt. George Stillwell, every so often his memory came rushing back with the same result. Elizabeth would become distraught and agitated. She would shake her head, as if trying to rid herself of a bad dream. As much as she would have liked to share her thoughts and emotions with her mother, the young girl was reluctant to bare her soul to anyone, and kept everything hidden within her breast.

When Christmas time came, it was Elizabeth who entreated the Commander to be allowed to decorate the hall with greens, and plan a festival. Together with her other young friends, they gathered fresh boughs and strung them from every post, window, and doorway, and busied themselves making special candles, then added ribbon bows to make quite a remarkable scene.

Runners were sent to the settlers in outlying areas, inviting them to come to the Fort on Christmas Day for worship services and the festival. Elizabeth worked for days baking goodies and coordinating the event with the other women of the fort.

"Even though we are far from our homeland, we shall try to continue a few of our traditions of the holiday for the men who are so far from home," Elizabeth explained. "Let us try to celebrate our Lord's birth here in the new land just as we have done before."

All the ladies and young children enthusiastically joined in, and in no time were excitedly deep into plans for the festival. It was a good break from the monotony of everyday life at the fort. Soon, the aroma of baking breads and plum puddings spread over the fort, and there was an air of excitement everywhere.

When the day arrived, the settlers began assembling, filling the church to overflowing. A lucky break in the weather allowed most of the settlers to make the trip with little difficulty. Elizabeth beamed with pride when she saw a large turnout at the chapel. Dutifully bowing her head in prayer, she gave thanks for everything dear to her: for her parents, life in the New World, and for new friends she had made. The young girl prayed earnestly that God would guide her to a good companion with whom she would spend the rest of her life; for she was already getting to an age that if she did not marry soon, she might miss the chance once and for all, and become a spinster.

"Lord, in your infinite wisdom," Elizabeth began, whispering to herself, "please help me to know when the right young man comes into my life. Guide him to me, and I ask you to forgive me for my youthful foolishness and wayward heart. I am easily swayed, and I pray I will not be taken in by someone like George Stillwell. Please help me find someone who is good and straight of heart. Someone who will love me totally in return, one to whom I can give my whole heart and soul."

Momentarily, the young girl halted, wondering if she was being too presumptuous. A small wave of guilt washed over her, and she then sought forgiveness for asking God for too much of a personal quest. "Forgive me, Lord," she prayed to herself, "for I know it is not proper to ask for things for myself, but Lord, I cannot help it! I need you to guide me and be with me always. Show me the one, Lord. Of all these nice soldiers who have been smitten and are so attentive, please show me the one. I am sure he is near. Open my eyes so I may see beyond the ordinary, and may look deep into their hearts. Show me, Lord, Amen." Elizabeth earnestly prayed.

Thus refreshed, she lifted her head, and opening her eyes, stared across the room directly into the melting eyes of Nathan Herrington. With a start like a thunder-

bolt, color rose to her cheeks, and her hand flew uncon-
sciously to her mouth, while she continued to stare.

Nathan tilted his head in greeting to her, and
flashed a white-toothed, dimpled smile her way.
Quickly Elizabeth lowered her eyes and looked down
at her lap, twisting her kerchief into a tight knot. Shyly,
her eyes peeking from beneath her lashes, the young
girl glanced his way again, as if to convince herself that
he was really there, and she had not daydreamed the
whole episode.

But, sure enough, there was Nathan, sitting beside
his twin brother, gazing her way, a grin still upon his
face. Despite herself, Elizabeth could not help the smile
that crossed her lips, as she reluctantly turned her
attention to the man in the pulpit, all the while feeling
Nathan's eyes upon her. She dare not look again. *Dear
God*, she thought, *are you answering my prayers already?*
Her breath came faster, and she was truly startled,
amazed, and greatly puzzled.

Chapter Ten

It had not taken much urging for Nathan to decide to journey to the Fort when the two became aware of the planned Christmas festivities. Jonathan smiled to himself as he watched Nathan prepare for the trip. Snow had ceased for the moment, and they were able to make their way down the mountain and to the Fort in record time, considering they had to battle drifts and fallen trees that hampered the going. The sun even peeked weakly through the clouds as they entered the worship place.

Nathan blinked in the darkness, trying to clear his vision, and his eyes searched for the golden hair his heart so much wanted to see. At first, he did not recognize Elizabeth, for her head was covered with a lacy cap, but then he spotted her, and his heart gave a little leap. Quietly, he took a seat directly across from her, noting that the young girl's head was lowered in prayer. Nathan, too, lowered his eyes for a few moments of thanksgiving and praise to his Lord.

When once again Nathan lifted his eyes, a thrill surged over him as he gazed upon Elizabeth's beauty. Silently, he willed her eyes to open. Nothing. Again, he willed those hazel eyes to open, harder this time. Suddenly, Elizabeth's eyes flew open and stared directly into his. Nathan saw her hand fly to her mouth, and noted the strange shock appearing in those orbs, which at this moment puzzled him.

Tilting his head toward her, Nathan smiled. He saw how quickly she looked down, and thought he saw color rising into her cheeks. He sighed deeply, satisfied, knowing that he would have the opportunity to be with her today. Yes, Jonathan had already told him, and now Nathan was certain, that he had lost his heart to this golden-haired girl. He was tumbling down into the delicious state of everlasting love, and nothing could stop the fall.

A great feast had been prepared that day, and the guests ate their fill of roast venison and other wild game, and were treated to sweet desserts baked by the women. The day flew by too quickly to suit Nathan, for he relished every moment he could be close to the lovely Elizabeth. Shyly, they gravitated toward each other, and chanced to meet over the punch bowl. Their fingers touched as he handed her a cup of the sweet nectar, sending a tingle through Elizabeth's heart, and at the same time a thrill shot over Nathan like an exclamation point. "It is so good to see you again, Mistress Wood. I hope you have fared well since last we met?"

"Quite well, Sir," she smiled, and her hazel eyes changed to a flickering violet in the mellow light of the candle-filled hall. Why was she so tongue-tied? Elizabeth wondered. Angry with herself, she could not think of a single question to ask Nathan in order to keep the conversation going, yet she longed to extend those moments with him. She found she was enormously attracted to this young man. Was it the wild borderman image he imbued? Or was it just that he was so handsome, and somehow romantic, garbed in the fringed buckskin?

"My brother and I are quite snug in our cabin," Nathan volunteered. "However, we are high up on the mountaintop," he said, gesturing to the northeast. "There is a lot of snow up there, but we made the trip down to the Fort just fine. Thank you for inviting us to this wonderful Christmas celebration. I understand you had a great deal to do with this event."

Elizabeth brightened, and seemed to come back from her momentary shyness. "Well, I could not see Christmas come and go without some tradition, so I begged the Commander to let us have this festival."

"I can certainly see your hand in these lovely decorations in the hall. Surely you were the one who did this, Mistress Wood?"

Elizabeth blushed slightly. "Yes, the other girls and I brought in the greens and did pretty it up some. But, please, Mr. Herrington, you may call me Elizabeth."

"Thank you, Mistress Woo -, I mean Elizabeth." He loved how her name rolled off his lips, and he looked intently into her hazel eyes. "Please relay to the others how much we poor woodsmen appreciate a little part of England and the season so well displayed."

"I shall, Sir." By now, Elizabeth was breathing harder, suddenly flustered at being in his presence.

"And please call me Nathan, for I am not used to so much formality."

There was a pause.

"Nathan," Elizabeth mulled the name over on her tongue, as if tasting it. "However in the world can I tell you apart from your brother? I mean no disrespect; I believe you to be Nathan, the man I met aboard ship, but perhaps you are playing a trick on me, and you are really... what is his name... Jonathan?"

Nathan smiled down at her. "I certainly can understand your confusion and frustration, Elizabeth, but there is an easy way to tell us apart, once you get to know us well. You see, my brother, Jonathan, has a scar on his neck under his left ear. A legacy from being captured by the Indians a few years ago."

"Oh, my! How dreadful!" Elizabeth's eyes grew wide. "Was he hurt badly? How did he escape?"

"Even I do not know the whole story yet. One day he will tell me. Enough about Jonathan, I want to hear how it came about that you ended up here in America, on this wild frontier."

Nathan took her by the elbow, and guided her through the crowded hall until they found a quiet place off in one corner by themselves. Elizabeth straightened her skirt as she settled onto a low bench, and continued, "As you probably would surmise, I am here because of my father, who is a Captain in the British Army. He was assigned to this new post. I understand that a new General will be arriving soon for some kind of an extended mission."

Nathan raised his eyebrows at that news, anxious to relay that tidbit on to Jonathan. Changing the subject, he said, "It does not seem as though so many months have gone by since we arrived in this new country. The time has gone by so quickly."

"We have been here four months already," she remarked. "And I believe I have already forgotten more than I wish about my homeland. It is so different here. So crude and wild, and in a way exciting."

"I know I have learned a great deal about life in the wilderness," Nathan said. "Jonathan has been a good teacher. I have acquired a good many skills I would never have dreamed of doing, were I still in England."

They chatted animatedly for a long time, relaying bits and pieces of their childhood days, and the common remembrances of their beloved England. Finally, Elizabeth took his arm and led Nathan away from the corner. "Come, meet some of my friends."

The rest of the day went quickly, and Nathan found it an exhilarating time, for his spirits were soaring after spending those long precious hours with Elizabeth. They talked, and strolled, and as the hours ticked away, became more and more at ease with each other. In the evening, musicians struck up some tunes, and soon there were couples whirling upon the floor of the hall. Nathan welcomed the opportunity to put his arm around Elizabeth's waist as they glided to the music. Her touch sent a thrill through him, and he longed to hold her in his arms forever. Elizabeth, too, was very well aware of Nathan's strong arm around her, and felt herself yielding to the giddy sensations of infatuation that were coursing through her.

All too soon, the evening ended, and reluctantly, Nathan found himself escorting Elizabeth to her quarters, wishing silently that the day would never end.

"Do you have a place to sleep tonight, Nathan? Surely you will not be able to return to your cabin this late at night?"

"Yes, Jonathan and I will sleep in the barracks tonight. Shall I see you in the morning before we leave?" He held her hand in his.

Elizabeth looked up at Nathan, drawing her shawl closely about her shoulders in the evening chill. She felt warm and safe with Nathan, and wished, too, that the day would not end, for it had been one of delight and happiness for her. Emotions that she thought had long been buried started to come to the surface, and she felt a delicious sense of warmth flood her.

"I would like that very much, Nathan, but I am not certain I shall be about in the morning. I must care for my mother. She has not been well."

"I am most sorry to hear that. Please give her my warmest regards, and wish her a speedy recovery for me."

"I shall," Elizabeth murmured, her voice suddenly faint and far away.

At that, Nathan took both of her hands in his, and held them for a lingering moment. "Good night, Dear Elizabeth," he said, barely able to see her face in the darkness. His heart quickened as he dared utter that one word of endearment, and he wondered if she had heard it.

"Good night, Nathan, my friend. Glad Tidings of the Season." Elizabeth's voice was soft as an evening breeze. She gently withdrew her hands from his, and reached up to lightly brush his cheek with her fingertips.

A shiver went up Nathan's spine.

Chapter Eleven

Martha Wood's health was failing. No matter what the medical officer of Fort Mount Pleasant could do, nor what medicine and powders he administered, Elizabeth's mother was slowly fading. Elizabeth was constantly at her mother's side, tending to every need. Martha's fever would not break despite all efforts, for a cough wracked her body and sapped her strength. The doctor had bled her many times, to no avail, and he now looked into Elizabeth's eyes and shook his head, signaling no more could be done.

Elizabeth wrung out a cloth and placed it back on her mother's feverish forehead, soothing her cheek at the same time, noting that the skin felt very hot and dry. The woman moaned and moved her head aside. When she opened her eyes, Elizabeth became alarmed, for Martha's blue eyes had become pained and glazed. They sank back into the woman's head, and the whites had become a frightening grayish color. Black shadows appeared to deepen below her eyes, and the woman's cheeks were sunken. A deathly pallor spread like a shadow over the older woman's face, and her lips were cracking from dryness.

Again, Elizabeth tried to give her mother water, but Martha clamped her teeth together and refused. Her pained blue eyes looked into her daughter's, pleading silently with an unnamed request, which the girl could not comprehend. She wrung out the cloth once more, and attempted to moisten those lips which were so dry.

Her mother had been Elizabeth's constant companion over the years, for she was an only child. Martha had heaped love and attention upon the girl, and now Elizabeth was silently grieving, for she could not even begin to think of life without her dearest mother.

Exhausted, Elizabeth brushed away a strand of hair from her temple with the back of her hand, and reapplied the cool cloth. She had been caring for the failing woman day and night for three weeks, ever since the Christmas Festival, with little or no sleep. There had been practically no time for Elizabeth's thoughts to wander and try to recapture the warm feelings she had experienced while being with the tall woodsman on Christmas Day, yet Nathan's name seemed always on her mind.

At that moment, Captain Wood opened the door and stood silently at the bedside. The lines of his face showed grave concern and he put a compassionate hand upon his daughter's shoulder. "Any change?"

Elizabeth shook her head. "The doctor said we have done all we can for her."

Martha had another coughing spell. Deep, rasping heaves wracked her chest, and one could hear the phlegm clogging her air passageway. Elizabeth helped the older woman lie back into a new position when the coughing finally ceased.

"Let me sit with her tonight, Elizabeth," The Captain said.

"I cannot leave her, Father... I need to be here for her." There was anguish in the girl's voice.

The Captain patted his daughter's shoulder. "It's all right, Dear Girl. You need some rest. I will care for your mother."

Tears welled in Elizabeth's eyes as she gazed upon her mother's pinched and pained face. The young girl put her cheek against her mother's thin hand and blinked back tears. Slowly, she rose, lingering at the bedside, whispering, "Please call me if you need me. I shall just take a little nap."

"Rest, my Dear, rest," he uttered. Captain Wood, though stoic, was hurting, too.

With every fiber of her body aching from exhaustion, Elizabeth lowered herself upon her bed in the next room, and pulled a comforter up to her chin. She closed her eyes, but sleep would not come, for thoughts were whirling in a blackness in her mind, and a sense of dread came over her. Images flashed before Elizabeth's mind, disjointed and dream-like. She imagined herself as a child again in England. A little girl standing in a garden, filling a flower basket with blooms. Irises, daffodils, tulips and roses overflowed the white basket, and it became almost too heavy for the girl to carry. With both hands, she carried the wicker bundle to the back stoop, calling out, "Mother! Mother! I have something beautiful for you!"

Elizabeth's mother appeared in the doorway, tall and young, and clasped her hands together at her chest, exclaiming, "Oh, my little Beth, how simply lovely!" The woman stooped to kiss the child on her cheek, taking the flowers into the kitchen. Beth beamed, her heart swelling with pride.

The dream picture faded and dark images of nothing invaded Elizabeth's tortured mind, swallowing her downward, and she found herself spiraling down... down. Flashes of an ocean voyage blurred together, and a figure in buckskin emerged, tall, with wavy black hair flowing to his shoulders. The man was smiling at her, dimpled lines on either side of his mouth, white teeth flashing.

Elizabeth's heart ached with longing for him. She called out, but no sound came out of her lips. Soon, in her dream, there were two buckskin clad men, their faces intermingling... identical. Elizabeth panicked, for she could not distinguish which one was Nathan.

"Nathan?... Nathan?" the girl called out, and the images faded. Then a sweet female voice faintly called, "Elizabeth!" and she saw her mother once more, tall, young and beautiful, smilingly move forward, reaching out her hand to the girl.

"Do not be afraid, my love, for I am all right now, my dear, sweet Beth." The woman smiled at Elizabeth, and the image slowly faded into the shadows.

A hand gently shook Elizabeth's shoulder.

"Elizabeth... Elizabeth, my dear," the Captain's voice was low and hoarse.

With a start, she opened her eyes to see her father bending over her. It took a moment for reality to hit. When it did, the young girl felt as if a blow had been struck to her mid-section. Frozen, she stared into her father's face. Then she knew. With her hands clasping her mouth, and tears welling into her eyes, she started to shake.

"She's gone, isn't she? She's dead!" Elizabeth sobbed. The Captain nodded his head. "Oh, Father! No!"

Elizabeth ran to her mother's bedside, and throwing herself across her mother's lifeless body, collapsed into wracking sobs. She dug her fingers into the blanket, and screamed, "Mother! Mother!" until blackness engulfed her, she slid down, and knew no more.

Chapter Twelve

S pring came to the mountain with welcome relief.
The earth awakened under a warming sun, and
tiny green leaves began to burst open upon the bare
tree limbs, assuring that once more the resurrection of
the life cycle was complete. Snow still lurked in patches
where dark shadows lay, and everywhere song birds
were returning again to take up residence in the forest.
Dogwood trees, flowering with great white blooms,
spread their branches almost to the ground. Rhododen-
drons and azaleas blazed with purple, pink and
magenta blossoms, splashing brilliant color across the
landscape.

Nathan was quite impressed, having a keen eye for
color and all things of nature. As he soaked up the

warmth from the sun, he felt rejuvenated and invigorated by the change from the grayness of winter to the brightness of spring. Walking among the azaleas, which were totally in bloom, with not a green leaf yet showing, Nathan's thoughts turned to Elizabeth, as he gazed upon the blaze of the blossoms' colors. It was easy to think of her when he saw the beauty of the blooms. *She belongs with these beautiful things, and they belong with her,* he thought. He could picture her with her arms piled high with branches from the flowering shrubs, smiling and delighting with every step.

Jonathan's call interrupted Nathan's reverie, and the young man's attention turned toward the sound. Jonathan was grubbing out a tree stump in the area they were to make into a vegetable garden.

"Lend me a hand here, Nathan," Jonathan grunted, as he leaned heavily against the stubborn stump.

"Right!" Nathan said, grabbing a rope, and, encircling the stump, he pulled mightily as Jonathan pushed from his side. The stump groaned and suddenly broke loose with a snap, sending both men to the ground. They wiped their brows with their sleeves and smiled as they rolled the stump aside. Jonathan strode to the creek and gulped down the sweet liquid, letting the coolness trickle down his throat in refreshing waves.

"We need to go for supplies."

It was a simple statement by Jonathan, but one that caused Nathan's heart to skip a beat. The long winter had dragged agonizingly slowly for the frontiersman, while he had spent hour upon hour each day dreaming about Elizabeth Wood. No matter where he was, or what he was doing, her face appeared before him at every turn. In the woods, tramping through snow; at night, staring into the evening fire, she was there. Her image blazed into his mind.

Many times Nathan had stood on the outcropping of rocks upon the brow of the mountain, gazing down into the valley, wanting more than anything to plunge headlong down the steep slope to Elizabeth's side. Nathan would watch an eagle soar and loop, and wish that he could be that great bird, to sail effortlessly across the valley and swoop low into the fort to land at Elizabeth's feet.

The brothers gathered all the fur pelts they had accumulated over the winter's hunt, and bundled them together for transport. It turned out the load was heavy.

"I hope we have enough to trade for a horse," Jonathan said. "We need one, for sure."

He grunted under his load. Then an idea struck him. The borderman went into the woods, and with a few swift blows of his ax, felled a sapling tree. Quickly, he lopped off the sparse branches and chopped the sapling in two. With deft fingers, he lashed the two long poles together, and made a carrying sling between them. The two men heaped the fur pelts upon the sling and tied them down.

"Now we are ready," Jonathan exclaimed, puffing slightly.

"What is this?" Nathan inquired.

"It is called a travois. Indians use this mode to carry burdens. Sometimes they use dogs or horses to pull the travois. Since we have neither, we will take turns pulling it ourselves."

"How do you propose to drag that through the forest with all the brambles and underbrush blocking the way?" Nathan seemed unconvinced.

"We might as well just hack a pathway through, and then it will be easier the next time we need the trail." Jonathan's voice was bright and eager.

Nathan raised his eyebrows and rolled his eyes, not believing that such a little miracle could take place without major effort on their parts. Shouldering his rifle, however, and securing a hatchet to his belt, Nathan lead the way into the forest. Periodically, they stopped to hack away underbrush and small trees. The going was indeed slow, as Nathan chopped his way forward, tossing aside the refuse. From time to time, they stopped to plot the best route, weaving in between giant trees and rocky terrain. Hours passed as they made their slow progress. Where they might have scrambled down precipitous slopes, were they on foot with no burdens, now they had to circumvent certain areas for a better foothold on the trail.

On one of the detours, the two came upon a surprise opening in the forest. A quiet glen was situated beside a trickling stream. Glancing up at a moist, craggy wall, they discovered a spring was oozing from the moss laden rocks. The clearing was oval shaped, relatively flat, and had abundant grass. Willows and myrtle lushly crowded the perimeter, and ferns as tall as each man were arching gracefully, the light yellow-green color a contrast to the surrounding darker foliage.

The stream formed a deep, dark pool a few rods from the rocky ledge before meandering farther down the mountainside. Jonathan followed the craggy wall, and to his surprise, discovered a small cave, whose entrance was hidden by thick underbrush. He and Nathan explored the small area, and found the dry cave held enough room in which to stand upright, once they squeezed through the entrance.

"This would make a good hiding place for renegades and redskins," Jonathan remarked, "if they knew about it."

"Why would they need a hiding place?" Nathan queried.

"Well, it would be an excellent place to keep an eye on what goes on in the valley. Actually, we are not far from a good overlook. Come, I'll show you."

The two made their way through a tangle of wild berry bushes and suddenly burst though to a rocky outcropping. Below, they saw the river and could see the fort and settlement that surrounded the area. Nathan could make out tiny figures moving about and saw horses and oxen traveling to and fro. Shortly, they saw a long column of British soldiers, wagons, and equipment wind its way toward the fort. There seemed to be a good deal of excitement as more soldiers emerged from the fort and seemed to form a double line, greeting the incoming troops.

"There, see that black horse and rider?" Jonathan said, pointing to the one who was leading the British troops as they were approaching the fort entrance. "Looks like someone of importance is coming into the fort."

Nathan nodded, watching the procession as it disappeared behind the confines of the huge wooden walls.

"Wonder what that is all about?" he asked, his hands upon his hips, a puzzled look upon his rugged face.

Jonathan heaved a long sigh, looking at the burden they still had to convey, and muttered "We'll find out soon enough. Let's get going."

Chapter Thirteen

General Edward Braddock arrived at Fort Mount Pleasant amid a flurry of military pomp and ceremony. Troops greeted him smartly, lining each side of the roadway in salute, as the entourage passed through the entrance to the fort. The General rode a magnificent black stallion, whose coat glistened in the sunlight, highlighting the horse's rippling muscles at every prance. A full blue-black mane flowed over his powerful neck, and the animal's long tail almost fell to the ground. The stallion's nostrils flared as he arched his neck, and with hooves stepping high, bore the rider inside the wooden bastion almost in time with the drums and bagpipes.

Elizabeth watched from the doorway of her quarters as her father and the fort Commander greeted the General. There was a short, formal ceremony of greeting, and the General dismounted, handing the reins of his mount to an eager young trooper. After trading salutes, the officers escorted General Braddock swiftly into the command room. Elizabeth was excited, as the flurry of activity broke the monotony of daily life at the fort. That night, she would take her place at her father's side at the banquet that had been planned for the General's arrival.

Now, she must quickly finish arrangements for her part of the banquet plans. Taking a large basket, Elizabeth emerged from the fort and followed the path along the river. She intended to gather wild flowers for the banquet table as a surprise for her father and the General, since the young girl was performing the hostess duties that would have been her mother's place, had she yet been alive. Tears still stung Elizabeth's eyes, and her throat choked frequently when she thought about her mother's illness and tragic death. But, today, she did not let memories interfere with the beauty of the day.

The spring air was warm and delicious as Elizabeth walked along the river. Trees were leafing out, and wild flowers bloomed everywhere. The young girl felt a surge of well-being flow through her body, and for the first time since her mother's death, she was happy. She drew a huge breath of fresh air and glanced up at the sky. It was a clear, brilliant blue that played hopscotch between the tree branches. Little wisps of white clouds drifted lazily across the horizon.

Elizabeth began picking flowers to fill her basket. In her joy, she left the trail to follow the colorful blooms, picking first here, then there, when another colorful bloom would catch her eye a short distance away. Soon, without realizing, Elizabeth had lost track of the main trail. Suddenly, growing frightened, she turned first one way, then another, and could not find the way back to the river. Panic crept in, stealthily overtaking the frightened girl, and she scrambled through thick underbrush and briars, still clutching the basket, pushing her way to somewhere, she did not know where.

Like fingers of some devil, thorns clutched at her clothing, tearing at her dress, causing her to get angry. Elizabeth tried to blink back tears of frustration, and finally rested for a moment under a large pine tree. Attempting to calm herself, trying to remember in which direction the river must be, she sat trembling upon the ground, gasping for breath, her chest heaving, and her heart pounding loudly in her ears. If only she could find the river, Elizabeth knew she would be safe, but the lush growth of trees and brush prevented the girl from seeing more than twenty feet away.

The afternoon sun grew warm as the day wore on. By now, Elizabeth was in total panic, as she still tried in vain to find her way out of the trees and underbrush. She was getting thirsty and terribly tired. Eventually giving up, with a desperate little cry, the distraught girl sank upon a fallen log and dissolved into tears.

"Why was I so foolish?" she reprimanded herself out loud. "Why did I not remember the way? I should have listened to the warnings of those at the Fort about not going out alone."

She rested her forehead against the tree in utter dissolution as the panic spread in earnest. By now, tears stained her face, and she lost control, fearing she would never find her way home. She wished that she could transform the past few hours and magically be back to the safety of her room. Oh, if only!

All of a sudden, the forest grew frightfully silent, as birds stopped their twittering, and all became deathly still. Elizabeth became even further alarmed, as if she could get any more upset than she already was.

Thinking she heard a sound off to her right, and straining her ears, the small frightened girl scarcely drew a breath. There! Again! A twig snapped, and there was a rustling in the brush. At this, the color drained completely from Elizabeth's face, and she felt about to faint. With her heart pounding wildly, now she heard a crashing sound in the woods.

This time, the girl was sure it must be a bear or some other vicious wild animal! She whirled at the sound, and screamed hysterically as two buckskin clad figures came bounding toward her. Indians! Elizabeth screamed again, and her vision blurred, as she felt herself sinking to the ground. Great strong arms surrounded her and swooped her off the ground just as she fainted. Nathan cradled the limp girl to his breast and he gently patted her face.

"Elizabeth! Elizabeth, wake up. 'Tis I... Nathan... and Jonathan!"

The girl's eyes fluttered and opened. Nathan could see deep fear in those hazel eyes, and how quickly they changed the moment that she recognized him.

"Oh, Nathan! Thank God!" She threw her arms around his neck and hung desperately to him.

Nathan enfolded her more tightly, not wanting to release the trembling girl, for it felt so right and wonderful to hold her close.

"'Tis all right, you are safe now," he murmured, his lips against the girl's golden hair.

After a time, Elizabeth slowly drew back, her eyes glistening, lips trembling, and the pathetic look she gave melted Nathan's heart.

"I was lost! I could not find my way back to the river. Oh! Nathan! I was so frightened." Her voice was shaking. She glanced at Jonathan, who was standing close, leaning on his long rifle. "How did you find me?"

Reluctantly, Nathan slowly released the girl and helped her to her feet. "Jonathan saw fresh footprints in the sandy path near the river, and noticed that it was a small foot, with a square heel. Surely a woman's foot, and all alone, too. He saw where the prints went into the woods, but never came back out to the path. We followed your trail and noticed that you must have been confused, going in a circle, and were probably lost. Then we found you."

"Oh, I am so grateful!" The girl looked from one to the other. "I thought I heard a bear, then when I saw your buckskin clothing, I was sure that you were savages, and I guess I fainted."

She approached Nathan, and again threw her arms around his neck, hugging him. Then, standing on tiptoe, she kissed him on his cheek, and turned, doing the same to Jonathan.

"Thank you," she breathed. Nathan took Elizabeth by the arm and helped to guide her back to the pathway, relishing the very touch of her. He would never forget her embrace, nor the kiss she gave him on his cheek. Jonathan carried the basket of flowers until they reached the path where they left the travois. All three entered the fort together.

"Please do not tell my father about this. He would be furious with me." Elizabeth's eyes pleaded as she approached her quarters. But it was too late, for Captain Wood met them at the door, concern clouded on his face.

"Elizabeth?" He need not ask further, for his brows were skewed in a puzzled manner.

"Papa, you remember Nathan and Jonathan Herrington, don't you?"

The older man nodded.

Elizabeth briefly told her father of the near disastrous adventure that she took to gather flowers. He could not help but admonish the wayward girl for her foolishness of the moment, but then reached out a warm hand to greet the two woodsmen.

"I am beholden to you both for rescuing my daughter. Please forgive her thoughtless behavior. I swear she really does know better than to go out alone. It was a foolish thing to do, and perhaps she has learned a valuable lesson. I do not know how I can repay you for bringing her back. Gentlemen, please come inside."

Chapter Fourteen

C aptain Wood would have it no other way but that the two young men should join them that evening at the banquet. Once there, they were introduced to General Braddock and the other officers. Both men were quiet and a bit ill at ease as Captain Wood explained how they had rescued his daughter that day. The two woodsmen blushed with an awkward embarrassment despite how warmly they were accepted, as the other officers and men at the tables good-naturedly clapped each on his back, and pushed tankards of ale into the brothers' hands.

During dinner, Nathan and Jonathan were seated at the middle of the long table beside Captain Wood, while Elizabeth was at the far end of the long expanse, with General Braddock at one elbow and Colonel Innes at the other. Nathan watched the girl's face as it was bathed by the glow of soft candlelight. She was animated and smiling as she chatted with her dinner companions. Nathan couldn't help but admire her regal bearing, and noted she was not the least bit intimidated by the presence of such a high-ranking personage as the General.

From time to time, Elizabeth's gaze also wandered Nathan's way, and their eyes would meet. There was an instant bonding, and her eyes noticeably mellowed when she met his gaze. Nathan's heart leaped within him, as he dared to interpret that look. The softness of the candlelight danced in her eyes as Elizabeth's gaze boldly lingered on his. Nathan scarcely touched his meal, for his mind was racing, trying to assess the meaning of those glances, hoping beyond hope that it meant she thought of him as special.

Jonathan was saying something, jolting Nathan out of his daydream. Tearing his eyes away from the far end of the table, the young frontiersman tried to exchange pleasantries with those seated near him, and Nathan attempted to concentrate on the conversation at hand.

"I have not noticed any increased activity of the redskins up on the mountain," Jonathan was saying. "But I certainly will keep a sharp eye out this summer."

"I think there will be Hell to pay, for we have reports of the French and their renegade Indians making a lot of trouble on the border," Captain Wood was saying. "There have been occasional strikes against some of the settlers' cabins, and some mighty gruesome murders. More and more people are coming west, and soon they will be going over the mountains. We have to protect them."

Jonathan nodded, silently mulling over the news. The discussion continued for some time. At last, General Braddock rose, and lifting his glass, turned toward Elizabeth.

"Gentlemen: To the lovely lady, a toast for bringing a great bit of charm, civility, and beauty to this gathering."

He bowed to Elizabeth, and quickly all the men rose, their glasses held high in her direction.

"To the Lady," they all said in unison.

Nathan locked his gaze upon Elizabeth's, as again their eyes met, and he smiled, lifting his glass and tilting his head to her. He saw color rise slowly to her cheeks, and noticed that her return look did not falter, but held his, and she smiled back at him. His heart was lost forever that night, as the borderman realized he was totally in love with this golden-haired lass. The moment was forever etched upon his mind.

"Thank you, Gentlemen," Elizabeth said softly in a breathless voice, as she rose from her chair. "I shall leave you all to your military talk," and she tilted her head and curtsied to the assembly. "Good night, Gentlemen."

With that, she swept from the hall, glancing back over her shoulder to meet Nathan's eyes. She smiled again, and his heart leaped, as warmth filled his chest.

With difficulty, Nathan returned his attention to General Braddock and tried to concentrate on what was being said, though he really wanted to push back his chair and follow Elizabeth out of the hall.

The General continued, "As of today, I am renaming this fort. From this point on, it shall be named Fort Cumberland. A far more formidable name, I dare say, suited to the grandeur most befitting this great, solid edifice."

He paused, letting the idea sink in. "Now, Gentlemen, to the task at hand.... The French occupy Fort Duquesne, at the fork of the Monongahela and Allegheny rivers, and we need to establish a presence there ourselves. We are commissioned to build a military road from our Fort Cumberland, over the mountains to the Ohio River. A road on which we will be able to transport military supplies and troops quickly. That is our mission, Gentlemen!" The General said in a forceful and gruff voice. "In order to do that, we will need the assistance of the Colonists as well as our own military troops. So, by the order of His Majesty, The King, I am to conscript militia men to temporarily serve with His Majesty's brigade."

Turning to Nathan and Jonathan, the General directed his next remarks straight to them. "It has been brought to my attention that you, Jonathan Herrington, have quite a reputation as a borderman, woodsman, tracker, hunter, and rifleman."

Jonathan moved uneasily in his seat, looking down at the table before him, slightly embarrassed by the attention, and the fact that all eyes were presently upon him. He was far more comfortable alone in the woods with his rifle than being the focus of attention.

The General continued, "It would be our pleasure, Sir, if you would be in charge of enlisting the Militia troops which we will need for this project."

Jonathan was flattered, and slowly rose from his chair. "General Braddock, Sir, I would be honored to help in any way to drive the French out of the area. If building the supply road would help speed up that process, please count me in."

He paused, taking a deep breath. "However, Sir, I will need my brother Nathan's help. We are a team, you see. Inseparable." Grinning, Jonathan looked fondly toward his twin. "It's two for one, or none, General!"

The General nodded. "Done, Sir! Please report tomorrow, and I shall lay out the details."

With that, the assembly was dismissed, and the two bordermen retired from the hall, going out into the cool evening air. A half moon was rising over the brow of the mountain, illuminating a shimmering, soft scene, and the two slowly strolled down to the river. Silver slivers reflected off the water, and the trees took on ghostly shapes in the muted light. Dark shadows seemed to move and stretch in unimaginable shapes, giving an eerie quality to the landscape.

Jonathan sat on a log and took out his pipe, offering Nathan tobacco from his pouch. The two lit their pipes and sat smoking quietly for a long time. Each time they drew from their pipe stems, a small orange glow appeared in the bowl of the pipe. The brothers were bound together by a great love for each other, and were so in tune to each other that they seldom needed to speak, for each knew the other's thoughts so well.

Nathan finally broke the silence. "How far is it to the Ohio River?" he asked, a wisp of pipe smoke curling about his head.

"Depends on how you cut over the mountain range, but I allow as how it would be some hundred miles, give or take."

"It sounds like a huge undertaking to me, building a road that far. And over the mountain range, you say?"

Jonathan nodded, mulling over in his mind how he was going to gather the number of men and equipment needed to fill the roster.

"We will find out more tomorrow when we meet with the General."

Nathan stretched and yawned, looking back toward the fort. It stood as a silent sentinel in the semi-light, the silvery edifice resembling a shadowy castle. The block-houses at the corners could have been castle turrets. Nathan wished he had a white horse on which to ride through the gates, and sweep the Princess Elizabeth Wood off to a secret place in the forest. He smiled to himself, knowing that such a wild daydream surely was an indication that he was losing his mind! And all because of a wonderful, golden haired girl, who at this very moment was sleeping behind those castle walls. His heart warmed at the thought, and Nathan felt it fill his chest to bursting.

Jackie Gould

Chapter Fifteen

Elizabeth sat on the front stoop for a long time after she returned from the banquet hoping... no... even more than that, wishing that Nathan would come to her. She thrilled every time that she recounted when their eyes had met that evening. A special spark seemed to jump to her when she saw Nathan looking at her. The young girl had tried to carry on a normal conversation with her dinner companion, General Braddock, but had to admit that her mind was on the opposite side of the table.

Elizabeth was happy that she had forgone her black mourning dress in favor of the light blue gown she wore that evening. Her father had given her his approval to come out of mourning a few days ago. She had been surprised and pleased to find that Nathan and Jonathan were included as dinner guests. Taking great care, she had fastened her long blond hair up, and adorned it with matching blue ribbons, which fell from a tiny lace cap. She had pinched her cheeks to bring out a glow to her face, and knew that the soft candlelight was most becoming to her. From time to time, she had bitten her lips discreetly to cause them to have a rosy gloss that framed her mouth.

The young girl had hardly been able to keep her eyes from wandering to Nathan's, and Elizabeth had felt her insides warm at his gaze again and again. His dark eyes seemed especially large, and she noticed a mellow sparkle in them, which she hoped was meant just for her. She could feel herself melting under each glance and by the end of the evening, was sure she was falling in love. A giddy, whirling exuberance filled her very being, as waves of excitement washed over her.

When Elizabeth had left the table and bade good night, she glanced back over her shoulder at Nathan and smiled, sure that he would come to her. But now, as she watched the half-moon peek over the stockade walls, and the hour grow late, a feeling of disappointment replaced her anticipation.

Elizabeth's thoughts wandered to the events of the day, recalling the panic she had felt when realizing she had been lost in the woods. Again, she experienced the terror of sighting two buckskin clad figures rushing toward her, and even now, felt a sensation of faintness when recalling being swept up in Nathan's strong arms. She remembered the feel of warmth and strength when those sinewy arms enfolded her and lifted her up. She had been powerless to move, and was limp as a rag in Nathan's embrace. She remembered coming to, and the surge of relief that came when recognizing Nathan. She recalled clinging to him, trembling with emotion. Had she been too forward when she had reached up and kissed his cheek?

With a sigh, Elizabeth turned and retired to her room. There, she carefully put away her blue gown and donned a long nightdress. Brushing her long hair, she left it loose, letting it flow over her shoulders to her waist. Blowing out the candles, the girl paused by the window before climbing into bed, and as her eyes adjusted to the darkness, thought she saw two shadowy figures move past the opposite wall, but was not sure in the dim light. She heard her father come into the adjoining room and listened as his door closed.

Disappointment still tugged at her heart as Elizabeth climbed beneath the covers and snuggled into her bed. But sleep was not possible, for images of Nathan's handsome, square-jawed face invaded her consciousness. Try as she might, she could not get the memory of his flashing dark eyes from her mind. Each time Nathan's image came back to her, the young girl thrilled again and again, and fell more deeply in love.

Elizabeth thought that she had not slept at all, yet the next thing she knew, light was creeping into the window, and she heard the fort stirring to life. The slim girl rose, bathed her face and brushed out her hair, fastening it back with a ribbon and cap. Donning a simple green dress and apron, she proceeded to make breakfast, her heart singing, and her spirits high. Surely, she would see Nathan and Jonathan today.

❧

The two bordermen met with General Braddock for most of the morning. It would be a formidable task, they found out, for upward of two thousand men were needed for the expedition. Less than half would be military. Supplies had to be assembled, including wagons, tools, horses, mules, and oxen. They guessed that it would take two months, at least, before they would be ready. The General wanted to begin in early June, giving Jonathan what he felt was ample time to amass the necessary men.

"Herrington," the General boomed, addressing Jonathan. "You will undoubtedly need a horse and other gear. Go to the quartermaster and pick out what you need. I will personally sign the requisition for anything that is required. You and your brother decide between you how best to assemble the Colonists. You can use the grounds south of the fort to set up a staging

area. Place tents there where the recruits can be temporarily housed. Be sure that they bring their weapons,
blankets, and any tools or wagons they might have. If
you have any questions, Captain Wood will be your
direct contact, and you will report to him. Good luck."

With that, General Braddock dismissed the two,
and they emerged from the meeting into the courtyard
just as a dark spring cloud rolled overhead. A sudden,
brief shower quickly turned the open area into a
quagmire. Hastily taking shelter under an overhanging
porch roof, the pair watched hail stones pop and jump
in front of them, making a clattering noise against the
wood shingles. A door opened behind them, but they
did not hear Elizabeth's light footsteps as she
approached the porch rail.

"Nathan! Jonathan!" she called, above the noise of
the storm. "Come in out of the rain."

The wind whipped raindrops onto the porch as she
spoke, and the girl had to hold her skirt to keep it from
billowing about. The two men ducked their heads as
they followed Elizabeth through the low doorway,
brushing the wetness from their buckskin clothing
before seating themselves.

"I was about to make lunch. Won't you please
stay?"

Shyly, she looked from one to the other, satisfying
herself that she could pick Nathan out as the twin who

was seated nearest the door, and her eyes lingered on his face.

"That would indeed be a great pleasure, Miss Elizabeth, if it is not a bother for you," Nathan said quickly before his brother had a chance to decline. At the same time, he returned her intense gaze with a bold look of his own.

"No bother in the least! Please make yourselves comfortable, gentlemen, while I prepare something for you."

Nathan leaped to his feet. "May I help you in some way, Elizabeth?"

The girl smiled broadly and shook her head. "Thank you, but no... I shall be but a moment."

It was not long before Elizabeth brought a tray of freshly sliced bread, meat and cheese, placing it on a table in the corner of the room. She poured mugs of hot tea.

"It turned so cool after the rain, I thought perhaps you two would care for some hot English tea."

Nathan was quick to respond. "I fear we have had scarce little of that luxury in our mountain home. Indeed, what a delicious pleasure. Right, Jonathan?"

Jonathan nodded, politely, but failed to explain that he had been away from the habit of enjoying English tea for so many years, that he had actually outgrown the desire. However, after taking a couple of swallows of the strong brew, he felt a twinge of the old, warm feeling as he let it travel down his throat. For a fleeting moment, Jonathan regretted his lonely woodsman life, and could have hoped for a more civilized existence. But that feeling soon faded.

Nathan proceeded to tell Elizabeth about the assignment that General Braddock had bestowed upon them. He explained the task of gathering men and supplies, and her eyes grew wide with excitement when he told of having to work in the fort area for the next few months. Elizabeth's heart jumped for joy, knowing that he would be close at hand, and she relished the fact that they might see each other often.

By the way he was looking at her, the young girl was certain that Nathan's interest in the expedition somehow included her, though neither had been so bold as to speak of feelings for each other yet. Secretly, Elizabeth smiled to herself, and excusing herself, almost skipped to the kitchen area where later she reappeared bearing a plate of little cakes to place in front of the men.

Chapter Sixteen

Nathan felt embarrassed when he discovered in their conversation that Elizabeth's mother had passed away during the long winter. *What a clumsy, arrogant fool I have been!* Nathan reprimanded himself, *for not realizing what Elizabeth must have gone through in her grief.*

"Forgive me, Elizabeth," Nathan said, wanting more than anything to take her little hands in his... but not daring to touch this fair girl in his awkward embarrassment. "I had no idea that your dear mother had gone on."

"Of course, you could not have known," Elizabeth breathed, her voice choking slightly, and her eyes becoming misty. "Mother passed on last January of consumption. I nursed her for weeks after the Christmas Festival but nothing we nor the medical officer did could have saved my dear one's life."

This time Nathan reached out a warm, compassionate hand to lay atop Elizabeth's. "Please accept our deepest condolences," he said in a slightly strained voice. Jonathan also murmured his sympathy, and observed with a keen eye the attachment he knew that Nathan was showing for the golden haired girl.

With her lashes lowered for fear that the men could see the tears that welled from too fresh a grief, she softly murmured her thanks. With effort, she gave a brave smile, and changed the subject, wanting to hear more of the details of the road building project.

Jonathan cleared his throat and related the challenge that lay ahead, of recruiting Colonists, and procuring supplies. "Your father, Captain Wood, to whom we are to report... has he told you of the expedition?" Jonathan looked closely at Elizabeth as he spoke.

Shaking her head no, the young girl said in a low voice, "My father has been very distant since Mother's passing. He rarely speaks to me of anything, and spends most of his time at headquarters, arriving home late into the night."

This time a tear slipped down the girl's cheek. "I have been very lonely." It was uttered in a small, choking voice, barely audible.

Nathan's heart nearly broke for her then. He wanted to take Elizabeth into his arms and hold her close, to blot out that great sorrow she must be suffering. *Blast the old man!* he thought. *He could at least be here for her!*

Jonathan rose and headed for the door.

"Thank you, Miss Elizabeth, for your most gracious repast. I... we must be going, for I need to go to the quartermaster for a horse and supplies. Our assignment starts at once," Jonathan said, his cap in one hand, and extending the other to her.

Nathan followed reluctantly, and turning at the doorway, grasped Elizabeth's hand in both of his. He looked deeply into the girl's eyes and bent to kiss her slim fingers.

"Elizabeth... may... may I come calling on you soon? I should not like it, knowing that you are alone so much."

Again, tears welled in Elizabeth's eyes, and Nathan could see a grateful sense of relief come over her face. However, he could not have known that at that moment, her heart gave a lurch as she whispered, "Yes... yes, Nathan, please do come to call. I should like that very much." He only knew that he strode onto the parade grounds elated, and he felt ten feet tall.

❧

While Jonathan left Fort Cumberland on his mission of recruitment, Nathan, with the help of the British soldiers, set up a temporary camp outside the fort. Tents were erected in anticipation of both civilian and army troops which would swell the work force to almost two thousand bodies before General Braddock would be satisfied.

The General barked orders and became overbearing in his demands, for his temper was short, and he stubbornly demanded that the newly recruited Colonists learn how to march and drill. He attempted to have his soldiers teach the rough country men how to fight the British way by lining up in a civilized military manner. The Colonists only ended up jeering at the conventional military nonsense way of fighting, and tried to explain that in Indian country you best hide behind trees and brush, or else you will never see the fort again.

"Get me some different men!" the General bellowed at Jonathan one day. "These crude, rough, idiots will not learn how to be soldiers!"

Jonathan and Nathan cringed at the arrogance and hot temper of the man.

"Doesn't the General have any idea of how to fight in the wilderness?" Nathan asked in a hushed voice into his brother's ear.

"Looks as though he is stubborn and will not learn. But you, my dear brother, have never met the French and Indians yourself. They fight from every bush and tree trunk; on their bellies, and up in the branches, behind every log."

Nathan shivered, remembering some of the stories that Jonathan had told him over the long winter. "Heaven help us," he thought.

❧

It was almost a week after Jonathan's first departure when Nathan found time to call on Elizabeth. Indeed, he had intended to see her much sooner, however the demands of his duties prevented him from carrying out those precious wishes until this night. Even though he was wildly busy during those days, that had not prevented his mind from being constantly upon the girl. So, it was with great anticipation that he approached her doorway on one early summer evening.

Elizabeth was opening the door just as Nathan raised his hand to knock. They were both startled, stepping back, surprise echoing in their faces.

"Oh! Nathan, how good it is to see you," Elizabeth blurted out, finally stepping forward onto the porch. "I was about to venture onto the stoop to watch the sunset."

"I did not intend to startle you, Elizabeth. This is the first chance I have had to pay you a visit. I hope I did not come at a bad time?"

Nathan removed his cap, and stood awkwardly in front of the girl. Already, his heart was thumping rapidly under his rib cage, and his breath seemed caught in his throat.

"Of course not. Come, shall we sit on the steps?" Elizabeth said sweetly, taking his hand, and moving to the edge of the porch. There, she took a seat on the top step. Nathan rested his back against the opposite post so he could watch both Elizabeth and the sunset at the same time. He hardly could take his eyes off her wonderful profile. At first, they both gazed in silence as the sky blazed with rosy-peach colors, tracing edges of the wispy clouds. A brilliant robin's-egg blue shone between the ribbons of color. At each moment, the rose color changed from a peachy tint to crimson and orange, then almost to a blood red, before finally fading to lavender.

"It is almost too beautiful to disturb with conversation, don't you agree, Nathan?" Elizabeth whispered with reverence, referring to the majesty of the sunset.

"'Tis true, Lass," Nathan murmured, still captivated by the colorful sight before him. "But nothing compares to..." he broke off in mid sentence.

"To what, Nathan?"

His dark eyes looked boldly over at Elizabeth, hoping he was not being too forward as he continued. He took a gulp and went on. "To... to your beauty, Elizabeth!" he blurted out.

Color rose to the girl's cheeks, and she caught her breath. Momentarily, she dropped her eyes, studying her fingers, which lay in her lap. Her heart thudded, and there was an awkward silence as she grappled with Nathan's exclamation. She did not know how to reply, for words would not come to her. There was a rush of emotion that filled her, and she was left mute for the moment.

"Forgive me, Elizabeth! I should not have spoken so boldly. I meant it only as the highest kind of compliment. Do not think me brash, for... for I care for you!"

There, he had blurted out what was on his heart. But he was puzzled at her lack of response.

With her eyes still lowered, Elizabeth said in a shuddering whisper, which could barely be heard, "You are feeling only pity for me, Nathan. Pity because my mother has died... and my father has... has left me almost alone."

The girl could hardly speak, for sobs were choking her very words. Pent-up emotions she had held for too long now burst forth and she hated the tears that she could not stop.

"'Tis not pity! I truly care for you! I... I am in love with you, Elizabeth Wood!" Nathan cried out in desperation, wanting more than anything to rush to her side and gather the trembling girl into his arms. He wanted to hold her close, to assure her that he was sincere. But it was as if he was frozen to the very spot. And the world crashed around him when Elizabeth, with tears streaming down her face, gave a muffled cry, and fled to her room, leaving Nathan totally bewildered.

"Idiot!" he screamed to himself. "Now I have done it! I have spoiled any chances I ever dreamed of having that this sweet girl might care for me, too." His fist hit the porch rail in a rage, and Nathan stalked off into the twilight.

Chapter Seventeen

A s soon as Elizabeth closed the door of her room, she regretted having left Nathan, and knew she had made a horrible mistake. Throwing herself across the bed, the distraught girl gave way to sobs, as wave after wave of pent-up feelings were unleashed. A terrible longing tore at her chest, and her stomach was tied in knots, till the sobbing girl thought she would be turned inside out.

"Oh, Nathan! I love you! I truly do love you. And I want you to love me too, but not out of pity for a poor lonely girl. I want you to love me as a woman, with all your heart!" she sobbed.

"Why did I run away when he said he loved me?" Elizabeth was thinking out loud. "I have longed for and dared hope for that moment for months. But I am sure he only uttered those words out of pity for my situation. I cannot bear to think he was only trying to be kind. Oh, Lord, I cannot bear this! I wish I were dead!"

Again, sobs wracked her body, and Elizabeth clawed at the bed covers, till she almost tore the cloth. How long she lay there in the darkness, she did not know, yet she could not stop the sobs, and her head filled with a pounding ache.

Exhausted, the poor girl finally fell into a fitful sleep, with Nathan's name on her lips. Soon, in her dreams, she was being chased by a tall man, whom she could not identify. Dashing through trees and bramble bushes, she ran, terror gripping every part of her body. Somehow, a heavy burden seemed to weigh her down. Ahead, the young girl could see the fort; however, the faster she ran in her dream, the farther away the fort appeared to be. Thundering behind her, the huge frightening figure of a man gained on her as she struggled to run.

Still in her dream, Elizabeth was floating now, out of control, her feet not touching the ground. Ahead, the friendly walls of the fort meant safety, but she could not find the entrance, for there were only the heavy log posts, no doorway. Frantic, Elizabeth screamed, "Nathan! Nathan! Let me in!"

At that moment in the dream, a hand clutched at her long blond hair, and her hair broke off, leaving

Elizabeth with only skin-tight curls atop her head. Rows of laughing settlers were lined up on each side of the pathway, chiding her as she ran between them. She seemed to have a bundle in her arms, which the others wanted to grab from her.

Finally, the dream faded, and Elizabeth awoke, shaking, with a feeling of despair and foreboding filling her heart. The remainder of the night held nothing but scary, dark shadows for the girl, as she cowered under the bed coverings, trembling with fear and desperate longing. She wished she could relive last night's visit by Nathan. Oh, if only she could change what had transpired between them! She would not have been so shy. She would have gladly accepted his declaration of love, and returned the sentiment twelvefold. Oh, if only!

Elizabeth could not shake the dark dream, for even when dawn colored the eastern sky, relief would not come. The following day, she moved as if in a trance, the dream being a heavy presence from which she could not escape. A helpless feeling of sadness overwhelmed her as she went through the motions of her daily duties.

How can I face Nathan? Elizabeth thought. *Surely he will never return here now, for though I want to believe what he said was the truth, that he loves me, I fear those words were just so many words, coming from a deep sense of pity.* A dark anguish continued to spread over her, which she could not shake. *He pities me, for I am all alone. Would that his words were true! But I cannot believe they are, for he cannot be burdened by a girl such as I, almost an orphan. A girl who is virtually alone in this strange country. A girl whose father has practically abandoned her!*

Elizabeth felt overwhelmed with the realization that her father had stopped loving her ever since the death of her mother. Now, when hoping beyond hope that Nathan might care for her, she discovered that his love was one borne out of pity for her, not the kind of love that she wanted and longed for. In fact, she was positive that Nathan's declaration of affection was strictly a reaction to her plight of loneliness. A feeling of total abandonment overtook the girl, and she fell deeper into despair.

Nathan, meanwhile, fell into his own dark mood, carrying out his duties reluctantly. He snapped at some of the settlers and frontiersmen when they did not comply quickly enough to his directions. While setting up more tents, he pounded the tent stakes so hard, they splintered. Cursing, he had to replace them. Jonathan happened along just as Nathan was returning with more wood stakes, and noticed the icy reception he received from his brother. Dismounting, Jonathan placed a hand on Nathan's arm. Nathan shrugged it off, a dark expression brooding on his face.

"What in the world has gotten into you?" Jonathan asked, a frown furrowing his brow.

"Nothing!"

"Don't try to fool me. You certainly are in a foul mood, and are not hiding it very well. Tell me what is the matter."

Nathan's lips were tightly closed in a grim straight line.

"Come, on," Jonathan uttered, "let's take a walk down by the river. Looks like you need to cool off." He turned on his heel.

Nathan followed his brother reluctantly down the trail to the river. There the two perched upon a rock and sat in silence for some time. Jonathan knew that Nathan would speak when he was good and ready, and not before. Idly, he tossed some stones into the water, waiting for Nathan to calm himself enough to tell what was wrong, for surely something huge had caused Nathan's usual even-tempered manner to snap to such anger. They were away from the din of the fort, and only the sounds of the forest leaves rustling in the breeze and the river gurgling over pebbly rocks could be heard. A huge horsefly was buzzing nearby.

After some time had passed, Nathan muttered, "My stupid fault!"

Jonathan's eyebrows raised in question.

"I was dumb... stupid... an idiot!" Nathan spit the words out in a disgusted barrage.

"Whoa there, brother, sounds bad. Tell me what you were stupid about."

Nathan threw a flat stone into the water, and watched it skip the surface five times before sinking below the ripples. With his head down, the troubled woodsman slowly started to relate the events of last evening.

"Elizabeth... I was dumb, stupid, an idiot!"

"You have already established that, what happened? What did you do to the lass?"

"I... I told her that I cared for her. I was... I was too forward... too brash, I guess. She just up and ran away to her quarters. She was crying."

"Did you force yourself upon her?" Jonathan was frowning deeply now.

"No... no, not that at all. It was just the sunset, and her beauty, and I blurted out that I was in love with her. She said my feelings were only because I pitied her for being so alone since her mother's demise. But that is not it at all. I truly am in love with that wonderful girl!"

Jonathan was bewildered.

Nathan continued, "I just came out with it too fast. I think I spoiled any chances that there might be with Elizabeth because she must hate me by now for being too forward."

"It does not make any sense that the lass should be angry with you. You were only telling her of your real feelings for her. You were being honest."

"That is what I am trying to tell myself, but now that I embarrassed myself by proclaiming my love for her, I will not be able to face her again." Nathan was distraught and beside himself.

"I think," Jonathan started slowly, "that it was really a misunderstanding. Perhaps I can find out the real story."

"Do you think so?" Nathan asked eagerly.

Jonathan nodded solemnly.

"Can you find out about what Elizabeth is thinking, and tell me the truth?" Nathan brightened a little.

"I'll do my best, little brother." With that, Jonathan playfully shoved Nathan off the rock, where he splashed into the shallow water, coming up sputtering.

"You! Come back here!" Nathan yelled after his twin, as Jonathan, his long legs pumping mightily, ran up the hill to the fort sending a hearty laugh back into the wind.

Chapter Eighteen

B y the first part of June, the expedition members had assembled and were ready to embark upon the monumental task of carving out the military supply road through the wilderness to French-held Fort Duquesne, ninety miles to the northwest. Horses, wagons, men and equipment queued up, and with great ceremony, the column, led by General Braddock, filed out of the fort on the first leg of their journey. The General, riding his magnificent black stallion, headed the long line of red-coat clad British troops and brown-clad Colonial Volunteers, who followed smartly down the pathway. It took upward of one half hour for the entire assemblage to file past.

Elizabeth watched from a vantage point close to the roadway, as her father, who looked neither right nor left, rode past. Again, a knot grew tight in her breast as the girl felt the snub of his indifference, and it cut like a knife. Tears burned her eyes, as the ignored girl watched the stern figure of her father disappear down the road, his shoulders ram rod straight.

"Oh, Father," she whispered desperately to herself. "Please look at me... can't you see how my heart is breaking? Don't you know I am lonely beyond description?"

She was empty. As empty as she had ever felt in her life. Soon, her hazel eyes were searching the rest of the column for two tall forms she knew must be there. Dust started to obscure some of the figures, and Elizabeth moved even closer for a better look.

Flintlock rifles and shovel handles were slung over the volunteers' shoulders, bobbing up and down in an uneven cadence, while muffled drums could be heard as their feet shuffled in the choking dust. Elizabeth strained and stood on tiptoe to catch a glimpse of the two buckskin-clad figures. There! On the far side, barely visible through the dusty haze, were the two woodsmen. She could not make out their facial features, and was unable to see if they were looking her way, searching for a sight of her. But once more, she was disappointed, for it appeared they were not trying to find her. Great despair slammed into her heart as she watched the two dark heads, which rose above the others, bob up and down and out of view.

Suddenly they were gone, and a deafening silence replaced the din of men and equipment, horses, and wagons. Now the shouts and loud deep voices were silent. No horses whinnied, nor stamped their feet. There was no clang now of metal, nor smell of campfires. No cursing or hoarse laughter. Only the soft moan of an early summer breeze as it wafted through the quiet buildings.

Elizabeth followed the path to the river in a hushed daze. She could not shake the feeling of doom and terrible loneliness that gripped and held her as if in a vise. Perching upon a rock, the young girl stared, unseeing, into the water, thoughts all a jumble in her head. Why, she asked herself, had she not been able to swallow her pride and go to the camp to seek out Nathan before it was too late? Why had she not gone to him to try to explain what was on her heart?

"I don't want your pity, Nathan. I want your heart for my own... and now you are gone." Tears spilled down her soft cheeks as she spoke out loud to the river. For a fleeting moment, Elizabeth wanted to rush down the path where the hundreds had marched into the gloomy forest, and catch up to the tall woodsman. She wanted to fling herself into his arms and cling to his muscular frame, all the while declaring her undying love for him. She ached to beg his forgiveness for being such a foolish girl, to explain that her pride had kept her away so long.

Doubts started to cloud Elizabeth's mind. Perhaps she had been right in the first place, for Nathan had never come close to her in the weeks before he left. Perhaps, she indeed had hit the nail on the head, and he was embarrassed at being caught in the lie of declaring his deep affection for her, only realizing later that it was really because he felt sorry for her. Then sadness overwhelmed the girl as she came to the awful conclusion that Nathan must surely have made the decision to forget her. The fact that he never came back to see her was proof to her that his words were only lightly given, in a moment of deep pity and sympathy for the grieving young woman.

"Oh, I cannot bear this!" Elizabeth groaned out loud. "My heart is breaking... Nathan! Nathan! How I love you! How foolish I was to run from you. Had I stayed that evening, would it have made any difference?"

Elizabeth wrestled with her ragged emotions, first twisting one way, then another and in the end was left in total confusion. Finally, her mind completely numb, the heartbroken girl collapsed upon the rock and dissolved into sobs.

How long she had lain there, Elizabeth could not tell, for there came a sound that roused her from her mind-numbing despair. The sharp snapping of a stick and the thud of horses' hooves jerked the tear-stained girl to alertness, and she slipped off the rock to take refuge behind a bush. Peering between thorny branches, she saw three figures on horseback approach the opposite riverbank and pull up to a halt.

To her horror, she recognized one as Lt. George Stillwell. He was flanked by two bronze Indian braves, riding bareback upon their paint ponies. Stillwell was not in uniform, but clearly, Elizabeth could not mistake the finely chiseled features of his face, the slim nose, and fine light hair. A shiver ran through the girl as she sensed that this British Officer was somehow casting a sinister figure. Why was he out of uniform? Why was he with those savages?

Elizabeth barely breathed as she watched the tall blond man study the ground and make some motions with his arms. He pointed and gestured, and without a word, the three carefully and quietly waded across the river at a point that kept an overhanging branch between them and the fort, and disappeared into the thick forest behind the stockade.

With her heart racing, Elizabeth flew up the path to the safety of those imposing huge stockade walls, and did not stop until she had slammed shut the door of her quarters. Trembling, the young woman sank into a chair by the window, and attempted to calm the fluttering that churned inside her. Her mind raced, and she tried to determine the reason for the unexplained reappearance of George Stillwell. Why were his actions so suspicious? Elizabeth only felt the cold hand of fear as she dealt with the scenario she had just witnessed. If he were not trying to hide something, then why did he not approach the fort by the usual route?

Shaking her head in disbelief, Elizabeth suddenly became aware of something that lay on the floor inside her door. Frowning, she slowly crossed the room, and picking up a folded piece of yellowed paper, turned it over several times, puzzled and a bit frightened. Where had this come from? Her eyes glanced to the door, and she determined that this piece of paper must have been shoved under the doorway, and in her rush to get inside, Elizabeth's skirt must have scattered it in to the room. Slowly unfolding the paper, Elizabeth began to read:

> *My Dearest Elizabeth;*
> *I cannot leave on our long assignment without attempting to right what appears to be a horrible misunderstanding. At our last meeting several weeks ago, during a lovely twilight encounter, what I said to you was the truth. I am helplessly in love with you.*
> *I have dreamed of nothing but your beautiful face for months, and how I was going to try to tell you of my feelings for you. I planned and dreamed of the*

perfect way, but it just all came out in a rush. Now, I fear I have lost you forever, because I was too brash.

I even hesitate to write this letter; however, I cannot leave on this journey, no matter what you think of me, without telling you from my heart... I love you, Lass. Though I may be unworthy, my heart is filled with love for you, and I cannot even dare hope that you somehow might care for me a little. My thoughts and my love will be with you always, my sweet Elizabeth.

However you must think of me now, I shall love you until the day I die. If you can find it in your heart to forgive my blundering, blunt admission of affection, I shall be ever thankful, and would be at peace.

Your servant, Nathan Herrington June 1, 1755

Tears flowed in earnest then as Elizabeth hugged the letter to her breast.

Jackie Gould

Chapter Nineteen

Nathan and Jonathan strode side by side along the roadway as they left the fort behind. The trail was dusty, and Colonist regulars were soon coughing and choking as they brought up the rear ranks. There was a muffled shuffling sound interspersed with the jangle of metal and squeak of leather. Low voices mumbled words that could not be distinguished except for an occasional outburst of profanity, as the entourage trudged forward.

The afternoon wore on and grew hot, and dust continued to rise in choking clouds, while thousands of feet churned up the dry ground. Soon, the going slowed, as the lead troops had to hack their way through the ever thickening forest. Men, animals, and wagons groaned their way out of the valley toward the mountain range.

"God's heart! I can't even spit in this dust!" a grizzled old Colonist said, with a mighty emphasis. "Don't dare to! Might come out a mud ball!" He ended with a choking fit of coughing.

The sun was a hot, white sphere of light flashing between leaf-laden branches of oak and walnut trees. Nathan was happy for any patch of shade as the column snaked its way forward. Soon, they were using picks and shovels, carving out the roadway, smoothing a wide avenue in the wilderness. Nathan worked methodically, his mind a few miles back at the walled fort, wondering if Elizabeth had found his letter. The young frontiersman had searched for her face in the crowd when they left the fort, but did not catch a glimpse of her. There had been only a short bit of time to run to her quarters and slip the letter beneath her doorway as the expedition was taking off. He felt disappointed that he had not been able to speak with her, and a certain sadness now crept over him as he trudged along.

By now, surely she should have read the note. Nathan's heart swelled with love for the golden-haired lass, and he dared hope that she would one day return that love. "Perhaps time will heal all," he mused to himself, swinging a pick ax and dislodging a large stone from the roadway. He tried to convince himself that once the road building project was completed, he could return to the fort, and perhaps, if the Heavens allowed, Elizabeth would accept his love.

Nathan stopped to mop his brow, and looked back along the road toward the fort, now some five miles distant. It was like a dark tunnel, looking down that road, for tree branches met above, forming a canopy of dark green shade. A mixture of hickory, oak, walnut and maple trees, and an occasional pine tree towering above as a sentinel choked the way. Nathan longed to trot back down that road to Elizabeth's side, but realized the folly of such a thought, so he resigned himself to the task at hand.

"Time... give it time," he said out loud.

"What did you say?" Jonathan asked, working a few feet from his brother.

Nathan shook his head. "Oh, nothing, just thinking out loud."

Jonathan knew without even asking that his twin was thinking of the girl back at the fort. He heaved a sigh, and silently his heart ached for Nathan's anguish. He, Jonathan, knew only too well the heartbreak of a lost love. It was not fair, he thought to himself, for his brother had already lost his first love, Sarah, to a horrible accident. How happy Jonathan had been lately that his brother had now found a new love, one to replace the devastation of that tragic loss. But now there seemed to be an insurmountable obstacle between those two.

If only he, Jonathan, could think of some way to help them. Perhaps if he could put his mind to it, he could hatch a plan to get the two together. He resolved at that moment to make that his first priority. He loved his brother, and would do anything to see to his happiness.

❧

By the end of the third day, the expedition had only traveled nine miles. It took much longer than anyone expected, for the British Command demanded that bridges be built across every stream and gully, and causeways be created over swampy areas. Besides, every bump had to be smoothed, and every rock removed from the right-of-way. Great trees were felled, stripped, and cut for the crossways, leaving a twelve-foot-wide road, smoothed and leveled. At the beginning of the second week, they endured three days of steady rain, which stopped the entourage and turned everything into a muddy, slippery quagmire, halting wagons, men and livestock.

Thanks to Jonathan's knowledge of wilderness living, he and Nathan took refuge under a quickly erected lean-to on a rise above the roadway, away from the main body of the camp. While those two were snug and dry, most of the other men were miserable, soaked to the skin, and unable to even make a fire to warm a meal. One night, as the relentless rain pattered down outside their shelter, Nathan entreated his brother to tell the tale of the Indian Girl named Blue Water. So, reluctantly, painfully, Jonathan began to narrate the story that he had kept so tightly locked within his breast.

"Well, as you know, I had been captured by the Indians while trying to rescue two white young 'uns," Jonathan began. "I was unconscious for two days, and when I finally awoke, I found myself a prisoner of the Delaware Chief. There was a disagreement amongst his council, for some wanted to kill me immediately, and others were reluctant to do so. They wrangled with each other. All the while, I got the mighty Fever, and knew not how many days, nor even weeks had passed that I was held captive.

"The Chief's daughter, Blue Water, nursed me back to health. She would not leave my side, putting herb poultices on my wound, and hand-feeding me soups and stews which she had made. Slowly, after many weeks, I began to get my strength back. I was weak as a babe at first, but Blue Water helped me... made me get up and walk... forced me to bathe in the icy river." Jonathan paused, re-lit his long stemmed pipe and continued.

"There were still those in the village who wanted my scalp, but Blue Water protected me, claimed me as hers, and being the Chief's daughter, no other could touch me. Gradually, I became stronger, and went for longer walks into the forest.... but not alone. Blue Water was always by my side. I was never allowed to be alone." Here he stopped for a moment, then continued on wistfully. "She was incredibly beautiful, with her raven hair, and great shining dark eyes."

Again there was a pause, as Jonathan brought the picture to his mind.

"Well, I fell head over teakettle in love with this wild girl, who was as free as a bird, who ran and laughed and got such joy out of every bit of life. She taught me to revere Mother Earth and Father Sun, and the miracles of natural things. Like grass and plants and trees. Blue Water taught me how to extract all that is necessary to fulfill any need from the earth.

"It turned out that she wanted me for her husband, and I did not put up much resistance, so she took me to her lodge... and we were married... Indian style. I became part of the Delaware Village... sort of. I was still closely watched, for the Indians thought I might someday try to make a run for it. They were right, indeed, for I watched my chances. I still meant to escape the village and get back to the white man's world. Even though I had lost my heart to the sweet Indian Maiden, and truly loved her with a love stronger than I could ever realize possible, I did not want to remain in the Delaware Village for the rest of my life."

Nathan listened with rapt attention, picturing the scenes that Jonathan's words were painting. It was unusual for Jonathan to speak at such length, for normally, he was quiet and reserved. Nathan did not utter a word for fear of breaking the spell. Jonathan shifted his position, stretching out his legs, and took a pull on his pipe. The ashes in the bowl turned orange, and a curl of blue-white smoke wafted around the borderman's head. The rain incessantly continued to patter and splash outside the lean-to with a steady cadence, and the dampness crept inside.

"I was completely happy, learning the Indian way of life," Jonathan began again. "So very happy living with and loving my Indian Bride, whom I adored. Yet, I knew in my heart, someday I would have to leave, for I could not, nor would not stay there forever.

"I was there a little over a year, all the while plotting in my mind how we would escape. Blue Water, it turned out, was willing to go with me, and we made secret plans to leave. One morning, I took my flintlock rifle, knife, and bow and arrows to go hunt, while Blue Water took a basket to pick berries. Inside the basket, she had hidden some provisions. We met in the forest, and ran for most of the day, as much as we could, for Blue Water was in her sixth month, big with my child.

"We knew the Delawares would be after us as soon as they discovered we were missing, so Blue Water taught me well how to cover our tracks. But not well enough, for on the fourth day, as Blue Water was resting near the edge of a waterfall on the river, I was across the water trying snare some rabbits. A small party, led by her father, the Chief, surprised her."

Jonathan paused, and gulped hard, his voice cracking. "She screamed, and put up a fight, even slashed her own father with the knife I had left with her. I could only watch helplessly from the cover of underbrush on the opposite side of the river, as they quickly cornered my black-haired beauty. Oh, how she fought, her dark eyes blazing, as she struggled, twisted, and lunged... and there I was, hopeless, for I could not reach her in time.

"I was sure they would capture her, and return her to the village, where, perhaps, I would be able to someday rescue her. But that was not to be, for in horror, I watched as my Beautiful Blue Water backed onto a rocky ledge, still slashing and fighting, like a caged cougar. I do not know if she was struck, or if she slipped, but with a warning scream caught in my throat, I saw her tumble over the edge and fall to the rocks below, striking her head before she disappeared into the foaming water."

There was a long pause, and Jonathan's throat tightened to a husky whisper. "The Chief found her a few feet downstream. His mournful howl was like a knife to my chest as he lifted her lifeless body above his head and screamed the death chant from the depths of his soul. I... I was struck numb, feeling my own life drain within me, for I loved my Indian Princess with all my heart."

Again, a long pause caused Nathan to hold his breath.

"So that is the end of my story, Nathan."

In the dark, a tear slipped over the rim of his eye, and slid down Jonathan's cheek. Nathan struggled with a wrenching feeling in his own throat, his heart now aching for Jonathan's loss. Rain continued to fall outside the lean-to, as both men fell silent, each deeply immersed in unthinkable thoughts.

Chapter Twenty

T he expedition inched forward, by this time well
spread out nearly a mile along the trail. The British
Officers, including General Braddock, refused to take
any advice from the knowledgeable Colonists regarding precautions to take against a possible attack by
Indians. It turned out that Braddock was stubborn and
arrogant, preferring to turn a deaf ear on all advice
from what he considered were lowly, ignorant Colonial
Irregulars. The man ignored all pleadings from the
colonial leaders including young George Washington,
the man who had surveyed the area two years prior,
and was now along on the expedition as an Aide de
Camp to General Braddock. Time and again, the tall
young surveyor tried to reason with the General to be

aware that Indians and French hid and fought from behind every tree and stump, and consequently, surprise would be the enemy's greatest strength. He entreated the General not to spread out so far in a single line, for they would easily get picked off, one by one.

Jonathan shook his head at the stupidity of the commanding officers. Many of the Colonial Irregulars had become alarmed at the way the expedition was being handled, and at first a few, then many turned their backs and returned down the road toward Fort Cumberland.

"Can't say as I blame them," Jonathan muttered. "The General seems Hell-bent on a suicide track. Well, the man is surely almost handing this expedition and all the men to the savages on a platter, it seems."

"Don't try to scare me, Jonathan. Are you toying with me, or are you serious?"

"Dead serious, my brother. All I can tell you is, keep your eyes peeled and watch for all the things I taught you. Notice every tree trunk and fallen log. Watch for a suspicious lump or bulge that could be an arm or a shoulder. Take notice of how the birds are acting, and listen for any strange sound or call you may hear. Above all, keep your rifle loaded and ready."

Nathan could not help the goosebumps that rose on his arms, sending the little hairs straight up. He swallowed hard, and glanced around into the dark recesses of the forest, sharpening his senses to be in tune with every leaf that swayed and branch that moved.

The expedition came to a halt on the third week out at a place called Little Meadows, where several men and officers fell ill with fever and dysentery. It was here that Braddock ordered Jonathan back to the fort to try to retrieve those Colonists who had deserted, promising to wait for him for one week.

Without mentioning it out loud, Nathan conveyed with one glance his desire for Jonathan to meet with Elizabeth and explain his position. Jonathan's returning gaze into his twin's eyes, and his sure handshake assured Nathan that he would indeed speak on the anguished young man's behalf when he, Jonathan, reached the fort. Nathan watched as Jonathan mounted a big bay gelding and disappeared down the road.

"Godspeed," Nathan breathed as Jonathan rode out of sight. Nathan's heart rode on that bay gelding with his brother as surely as if he were in the saddle himself.

❧

The newly built roadway was so smooth and easy that it only took Jonathan two days to traverse the sixty miles back to Fort Cumberland. He had to admit that the bridges and causeways that were so time-consuming to build were certainly time savers in travel now.

He alternated between a trot and a slow lope, not wanting to spend the fine animal he rode.

Reaching the fort at twilight of the second day, Jonathan dismounted at the stable, handing the bay over to an orderly to be cared for, and immediately headed for Elizabeth's quarters. The thought uppermost in his mind was to try to patch things up between Nathan and the lass. As he neared the quarters, Jonathan heard a low cry, a sudden rush of skirts and patter of feet, as the golden haired girl ran toward him and flew into his arms, grasping him around the neck.

"Nathan! Nathan! Thank God you have returned!" she cried, and covered Jonathan's cheeks with kisses.

Embarrassed, Jonathan gently removed the girl's arms from his neck, and pushed her back slightly, holding her by the shoulders.

"Lass, 'tis I, Jonathan," he said gently.

"Oh!" Elizabeth's face grew red. "Forgive me, Jonathan. In this light, I thought you were Nathan." She visibly shrank as if a blow had been struck. The young girl tried to hide her disappointment, and looked over his shoulder, searching for his twin.

"I am sorry to disappoint you, Lass, but I am alone."

He took her arm and steered her to the front stoop where they both took a seat. The tall frontiersman leaned forward, with his fringed buckskin elbows resting upon the well worn leggings. He could see the disappointment on her face, and felt a tug at his heart while she watched him, becoming more alarmed. Now she was frightened. Something must have happened to Nathan.

"Do not be frightened, Lass. Nathan is well and would have come if he could, however it was I who had to make the trip back for the General."

Elizabeth tried to calm herself. There was a discernible relief in her face, which Jonathan easily detected.

"How is Nathan?" she asked in a faint voice.

"He is getting strong as an ox, and almost as stubborn."

A smile appeared at the corners of Elizabeth's mouth. "I fear I have embarrassed myself by kissing you, Jonathan. Please forgive me, for I do not want you to think that I am a thoughtless, loose girl."

"Not at all, Lass, for you have just answered the question I came here to find out."

He paused, shifting position, trying to word his next utterance correctly. "Nathan felt there was a terrible misunderstanding between you two when he left on the expedition. I came to see if somehow I might right the situation... but I think you answered already by how you greeted me."

Elizabeth sat in silence, almost holding her breath in anticipation.

"Nathan has been miserable, to be honest with you, for he is..." Jonathan paused and took a deep breath.

"He is very much in love with you, Elizabeth. So much so that he is beside himself. He fears he offended you gravely when he blurted out his feelings for you. He is sick with love for you."

Elizabeth's eyes were big and shining as she put her hands up to bury her face, and waves of excitement washed through her body.

"I came here to intercede for my brother; however, it appears as though I need not beg for his cause. The way you greeted me, when you thought I was Nathan, tells me that perhaps you care for him far more than he knows." Jonathan smiled and his eyes mellowed as he enjoyed seeing Elizabeth's reaction.

There was a long silence as the young girl struggled to maintain her composure, and she brushed at her misty eyes.

"Oh, Jonathan, I do love him with all my heart." Her voice was so soft, he had to lean close to hear. "It was my fault, for I thought that what Nathan was saying was just out of pity for me. I am virtually alone now, for Father has all but abandoned me in his grief over the loss of my mother. I do not want to be loved out of pity, I want to be loved as a woman. I did not understand what Nathan was trying to convey." Emotion overcame Elizabeth as she dissolved into tears, and leaned her head upon Jonathan's shoulder. He put a protective arm around her and drew her close.

"He does love you as a woman," he began, his voice very serious. "He thinks you are a sweet and wonderful, beautiful lady, and right now, his heart is breaking, for he fears you are angry and upset with him."

"Oh, Jonathan! Please tell him that is not so. I am not angry or upset with him." The girl sobbed. "I love him... I love him!"

Jonathan nodded, and kept holding the distraught lass tightly, as twilight deepened and stars began to appear in the darkening sky. In the distance, there was a flash of heat lightning, and night birds twittered their evening songs. Jonathan's heart stirred as he became aware of the warmth of Elizabeth's body pressing against his side. He knew he should release his hold, yet was reluctant, for the sweetness of her nearness awakened a long forgotten memory, and he thought of Blue Water. After all these years, a stabbing pain still came back to him, and Jonathan once again felt the wrench of her death tear at his guts.

The night grew black, and yet those two did not change their positions. Jonathan still had his arm around Elizabeth, and she still had her head against his shoulder. Each was wrapped in his or her own thoughts, for Elizabeth dreamed what it would be like when next she would meet Nathan, and Jonathan dreamed a dream that nevermore could be.

Chapter Twenty-one

Summer wore on, and General Braddock could no longer delay the expedition's mission. Jonathan returned to regretfully relay that he was unable to stir any of the Colonists to rejoin the force. Braddock was upset, and his rantings and ravings could be heard throughout Little Meadow Camp.

"What unpatriotic, slothful slackards!" the General bellowed, pacing to and fro, his hand upon the hilt of his sword. "We shall march ahead! Captain Wood, pick twelve hundred of the best men and be ready to march in the morning. Leave the rest here with Dunbar. We will use Little Meadow as a supply depot."

He turned on his heel and disappeared into his tent.

Jonathan and Nathan were among the twelve hundred who were to press on to Fort Duquesne. The terrain grew fearsome, as deep ravines and steep hillsides were cause for great effort from the brigade. Young George Washington re-joined the party, pointing out the trail he had surveyed two years prior. Again, the pickaxes and shovels started flying, and the horses and mules strained against the weighted sleds which were used to smooth the roadway. Men grunted and cursed once more as they heaved trees and boulders aside, sweating in the enormous effort before them.

On July 4th, with scarcely twenty-five miles to go to their destination, the party halted for two days while Braddock waited for an Indian Scout and some back-up provisions to come up in a convoy from Dunbar. Nathan and Jonathan took the opportunity to rest under a great pine tree, using fallen needles as a soft bed. Jonathan had taught Nathan how to scoop out an area in the ground to fit his hips, and pile the needles to cushion the area just so, before throwing down his blanket.

"What will you do, Jonathan," Nathan inquired, "after finishing all this?"

Jonathan was thoughtful for a moment. He had a long stem of grass clenched between his teeth, and lounged on his side, propped up on one elbow as he contemplated. A breeze ruffled a lock of his black hair, and it fell over his forehead in an unruly swirl.

"I allow as how I will return to the cabin and perhaps continue to improve the land."

Nathan nodded, rolling onto his back, looking up at the sky between the gnarled branches of the trees. Sunlight filtered through, glistening on each green needle, outlining the slender shafts with a tracery of silver.

"And you, Nathan?"

"I will try to win Elizabeth's hand, and build a cabin close to yours, I hope, if she will have me."

"There is no worry about that, dear brother, for I already recounted to you how she is dying of love for you and can scarcely await your return."

Nathan smiled as he could picture his beloved watching the trail diligently for a glimpse of him.

"You are a lucky man, you know, Nathan, to have the love of one so sweet and pure as that girl."

Nathan blushed under his bronze tan. "I could only wish that you, too, Jonathan, my dear brother, could have a love as dear."

Jonathan starred blankly ahead, a million thoughts racing unchecked in his mind.

"If I could have a love half as sweet, I would forever be grateful," Jonathan mumbled, his mind a far way off. "However," he continued, "I am too used to being a lonely woodsman. There is no room in my life for a woman. My life is too hard; I could not ask a member of that gentle sex to share such a rugged existence as I have. I am off hunting or trapping most of the time, as you well know. The stars, sky and moon are my ceiling, and the trees and hills my walls. The cabin is only a resting place and sanctuary during the hard winter."

Jonathan seemed to gain enthusiasm while he spoke, as an idea coursed through his mind, and said excitedly, "Nathan, why don't you take the cabin for your own when you and Elizabeth are married?"

"Jonathan, I would not dream of it, for you have put so much work into the building and clearing of the land."

"Nonsense!" Jonathan retorted. "I insist you keep it and work the land for me. I shall come and visit you every so often, in between my hunting trips, if you and your bride will allow."

Nathan's love for his brother was never greater than at that moment. He swelled with emotion, and his throat tightened. It took him a moment before he could speak.

"We have come a long journey, so far, haven't we, Jonathan? Growing up in our childhood in England, and the adventures we are having in this new, wild place. Especially you, who have had such an experience as being captured by the Indians." Nathan paused, heaving a big sigh. "Do you ever think of England and home?"

Jonathan nodded, chewing on the grass stem. "At first, I thought often of Mother and our sister, and you, of course. However, I knew when I left those shores, I would never see them again. At first, it was real hard, but as the years have gone on, I think less and less of them... only wonder sometimes if Mother is still alive... and whether Sis has made a good marriage."

Jonathan looked fondly toward his twin. "I am really pleased that you came to the Colonies, for of everyone I left behind, I could not have endured if you, my twin brother, had not joined me, for you are like my right hand. We are one... inseparable. Our thoughts and lives are like two beans in a pot."

There was a long silence. Then he continued, "I am sure we must have driven Mother crazy when we were tykes. Such shenanigans we used to pull! Remember when we tied the bell on the calf's tail, and the poor thing went bawling all over the pasture, kicking up his heels? And the time we smeared molasses on the cat?"

Nathan burst out laughing as he recalled the number of hours it took the cat to lick itself clean, and how the unfortunate creature ended up almost bald. "And how we would tip over the loo when Father was inside!" he added, laughing until his sides hurt.

"We were a handful, I guess. What one of us wouldn't think of, the other one would!" Jonathan chuckled, and there was a long pause as each twin laughed at the old memories.

Later, in a more serious vein, Nathan asked, "What do you think the French will do when we approach their fort on the Ohio?"

Jonathan pondered a moment before replying. "I have given that a lot of serious thought. It seems to me that they will put up a great deal of resistance. Although, there have been times when they just retreat, without a confrontation. But I don't think so, this time. Surely they will not roll over without a fight, and it will be a fierce one, Nathan."

"How can Braddock and the other officers be so stubborn? From how you describe it, Jonathan, it would seem that we English will not be prepared."

"I fear you are correct, my dear brother. I think we will have great trouble ahead. We must stick close together, for I should not like to see you off by yourself from now on."

The two clasped forearms, and a special meaningful look passed between them.

Again, the expedition continued pushing forward. Late in the afternoon of the next day, the road came to a sudden end at a precipice high above Turtle Creek. It would be impossible for the wagons and artillery to cross at this juncture. General Braddock assessed the situation, and determined to quit the ridge and make a crossing down the river at another point, opposite a ravine on the other side.

"Tomorrow," he mused, striding back and forth, atop the ridge overlooking the gap ahead, slapping his riding crop against his leg. "Tomorrow we shall cross the river and proceed up that ravine," gazing toward a dark slit in the opposite bank, not guessing what foreboding events lay ahead for the expedition.

Jackie Gould

Chapter Twenty-two

Elizabeth was ecstatically happy for the first time in months. The news that Jonathan had brought so thrilled the girl that she barely could contain her excitement, skipping through her few daily tasks, lost in a delicious daydream. The days seemed brighter and the sky more blue. Even the songbirds seemed more cheerful, sending trilling warbles piercing through the summer air. There seemed to Elizabeth to be a lifting of a tight band around her chest, and she could breathe more easily.

She was in such a mood one lovely late June morning while heading down the path to the river. Elizabeth had not ventured so far since the day the expedition left, but on this day, the freshness of the air beckoned, and she felt safe, for she could keep the fort in sight up the hill. It was cool and tranquil by the river's edge, with dark heavy foliage on towering oak trees providing a canopy of shade that gave respite from the midsummer sun.

Sitting upon a large rock, she drew her knees up to her chin, and gazed for a long time into the transparent water as it glided lazily past. Turning her gaze down the road into the forest in the direction her love had traveled weeks before, she thought for a moment that she saw a movement. Soldiers and settlers often used that road, but now she decided it had only been her imagination, and Elizabeth was not concerned.

When would that joyful day come when Nathan would stride jauntily down that road? Tossing back her long blond hair, she made the decision then that she would come every day to that spot to wait and watch for Nathan's return. Surely it would be soon, for Jonathan had indicated that they had almost achieved their goal.

The love-smitten girl let her thoughts drift to that wonderful day. She could picture Nathan swinging down that trail, flintlock rifle in hand, his shoulder-length hair flowing, and the fringe of his buckskin shirt swaying with every step. In her mind, Elizabeth saw herself running to meet him, skirts flying, arms open wide, to be swept up and swung around in his embrace, finally, to be kissed long and passionately on the mouth.

Her body thrilled at the very thought, and so intense was her daydream, that she was totally unaware of a sound behind her until it was too late. A hand of steel clamped over her mouth, and other arms like steel bands pinned her own arms to her sides, swinging her off the ground, while she kicked and struggled. The terror in her hazel eyes at that moment would have stirred a dead man's heart.

Quickly, a blindfold blotted out the light before Elizabeth could catch a glimpse of her captors. A distinct odor of sweaty male bodies, mixed with wood smoke and bear grease reached her nostrils before a hand cut off her very breath, and all went black. The helpless girl was unaware that three savages quickly carried her limp body unceremoniously over their shoulders as they trotted into the woods and swiftly put distance between themselves and the fort.

When Elizabeth regained consciousness, she was horrified to find herself a captive. Her wrists were bound tightly behind her back, and thongs cut sharply into her ankles. A gag was in her mouth, pulling against her jaw. With frightened, terrified eyes, the girl searched the surroundings, and with a sinking heart, spotted the nearly nude savages. She had already guessed the identity of her captors, and when she saw those glistening bodies with their hideously painted faces glaring her way, she felt faint and nauseous. All the stories of torture that she had heard now flooded Elizabeth's mind with the ferocity of a thunderstorm, lashing her, searing into her very bones.

They appeared to be in a glen high upon a mountaintop. There was a deep pool of cool water surrounded by willows on one side, and a craggy outcropping of rocks reaching skyward on the other side. Moss and ferns clung to the rock wall. A fourth Indian suddenly emerged from the rock wall itself, surprising Elizabeth. She surmised that he had come from an opening or cave well-hidden in the wall. Her heart was pounding and she could scarcely pull herself together, for she feared she would faint, yet dared not. She could hardly imagine what horror might be done to her, and though weak with terror, the young girl fought to stay awake.

The Indians talked and gestured among themselves, occasionally pointing in her direction. There seemed to be a heated discussion that continued for some time. Elizabeth grew stiff and sore sitting as she was, and tried to change position, but only succeeded in getting a cramp in her leg. She bit down hard on the gag until the cramp subsided. After more haggling, the Fourth Indian, who seemed to be the leader, approached the girl. She lifted frightened eyes to meet his steely gaze, and saw not a flicker of expression in the savage's eyes or demeanor.

With one swift movement, a knife flashed, and the fourth Indian cut the girl's ankle bonds, jerking her roughly to her feet. Elizabeth staggered, her head in a dizzy whirl. The Indian pushed her ahead, and the slim girl followed two other Indians as they started quickly away from the shady glen. She had to trot to keep up with their easy strides, and when she slowed, the two Indians behind her prodded her back with a rifle or knife tip.

They traveled thus for two hours. Elizabeth was growing weary and lightheaded, and feared she would topple over in a dead faint when the party finally stopped to rest. Perspiration beaded on the girl's forehead. Her dress was wet from exertion, and torn from brambles and sharp twigs. She slumped to the ground, exhausted, closing her eyes, shaking in every fiber of her body when they finally came to a stop.

Her captors hunched together and each reached for a handful of ground meal laced with maple sugar, which was stashed in their belts, washing it down with water from a nearby spring. When they were finished, the leader sauntered over to the prostrate girl and rudely pushed her shoulder with one of his moccasined feet, rolling her over onto her stomach. Elizabeth cringed, expecting a fatal blow to come. But with swift fingers, the Indian untied the gag, and while doing so, put his hands into her long blond hair, examining the length and curls. The terrified girl shuddered, knowing he would treasure her scalp as a prize all other braves would covet.

Then, the bronzed specimen, wearing only a breechcloth, brought the girl water and grunted as he motioned for her to drink, which she did promptly, gulping it down at once, for her mouth was parched, and her throat sore. Again, the savage reached his hand into her golden curls and yanked Elizabeth to her feet. She gave a cry of pain, and the savage whirled threateningly in front of her, brandishing a knife before her face, his evil eyes burning a warning into hers as she dared to stare back.

"Yellow Hair, go!" He pointed, once more taking a position behind the girl, and shoved her ahead along the trail. This time, there was no need for the gag, for they were now miles from the fort, and Elizabeth had lost track of which direction it now lay, as they had forged deeper and deeper into the wilderness. Her arms were still bound behind her back, which prevented her from balancing, and more than once she stumbled and fell. Each time the fourth Indian's fingers dug into her flesh as he yanked her to her feet.

Nighttime fell, and at last the party halted. However, Elizabeth dreaded this the most, for the very thought of spending the night in the wilderness with four savages terrified the girl anew. She could scarcely imagine the atrocities that might be in store for her before the night was over. She watched warily as the four went about building a fire, which they sat around on their haunches, roasting strips of meat. Her great hazel eyes never left the four figures from her vantage point under a large pine tree.

When the savages had filled themselves to satisfaction, the leader approached Elizabeth. She cowered, pulling back farther under the tree, but he yanked her up to him, and near to fainting, she felt his body touching her side. The poor girl quivered with fright, and almost slipped from his grasp, but he merely cut her wrist thongs, and her arms fell helplessly to her sides. This time, the Indian put a braided thong around her neck with a long tether attached, which he tied securely to the tree trunk. It allowed Elizabeth a little freedom, but she could not stray far. The brave then pushed some food into her hands, and turning on his heel, left her in the darkness beneath the tree.

The exhausted girl, on shaking legs, sank to her knees, making sure she could keep all four savages within sight, before she settled herself, forcing her eyes to remain open, for she was totally exhausted. She ate the meager food halfheartedly, then tried to untie the necklace, but was unable to budge it at all. Soon, Elizabeth felt her head bob, as those hazel eyes closed, and try as hard as she might, she could not open them again, and slid to the ground, fast asleep.

In the middle of the night, as a hoot owl called out in the dimness of the stars, a hand reached up Elizabeth's thigh beneath her skirt, startling her awake. Letting out a loud scream, she rolled violently away, crouching low on all fours. There was a brief shuffling sound of straining bodies, which ended shortly in a thud of someone being thrown to the ground. The trembling girl froze in terror, and all color drained from her face then as a hand grasped her arm, forcing her flat to the ground. She was sure, then, she was about to be ravaged by the savages, and dread filled every fiber of her body.

"Sleep," the fourth Indian said. "Yellow Hair sleep, no harm." He sat cross-legged a few feet from Elizabeth, on guard, while two other Indians snored in their blankets, and a third grunted in dissatisfaction as he rolled over to sleep.

Elizabeth's heart pounded so hard, she scarcely breathed, as she slowly tried to recover. But to sleep that night was impossible. She wanted to trust the fourth Indian, and did recognize that he had kept her from being molested by the others, yet she was too upset to relax. Dawn seemed a long time in coming, and the stars, peeping through the blackness of the night did little to comfort the frightened girl.

Chapter Twenty-three

Elizabeth and the four Indians traveled for three more days before they reached what she later would find was the Delaware Village. As they entered the campground, Indian women and children excitedly lined up in rows, chattering, brandishing sticks, and throwing stones at the hapless girl. By now her clothes were in tatters, and somehow, she had lost her shoes a long way back. Stumbling and faint, she limped on cut and bruised feet, following her captors, still leashed by the throat.

The women screeched and grabbed at her hair, yanking and pulling with such force, it brought tears to her eyes. They tore at her dress, and she almost gagged at the odor of their bodies. Elizabeth's worst fears were realized when she looked over the village at the wooden longhouses and smoky campfires. All the faces were hostile, and there was a helplessness that invaded her very soul.

Her heart ached for Nathan, and despair crashed upon her like a feeling she had never known before. Even though the fourth Indian had been her protector during their journey, now he cruelly yanked on her leash, forcing the girl through the village like a prize on a string. They finally came to a small hut at the far side of the village, and he motioned for her to enter the low doorway.

Once inside, Elizabeth blinked, trying to adjust her eyes to the darkness. The fourth Indian did not remove the throat leash, instead fastened the end high upon a pole inside. He grunted, "Here stay," and promptly left. The frightened girl sank to the ground, taking note of the interior. Several baskets were on a raised area on one side, and on another raised area, a bearskin and blankets were folded. In the middle of the hut there was a firepit of ashes, and Elizabeth could see the smoke hole in the ceiling.

Taking one of the blankets and placing it upon the floor, she gratefully stretched out, and, totally exhausted, fell into a fitful half-sleep, with sounds of the village pulsating in her head. She heard laughter and the singsong chatter of the women, dogs barking, low men's voices, and delightful little screams from children. Crazy images floated in a dream, of her mother, of Nathan, of hideous Indians, their faces painted, of cannons booming and rifles cracking, of blood and screams.

Elizabeth awoke a little later with a dreadful sense of doom. Scarcely had her eyes fluttered open, when a slim young Indian girl entered the lodge with a basket of food upon her hip. The dark-haired girl with dusky eyes shoved the basket in front of Elizabeth and motioned for her to eat. Now famished, Elizabeth wolfed down some parched corn and berries, and quenched her thirst with water from a pouch offered by the young Indian girl. The native girl curiously looked at Elizabeth's long hair, and timidly reached out to touch the blond tresses.

Putting her hand on her chest, Elizabeth haltingly said, "I am Elizabeth... Elizabeth."

The dark-skinned girl put a slim brown hand to her own breast, and shyly said, "Te-tak-wa-o-ee."

Elizabeth nodded and repeated, "Te-tak-wa-o-ee," as she looked closely at the girl, who was dressed in a fine doeskin gown, and had beaded moccasins on her little feet. The Indian girl was incredibly beautiful, having great dark almond shaped eyes, and flashing white teeth. Elizabeth guessed her to be about fourteen years old, for the little bumps underneath her dress were buds of developing breasts, and her hips had not yet filled out.

Elizabeth hoped for an outside chance that perhaps the girl would help her, but when she motioned for the young Indian girl to remove her throat leash, the girl firmly shook her head, turned and left the lodge, leaving a dejected Elizabeth to contemplate her fate.

❧

Late in the afternoon a couple of days later, there was a flurry of excitement in the village. Elizabeth drew close to the doorway, and could see children running, and women chattering with excited animation. It appeared that a very important party had arrived in the village, however she could not see who it was, nor how many were in the party. She only knew that Te-tak-wa-o-ee, with whom she shared the lodge, ran with glee out of the dark, smoky shelter toward the incoming party.

It was not long before the doorway darkened, and to Elizabeth's utter shock, a tall, blond man stooped to enter. He was clothed in buckskin, and had his arm around Te-tak-wa-o-ee's slim waist. Looking at Elizabeth, a crooked smile crossed his angular face.

"So, my braves did fetch my DEAR Elizabeth!" George Stillwell sneered.

Elizabeth went ashen, her huge eyes looked like the dying eyes of a doe that recognized it had been trapped, and was waiting for the fatal bullet to hit. Stillwell grasped her wrist and twisted as he pulled her up to him, his face close to hers, his hot breath smelling of rum, as he breathed into her face.

"Welcome to the Delaware Village," he hissed. "Now we will find out how sweet you can be, my dear."

He shoved her rudely away, and Elizabeth fell backward, cowering as far into the corner as her leash would allow. She could not control the trembling that permeated her entire body, and again she felt nauseous. *It is incredible,* she thought. *Stillwell, friends with the Indians!* All those months that he had been away from the fort... now it became clear. He had deserted and thrown in his lot with the Delawares, who were allies of the French. Elizabeth's mind raced... how could she escape? Who at the fort would even know that she was missing? *Oh! Nathan!* she groaned inwardly in anguish.

Stillwell turned his attention to the Indian girl, who looked up at him with adoring, smiling eyes.

"Come here, my little Princess," he cooed, pulling the dark haired beauty close to him. "I really missed you, you little tart," his rough hands fumbling all over the girl. In one flash, the dark eyed girl drew off her doeskin dress, and stood proudly naked before him, smiling as his eyes hungrily admired her nubile form. Stillwell groaned, his fingers grasping at her, and he lowered his head to roughly kiss her.

In horror, Elizabeth tried to turn her head, but not before she saw Stillwell grab the girl and roll her onto the blanket. She heard their bodies strain and heave, heard the girl give a delighted little cry, and Stillwell's grunting groan of completion. Elizabeth felt sick to her stomach, and with her back turned to the writhing couple, buried her burning face in her hands. Te-tak-wa-o-ee giggled, and Stillwell pressed his lips to hers as she wrapped her brown arms around him. Soon they strained and groaned again in pleasure.

"You are the hottest little shit I have ever had! And I've had myself a good many," he panted, spent. Then he looked toward the corner of the lodge at Elizabeth's back. "But there's another one I can't wait to have, and I mean to have her, too!"

Te-tak-wa-o-ee smiled, not understanding any word of Stillwell's utterance, but laid a gentle finger upon his face kissing him on his lips, her mouth open, tongue searching. She rubbed against him, pressing her body to his in a renewed invitation.

"No more, my Little Dove. God, but you can never get enough, can you? You could wear a man out before dinner. I've got to save some of my seed for others!" He looked at Elizabeth.

Stillwell slapped a familiar hand on the Indian girl's behind. "Go get me some grub, girl, I'm famished." He threw the doeskin dress at her and pointed to his stomach, making hunger signs. She giggled, slipping on the dress and disappeared out the doorway.

"Come, come, my proper Miss Wood," he directed the English girl, who was cowering in the corner. "Turn around here and be sociable!" He grabbed her hair and yanked her so that she was facing him. "So... here you are... and here I am! Isn't that just splendid! I vowed one day I'd have you, and it looks like today is the day! I mean to have you for my wife, Elizabeth."

Elizabeth's eyes were like darts. "Never!" she hissed through clenched teeth. "I shall die first!"

"Now, my dear," he soothed, "that is a pretty bold statement, and rather drastic, wouldn't you say?" running a finger along her cheek.

Elizabeth turned to gooseflesh at his touch, and pulled away. "You vile traitor!" she spat at him, her voice tight and strained.

Stillwell grinned. "I see I have a bit of taming to do. But you will come around eventually. You, Elizabeth," he said, staring directly into her eyes, "will come to me willingly one day, my dear. I can wait. It will be worth it."

His eyes stripped her naked then, as he glanced her up and down. Elizabeth shuddered and closed her eyes, clenching her fists.

Noticing her throat leash for the first time, Stillwell fingered it for a moment. "Oh, I see they have you well kept. For now, we will just leave that on your beautiful neck, for I should not want to see you slip away, Love. You perhaps have heard of the punishment that Indians can dish out. Well, now, just for the record, and to let you know what might be in store for you, should you try to get away, keep in mind that these Indians are my friends. They will do anything for me, including bringing you back, if you should escape. If that happens, my dear Miss Wood, you would not like the consequences."

Chapter Twenty-four

Elizabeth had to endure the sounds of George Stillwell's lovemaking to the Indian girl several times a day, and throughout the nights. She grew to dread the shadow of his form as it darkened the doorway every time he approached the hut. She tried to block out the excited little squeals and sharp intake of breath coming from Te-tak-wa-o-ee's lips as the young girl again and again shuddered in satisfaction. Elizabeth's only solace was that at that moment, Stillwell seemed so occupied with Te-tak-wa-o-ee, that he had not approached her since the first day of his arrival at the village.

Her presence, Elizabeth highly suspected, only heightened the former army officer's desire to humiliate her. If so, he was doing a fine job, for Elizabeth still flushed each time she knew that the two of them had their bodies locked together, and felt a sick uneasiness inside.

When Te-tak-wa-o-ee's moon phase came on, she, like all other women of the village had to retire to the Woman's Lodge until her flow was finished. It was during this time that Stillwell turned his attention to Elizabeth. So, one day, as she had dreaded, he came to the hut and the girl was alone with the man she had grown to hate. Stillwell took hold of Elizabeth's leash and pulled her up to stand before him. She stood with trembling limbs while he looked her over.

"I must apologize, my dear Elizabeth," he started. "My, indeed you do look a mess."

Elizabeth's hand went to the tangled locks of her hair, and she realized that it had not been combed in weeks. She felt ashamed of her appearance.

"I fear my little Indian Dove has been neglectful of her visitor. Look at you... clothes dirty and torn, no shoes, and filthy beyond belief! We shall fix that right now, for I cannot think that the woman I am to marry should be in such a sorry condition."

Elizabeth's bright eyes flashed as she tried to pull away.

"Now, now! Be still, you tiger, for I mean to get you cleaned up. Wait here." He disappeared out the door.

Elizabeth, her pulse rising, sank to the floor and put her hands on her throat leash, but still had no luck in getting it untied. Before she could even think, Stillwell returned with a bundle under his arm. Giving a little snap to her leash, he said, "Come on, we're going to clean you up, Elizabeth Wood, and make you present-able."

The young girl blinked in the bright sunlight as they emerged from the hut, and tried not to notice the giggles and laughter that came from the Indian women as they watched the white man drag his woman to the river's edge.

At least he was gentlemanly enough to pick a spot behind some bushes, out of sight of the village, to throw down the bundle he carried. Turning to Elizabeth, he motioned for her to remove her clothes. She was startled, holding her arms across her chest. "No, I will not disrobe!"

"My dear, you are going to bathe in that river, wash with this soap, and get cleaned up. Now, are you going in by yourself, or am I going to have to throw you in?"

Elizabeth hesitated, trying to avoid Stillwell's eyes.

"Give me your clothes!" Stillwell grew more intense. "Look," he said in a sudden pleading voice, "see, I brought you a new dress and moccasins."

He held up a soft doeskin gown, fringed at the arms and bottom of the skirt, and a pair of little beaded moccasins, decorated with colorful porcupine quills.

"Now, let's get you scrubbed up. Frankly, you disgust me as you are now."

"Then, turn your back or I shan't go in." She flashed back at him.

"Don't be foolish, little Miss Proper! You think that I don't know what your body must look like under that dirty facade? I can make a very good guess, and I know I will not be disappointed."

Elizabeth was near to tears. "Oh, please, Lt. Stillwell, for all that is good in you, I beg you to leave here now, and I shall bathe and change. But please go away."

Stillwell mulled over her suggestion, and with a sudden change of heart, sighed and said, "Tell you what, Love, I'll just be over there on the other side of that bush, if it will make you feel more at ease."

He moved away. Stillwell knew instinctively that taking Elizabeth could never be done by force. The only way would be to sweet-talk to her, so she would relax her guard. So for now, he backed off the pressure on the girl.

With her eyes darting about, Elizabeth stepped into the water, and while submerged, removed her rags of a dress. It felt good to wash her hair and bathe, for she had not enjoyed that luxury for some time. She let the cool water soak at her bones, and experienced a soothing, delightful refreshment. She almost felt human again.

"Lieutenant..." she called, suddenly becoming bold. "Lieutenant Stillwell, I cannot bathe properly with this leather necklace on."

Elizabeth was taking a chance that Stillwell's demeanor had changed slightly, and wanted to see how far he would bend. At the moment, he was even sober, not being under the influence of drink, which she had detected so many times recently.

"Please remove this, it is choking me."

Stillwell appeared from behind the brush, and approached the river's edge. With her back to the Lieutenant, and submerged as far as she could into the water, Elizabeth pulled her hair back from her neck. She hoped he would not see how her hands were shaking. She knew she was taking a great chance that Stillwell might overpower her on the very spot, but, suddenly, she felt confident that she could handle him with dialog. Perhaps she could win his confidence enough to gain some freedom.

George Stillwell's hand lightly touched Elizabeth's shoulders, tracing the delicate shape, and the girl froze, positive now that she had made a mistake.

"The neck leash, Lieutenant," she said, trying to keep her voice calm, all the while trembling internally. She closed her eyes tightly, expecting the worst. Again, Stillwell's hand traced Elizabeth's shoulders before testing the leash at her white neck.

"Now, my dear, why would I remove your leash? You would probably run, and we have already discussed how such a move as that would end."

"I promise I will not try to escape. Where would I possibly go, anyway? I do not even know where I am. And I well understand the consequences, Lieutenant. Believe me! Please remove my leash!"

This time Elizabeth was more emphatic, and hoped that Stillwell would be convinced. She tried to seem calm and in control.

There was the sensation of a cold steel knife blade at the back of her neck, and suddenly, the leash fell into the water. Elizabeth silently breathed a sigh of relief, and sank quickly to her chin, covering herself as she turned boldly to face her captor. Still attempting to calm the tremor in her voice, she asked the Lieutenant to retreat once more behind the brush.

"You are asking the supreme sacrifice of me now, you know," Stillwell said, his eyes upon Elizabeth's white skin shimmering beneath the surface of the water.

For a moment, Elizabeth feared she indeed had made a mistake, but continued to stare up at Stillwell's face, meeting his gaze straight on. He made a move to reach out for her, but changed his mind, and, pulling himself up to full height, retreated behind the evergreen.

As much as Elizabeth would have liked to luxuriate in the refreshing water, she felt compelled to finish her bath quickly, and slipped out of the river under the protection of a low hanging branch, swiftly donning the doeskin dress. It felt so soft against her clean skin, that she took a moment to run her hands down over her hips, feeling the suppleness of the garment. Though the moccasins were a bit snug, she was happy to have something on her callused feet.

Jackie Gould

Chapter Twenty-five

"**N**ow then, that is much better! You look present-able again, my little White Squaw!" Stillwell was impressed by how well the gown shaped to Elizabeth's form as she emerged from the bushes. Her long hair now hung in a loose braid across her right shoulder. "All we need now is a preacher, if there was one around," Stillwell remarked as he reached for the young girl's hand.

Elizabeth skillfully avoided his touch as she negotiated a path around him. Her mind was racing to find a way to escape from his overbearing presence.

"Not so fast, Little Squaw," Stillwell said, grabbing her wrist. "You going to come to me tonight, as my bride?" He leered into her eyes.

"I told you, Lieutenant, never!"

"Now, that is no way to treat a gentleman... especially one who is seeing to it that you don't get thrown out in the middle of the village for all those hot young bucks to take to their lodges, and get a taste of your sweet nectar. If it were not for me, Elizabeth Wood, you would already be with child by at least a dozen of these hotbloods!"

Elizabeth opened her mouth to speak, when a great commotion started in the village, distracting Stillwell's attention. He pushed her forward, ordering her to the hut, while he went to find out the cause of the big disturbance. She was relieved that she would not have to deal with Stillwell at that moment, for she had no idea how to escape his obsession of taking her for his wife. She knew only two things: that she must at all costs prevent Stillwell from taking her, and that she must try to escape the village. At that moment in time, the unfortunate girl had no idea how to accomplish either thing.

Watching from beside the doorway of her hut, Elizabeth saw that the Elder Leaders of the village were surrounded by near-naked braves, whose shaven heads, except for a top crest in the middle, glistened in the sun. There was excited gesturing and cheering coming from the gathering. The Chief, regal in his bearing, uttered some harsh words, and everyone about him abruptly sat down in a semi-circle around him, waiting for him to speak. Smoke rose from a dozen cooking fires, lazily spiraling upward, while women and children went about their domestic tasks, not paying any attention to the gathering of men.

At the center of the circle, sitting beside the Chief, were several white men in blue uniforms, which Elizabeth recognized immediately as the uniforms of the French Army. There seemed to be a lively discussion which lasted for some long time. She noticed that Stillwell was seated in the intimate circle of Indian Leaders. Then the Chief rose, lifting his tomahawk and shield far above his head, and gave a long, impassioned speech. One by one, the other leaders rose, and their voices were also heard. Soon, there was a resounding chorus of agreement from the savage warriors, who whooped war cries into the air, and started to make dancing steps. In moments, the entire gathering broke into a war dance and the drums beat furiously.

Stillwell was approaching the hut, and Elizabeth quickly ducked back inside to take refuge in the dark confines of the domed wigwam. She awaited his return with trepidation, twisting her hands together. Just then, Stillwell burst though the doorway and there was an air of excitement as he proceeded to gather his rifle and ammunition from the pallet he had shared with Te-tak-wa-o-ee.

"Well, my dear Bride-to-be, our wedding shall have to wait."

Elizabeth sat quietly in the corner, and appeared not to have heard the Lieutenant's proclamation. He approached where she was sitting, and hunkered down beside her, his body perspiring in the July heat. Elizabeth grew wary, and pulled back farther.

"Give me a kiss for luck, my dear, for I am embarking on a little journey to meet my old comrades," he uttered, a sort of glee in his voice.

Elizabeth shook her head, and tried, but was unsuccessful in avoiding his hands as he grabbed her below the shoulders, pinning her arms to her sides. He forced her to the ground and rolled half-way on top of her. Stillwell's face closed in on the frightened girl, his cruel mouth coming down on hers, forcing her lips to part, despite her efforts to turn her head. She struggled, trying to free her arms, and kicked to try to extricate herself from the weight of his body.

Her struggles, however, only succeeded in arousing the man, and she grew more frightened as his mouth continued to crush down severely on her lips. With all her strength, Elizabeth rolled and heaved him off, biting down hard on his lip in the process. Stillwell gave a yelp, and putting up his fingers, found that his lip was bleeding. With fire in his eyes, he struck her hard across her face, causing the girl to fall backward, where she quickly scrambled to her knees.

"Don't... ever... do... that again, you vixen!" he hissed in a hoarse, low, menacing tone, panting with effort. "You can count your lucky stars that I don't have time now, or I would claim my wedding rights this very moment! Who needs to wait for a preacher, anyway, out here in the wilderness?"

He grabbed Elizabeth's hand, and declared "I take you as my wife, Elizabeth Wood, forevermore. A husband has rights, and I intend to claim mine when I return from the engagement we are about to launch against the bloody British Army."

He pulled her rudely up against his body, and tilted her quivering face close to his. "Now, kiss me proper, like a good wife should."

Elizabeth was white with fright, and clamped her lips closed, trying to shake her head 'no.' He leaned close to her face.

"Your husband is off to do battle with the British Brigade that is chopping a road across the mountains. We aim to stop them dead in their tracks, and thank them for making a highway for us. The French will be most appreciative."

Elizabeth's heart lurched at the thought of Nathan and her father, who were with that British Army at this very moment.

"Kiss me luck, dear wife! I shall return very soon, and then we will have our wedding night. I shall look forward to that with a great deal of pleasure. You can be sure that every moment I am away, I shall have nothing on my mind but that very thought."

Elizabeth closed her eyes in horror as again his lips found her mouth. This time, she could taste the salty blood that her bite had drawn, and shuddered.

"You can do better than that, Love. But I will teach you how when I return. In fact, I will teach you how to do many things. Things that will specially please me. Te-tak-wa-o-ee knows these things. Perhaps she will teach you while I am away."

He kissed her once more, then was gone out the door. Elizabeth slid to the floor, her limbs trembling, and tried to wipe away Stillwell's kisses with the back of her hand. She had the uncontrollable urge to bathe again in the cold waters of the river. All the while there were the sounds of Indian war whoops, drums, and whinnies and snorts of the ponies coming from beyond her doorway. She watched as warriors and French Army men disappeared into the gloomy forest, with Stillwell riding near a French Officer at the head of the party.

The young girl sank helplessly to the ground, prostrate, as she contemplated the meaning of the band of Indians and French soldiers who were now on their way to seek out the very mission of which Nathan, Jonathan and her father were a part. Braddock's Army. Braddock's Road. Surely, Braddock's men could counter and defeat a bunch of straggling French and Indians braves. Elizabeth tried to take heart.

Chapter Twenty-six

The morning of July 9, 1755 dawned clear and hot in the wilderness, some twenty miles southwest of Fort Duquesne. General Edward Braddock, eager to make the fording of Turtle Creek, galloped back and forth on a large brown horse, rousing the advance troops to form up and begin the task of clearing the trail up the ravine across the creek. Inch by inch, foot by foot, the heavily tangled underbrush was cut, opening a twelve-foot-wide swath through the ravine's thickened undergrowth. Trees towered above, the branches in a seeming embrace, making a darkened tunnel of filtered light through which the troops cut their painstaking way forward.

It was hot, and the heavy, humid air was oppressive as the men struggled for every foot they gained. Insects were bothersome, with mosquitoes and flies a constant irritation, biting the men's necks and ears. The noise of whacks, thuds, and grunting curses reverberated up the ever narrowing ravine, as the expedition pushed up and up, away from the creek. The side walls of the ravine grew steadily more steep the deeper they penetrated the crevice, and trees grew more closely together.

Nathan and Jonathan worked side by side in the middle of the brigade. About one half mile of roadway had been cleared, enabling some wagons and teams to be brought forward. Braddock and his English troops formed in a loose defensive line; however, they were well strung out on the narrow trail. Jonathan, briefly taking a rest, looked around and declared in a low voice, for Nathan's ears only, "I don't like the lay of the land, Nathan. This is too dangerous." He stopped and mopped his brow. "Braddock is bringing up the men and wagons too quickly, packing the roadway full. If there should be an ambush now, there would be no escape."

The words no more than left his lips when there was a thunderous cracking volley of gunfire ahead. Screams and yells echoed throughout the ravine, as a sudden flutter of wings and noisy squawks erupted and dozens of birds rose from the treetops in fright. A huge cloud of white gun smoke obliterated the front lines, while hideous war whoops rang from the trees on either side of the ravine. White puffs of smoke from the ends of the blazing muskets appeared everywhere from behind tree trunks and fallen logs.

Everything was bedlam as the surprised British troops tried to form their attack lines. Braddock was galloping forward, sword raised, bellowing orders, frantically trying to organize the troop's fighting stance. Musket balls could be heard everywhere ripping through tree leaves and flesh. Screams of agony reverberated through the forest, sending chills down Nathan's spine, as he and Jonathan sprang forward to take cover in a small gully at the side of the road.

Peering hard at the trees, Jonathan strained to see movement. Raising his flintlock rifle, he fired, and heard the ball hit its mark with a sickening thud. There was a hoarse cry, and an Indian toppled forward, dead before he hit the ground. Nathan, with trembling hands, sighted a form moving behind the trunk of a large pine tree. He could see the barrel of a gun poking out, then there was a puff of smoke, and the musket belched forth its missile, whistling harmlessly over his head. As the figure momentarily showed itself from behind the tree trunk, Nathan fired. The musket ball hit the trunk above the figure's head, splintering bark, sending the enemy diving for cover.

Jonathan swiftly reloaded and whirled to his left, getting off another shot as Nathan tamped down his next load. Bloodcurdling yells from the Indians came from every direction, and the sound of muskets and hand-to-hand fighting rose to a deafening pitch. Horses and men were running helter-skelter. The Colonist regulars hit the cover of trees and underbrush, while Braddock galloped headlong, screaming at the men to form a military defense line. As he tore past Jonathan and Nathan, a shot rang out, and the General's horse pitched forward, quivering in a death throe. Braddock, unhit, ran to a second mount and once more yelled at the troops to form a line.

"Return fire, men! Fire!" the General bellowed, and the surprised British members sent off several volleys. "Form your line! Form your line! Attack, fellows, attack!"

The Colonists refused to form a line, knowing by instinct that they preferred to fight the invisible foe from the cover of the forest. Braddock was furious. He galloped his horse after the scattering frontiersmen, with threats and blows from his riding crop, trying to whip the Colonists back into line. Again, a horse was shot out from under the General, and he bounded up while an aide ran up with yet another fresh mount. Braddock, swinging up into the saddle, spurred the horse ahead to the front line, and rallied his troops.

The British then turned upon the foe, who, as they had guessed, were blue-coated French, and several hundred of their Indian allies. A ferocious counterattack was mounted, and momentarily the British drove back the enemy, sweeping away many with the first volley. The Indians turned to flee, but French officers rallied the savages, and turned once again upon the trapped British and Colonial expedition. The road, being so narrow, allowed little maneuvering, for behind the advancing British the provision wagons and teams clogged the passageway.

Scores of the hopeless troops fell, as volleys of muskets cracked, belching fire and smoke. There were screams of agony as hot lead tore into their bodies, and men ran in confusion. The army tried in vain to form their military fighting line... stand, shoot, kneel, reload; ...stand, shoot, try to step over fallen comrades, ...trip, ...take a volley. Musket balls went ripping into flesh, sending blood spattering onto white uniforms, soaking the red English coats with ominous dark patches. Horses screamed and fell as they were hit, their legs flailing, their eyes glazed over. Teams of mules dropped where they were in harness, still attached to the now useless provision wagons. Dying men, their bodies flopping, lay in every grotesque position imaginable.

"Higher ground," Jonathan yelled into Nathan's ear. "We must get to higher ground!" He scrambled out of the gully, and ran up to the first tree above, looking back to see if Nathan followed. The young Colonist sprinted up the grade, slipping once to one knee, but managing to take cover with the borderman. Again they ran, flintlocks held high, as they gained a few more feet.

Jonathan had his eye on a mammoth old log a few hundred feet away, which would offer them good cover. Up he jumped, crouching low, legs pumping mightily, to gain the steep ascent. Nathan followed, his thigh muscles bulging as he quickly tried to gain higher ground. The footing grew more treacherous, for wet fallen leaves made the going slippery.

A puff of smoke and the zing of a ball accompanied a loud crack off to the right, and Jonathan jerked and fell forward. Nathan heard the shot, and watched in horror as Jonathan's tall form crumbled and fell above him.

"Jonathan!" Nathan screamed, rising up to full height, running up toward his twin. "My god! Jonathan!" Another musket belched smoke. This time, Nathan did not hear the crack, he only felt a searing hot pain shoot through his ribs.

Chapter Twenty-seven

N athan sank to his knees. A weird redness enveloped his vision, turning the landscape into a grotesquely surreal sight of twisted, distorted trees and foliage. It was suddenly quiet, for he no longer could hear a sound. The stifling odor of acrid gunpowder seared his nostrils. As if in slow motion, he slipped ever so slowly forward, reaching a hand up toward his fallen brother. A pink froth bubbled from his lips as he attempted to call out.

How did you get here, my love? Nathan's mind asked of Elizabeth, as her vision appeared before him, her golden hair glinting with highlights from the sun. Her pale, beautiful face with the great hazel eyes smiled at him, and her arms were outstretched, reaching for the fallen man.

Elizabeth, my sweet love. Again Nathan's mind spoke. *Elizabeth.* He tried to form her name on his lips, but they did not move, and darkness crept over Nathan's vision, a slow-motion blackness, creeping like a long shadow passing. His big muscular body stilled. The hand holding his flintlock relaxed its grip, and slipped to rest upon the ground, palm up. Nathan's long black hair had fallen partway across his face. All color drained from what was once a bronzed and handsome face.

A shudder, and a long gurgling sigh were all that could be heard in the wilderness east of the Mononga-hela River on that hot July day, as Nathan's breath left him for the final time. A faint smile lifted the corners of his mouth.

❧

Jonathan cursed, raising a hand up to the spot where a ball had grazed his temple. Blood was running heavily down his cheek, and he raised up enough to see Nathan lying a few feet down the slope. His heart sank. There was a certain finality to the way Nathan's body was positioned.

"Nathan! Nathan!" Jonathan screamed. There was no answer.

Jonathan crawled on his belly down to his twin's still form. A cold steel band clenched the borderman's insides like a giant hand of ice, as he lifted his brother's shoulders to cradle in his arms. He checked Nathan's pulse, and finding none, waited what seemed an eternity to see if it would return. He shook Nathan, called to him, rocked him back and forth, while a scream rose up in his throat to wrack Jonathan's body as he tried to suppress his agony.

"Nathan! My dear Nathan!" Tears flowed down the borderman's face, streaking through the grime and blood. "Oh, God! No! NO! Not Nathan!"

Jonathan hugged the body to him, and closed Nathan's sightless eyes, rocking back and forth. "You are me, Nathan, I am you," the distraught man choked. "Without you, I cannot be whole, for we two are one. There has never been just you, never been just me. You know we are inseparable... one... now cleaved in two. You can't leave now... not now... not ever!"

The battle raged below him, yet Jonathan was not aware of the screams and yells... the volleys of shot... the twang of bows and arrows... the crush of bodies falling in clouds of white musket smoke. He was alone for the last time with this brother... and time seemed to stand still. There was no sound in Jonathan's world then, only a merciful numbness that kept the hurt from being unbearable. He didn't see the sunlight dappling through the tree branches, nor hear the clamor below.

"Tear out my heart! Tear off my limbs! Gut me in two... it is all the same... I am forever wounded!" Jonathan hissed, still cradling his likeness in his lap. He felt like something had ripped him in two, taking out the best of him. "Oh, God! Oh, God in heaven! Have mercy!" he cried. "I cannot go on!" Jonathan sobbed, waves of despair washing through and through him like a hurricane wind.

He hugged the lifeless form of his beloved brother again to his breast, shaking his head in silent denial. Nathan's head fell back over Jonathan's arm, and incredulously, Jonathan found himself staring at Nathan's Adam's apple, of all things. Jonathan felt himself go completely numb, and knew he was on the fringe of going mad. His face contorted in an anguished grimace as he gasped for breath.

He knew not how much time elapsed, but slowly he became aware of the battle still raging below. Somehow, he must bury Nathan's body, for if the savages should find it, the borderman knew all too well what atrocious mutilation might be take place. He must hide the body immediately before another minute went by.

Slowly, painstakingly, Jonathan pulled Nathan's still form up to the giant fallen oak log. He scraped a depression under the far side of the log, and after removing Nathan's knife and powderhorn, gently rolled the body beneath the log. Almost in a trance, he placed his brother's arms and legs out straight. All the while there was a tearing, screaming ache slicing through Jonathan's body and mind. A feeling of unreality. His movements became stiff and remote as a robot, and he was not at all sure he was actually in the real world. There was the curious sensation of standing beside himself, looking on as if he were some uninterested third party. With one more loving caress to his twin's face, Jonathan numbly covered Nathan's body with soil and packed it down with rocks. He bowed his head in a silent prayer. Satisfied that Indians would not find the grave, he picked up both flintlock rifles and turned his attention back to the ravine, where a sudden bedlam was taking place. He tried to clear his fogged senses back to reality.

There seemed to be mass confusion everywhere. British soldiers were running back down the trail to the creek, and brown-clad Colonists were scattering in every direction. A quick volley burst forth, and those in the rear fired into the smoke, not realizing they were firing on their own men. It was told later that fifty British army and Colonist regulars died in that one volley alone, by their own men's hands.

Like a madman, Jonathan raced, screaming down the hill into the fray, blood still oozing from his head wound. He fired, reloaded and fired again, ducking behind fallen horses for cover. As a man possessed, Jonathan, without regard for his own safety, leaped out and continued firing at the unseen savages and bluecoats, who were now pursuing the British troops in a rout.

Chilling screams and shouts echoed throughout the forest. Horses whinnied hysterically, trapped in their harnesses, and muskets ever continued to pop and crack, hitting their marks with rhythmic ferocity. The choking, acrid smell of gunpowder filled the ravine. The sound of the twang, whoosh and thud of arrows, and the resulting screams filled the air, accompanied by heart-stopping war whoops. Jonathan, finally out of gunpowder, grabbed the barrel of his long rifle and used it as a club, swinging wide, crushing a face here, and bashing in a skull there.

A few yards away, Jonathan saw Captain Wood take a bullet right between the eyes, and watched helplessly as the man fell dead from the saddle. Another shot, and his horse crumpled on top of the dead Captain, kicking furiously. In another instant, General Braddock fell from his mount, grasping his chest where a bullet had ripped through his lungs. By now, the soldiers and Colonists were in full retreat, that is, those of them who were left, for more than three quarters of the men who had traveled up the ravine on that July morning now lay dead.

British soldiers and American Colonists fled back down the ravine in headlong chaos. Braddock lay where he had fallen, weakly pleading for someone to carry him to safety. Several British officers and regulars ran or limped right past him without giving him a glance, as he lay on one side of the trail, bleeding from his chest wound.

Jonathan was heading toward the General to help when he simultaneously heard the whoosh of an arrow, and felt a searing, hot pain in his thigh. Looking down, he saw the shaft of a Delaware arrow protruding from his left thigh, the tip buried deeply into his muscle. The pain was excruciating, and he knew that the arrowhead was scraping bone.

Jonathan limped ahead two steps, wincing, when the crack of a musket sent a ball through his right side, and everything went black.

Jackie Gould

Chapter Twenty-eight

E lizabeth grew to respect some of the Delaware ways. They had taught her that everything had a spirit. The trees, grass, plants, rivers, mountains, and animals all had a spirit. She also observed the great love that family members had for one another, watching the laughter and happiness flow through the village. Even the children were delightful, and were much like the children back at Fort Cumberland. She wondered how such loving and kind people could possibly perform the tortuous atrocities that she had heard about. It must be that those stories had been magnified out of proportion.

Then on the day the first of the war party came back into the village, a dread crept back into Elizabeth's innermost recesses. With the war party's imminent return, she once more felt the long fingers of anxiety invade her being, for surely her problem with Stillwell would raise its ugly head once more. She watched as Te-tak-wa-o-ee ran to join the other women as they formed a line on each side of the returning warriors, and listened to their screeching greetings. Women and children shouted and jumped for joy. Dogs ran leaping and barking at the great commotion as the warriors entered the village.

Elizabeth did not join in the celebration, but chose to retire to her hut. A sick feeling wafted over her body as she thought of Stillwell. Soon, however, the screeches of happiness turned into wails of grief as the maimed, the wounded, and the bodies of the dead were brought into the center of the compound. The young captive girl put her hands over her ears, trying to block out the weird wailing.

One high pitched screeching wail grew louder, and suddenly, bursting through the low doorway, Te-tak-wa-o-ee came in, hysterically throwing up her arms, pulling her hair. Elizabeth was shocked as two braves carried in the limp form of George Stillwell, and deposited him upon the floor of the hut. He was terribly pale, and utterly still, as he lay upon the mats of woven corn husks. The Indian girl hovered over his prostrate form, still wailing at the top of her lungs. At first, Elizabeth could not tell where the man was wounded, for he showed no outward signs. Then, one of the Delaware braves said something to Te-tak-wa-o-ee, and gestured to the Lieutenant, turning the man on his side.

Elizabeth could then see the horrible wound in the man's lower back, and recoiled at the gaping, bloody spot festering near his spine. She quickly turned away, fighting the nausea that rose in her throat, trying to maintain her composure. Meanwhile, Te-tak-wa-o-ee quickly went about treating the wound, her wails now down to whimpers. She first removed Stillwell's clothing, then, rummaging through some baskets on the storage shelves, found some medicinal leaves which she put in her mouth. When she had chewed them sufficiently, the Indian girl took the wad from her lips and forced it into the large wound, repeating the process until the wound was packed with the mixture. Next, she covered the wound with sheaves of bark, and bound the area with braided fresh corn husks. Then she wrapped Stillwell in a bearskin covering.

Elizabeth stood helplessly by, knowing that Stillwell's wound should be properly cleaned, but dared not interfere. Te-tak-wa-o-ee fanned the fire in the fire pit and threw certain green herbs upon the flames, waving the resulting smoke about Stillwell's head. She softly chanted a healing song. Clearly, the Indian girl cared deeply for Stillwell, and she never left his side.

George Stillwell regained consciousness on the third day when his eyelids fluttered and opened. But the light in his eyes was gone. Those eyes, which had been so piercing and powerful, were now dull, and he seemed very far away. The injured man did not speak, nor did he move. Only his sunken eyes, staring at the smoke hole in the roof, gave any indication that he lived at all.

For all the hatred and disgust that Elizabeth had felt for this man, she could not help but feel compassion for his circumstances now. She, too, sat close, putting a cool hand upon his heated, feverish brow. As the hours went by, she helped Te-tak-wa-o-ee move him so the dark skinned girl could put fresh herbs into the man's wound from time to time. After a few days, Elizabeth was amazed to see that the wound appeared to be healing, and on the fifth day, Stillwell finally fully awakened.

Elizabeth leaned close as he hoarsely whispered, "I cannot move my legs." Then a wild look of horror came into his eyes, when the realization of his plight registered in his mind.

"Sh-h-h," Elizabeth soothed. "Try to stay calm. You have had a terrible wound, Lieutenant. Te-tak-wa-o-ee has dressed your wound, and you will be better soon."

He turned his head to look at the Indian girl as she lay a little brown hand upon his chest, and smiled at him with her eyes. "But I can't feel anything!" Stillwell yelled, thrashing his head back and forth.

"Be still, Lieutenant, let your wound heal. I am sure you will be better," Elizabeth said, not at all convinced of the truth of her own words.

Te-tak-wa-o-ee brought a bowl of corn soup, to which she had added fish and squash while it had simmered in the fire pot, bubbling into a nourishing mix. While Elizabeth elevated Stillwell's head upon her lap, the Indian girl spooned the brew between the wounded man's pale lips. He was able to tolerate a little nourishment, and swallowed some water from a goat bladder waterbag. Soon, he slept again.

And so for weeks, the two women, one white and the other one dusky brown, tended to the needs of the tall, lanky Englishman, who had turned traitor. It was pathetic to see the man, for he was paralyzed from his waist down, and his muscles were wasting away. True, he had regained some movement of his hands and arms, but his legs were useless. Elizabeth thought that by moving his legs herself, she could force some movement back into his body, so she spent long hours pumping the man's legs, bending first one then the other to stretch the muscles. His legs were dead weight, and it took a bit of hard doing for the girl to accomplish what she did.

The summer wore on, and crops ripened in the fields, yet Stillwell had only regained the feeling from his waist up. He was able to push into a sitting position and pull himself around the hut by his arms, dragging his useless legs behind him. His voice was strong, and he cursed with such profanity at his plight that it caused Elizabeth to cover her ears.

She hoped that he might have forgotten, but one evening the Lieutenant seemed more rational, and began talking about the 'wedding.'

"You are standing by me, like a good wife should, Elizabeth," he began.

She was suddenly alert, and stared at him, shaking her head. "We are not married, Lieutenant Stillwell."

"Yes, yes we are!" he insisted. "I declared us husband and wife, and that is all that is needed here in the wild Indian Village. That is the Indian way."

"Well, that is not my way," Elizabeth uttered with determination in her voice.

"Huh!" Stillwell grunted. "I suppose you are mooning over someone back at Fort Cumberland. Well, let me tell you, *Mrs.* Stillwell, there is no one left in Braddock's party, for we ambushed them, and scuttled them all. They are all lying dead up and down the ravine. I even saw Braddock take a hit. Saw soldiers and Colonists drop like flies. So much for their road to the French Fort Duquesne. They're all dead!"

Elizabeth turned white and ran from the hut.

Chapter Twenty-nine

The sun had set when Jonathan regained consciousness, and he woke to find himself high upon a hill on the other side of Turtle Creek, not knowing how he had gotten there. All around were moaning sounds from the wounded army, and Colonist volunteers. He found his head was pounding as he tried to raise up on one elbow. Pain shot through his leg like a hatchet blow, and he remembered the Indian arrow. With great effort, he pushed himself to a sitting position. That is when he realized he had been wounded in his right side, for he felt a warm wetness seep down his waist. Feeling gingerly with his fingers, he found it was merely a flesh wound. The bullet had gone though from the back, and had come out just under his rib cage in the fleshy area above his hipbone. Luckily it missed hitting any organs.

Jonathan winced as he attempted to move his left leg, discovering that the shaft of the arrow still protruded from his legging, which by now was soaked in his own blood. He scarcely remembered that there was a crease in his temple where the first bullet almost found its mark. Looking about, he discovered with horror that there were wounded men everywhere. Those who were fortunate enough to have escaped any bullet or arrow walked around in a daze.

Just a few yards away from Jonathan lay General Braddock, himself being attended by two officers trying to stem the flow of blood from his chest. Dozens of other Colonists and army regulars lay groaning with grievous bleeding wounds. Several died, or were dying as Jonathan watched, hardly believing his eyes.

The memory of the battle, or what could have been called the slaughter, came back to him, and Jonathan turned his gaze back across the stream to the dark shadows of the ravine. All was quiet now, for the French and Indians, for the moment, had withdrawn. But Jonathan's heart was back there under a log on the side of a bluff overlooking that dark ravine. Cold despair enveloped the wounded man, as he remembered Nathan's death, and he once more was filled with anguish that tore at his insides. He felt like half of him was over in that ravine, underneath the oak log.

Nathan... Nathan... His name came with every heartbeat. *My dear Nathan!*

"Let's see here," a gentle voice said, as one of the Colonist leaders, who himself had a bandage about his head, leaned over Jonathan. "Where are you hit?" Jonathan pointed to his side. The leg wound was obvious. Tearing a strip of cloth from his own shirt, and after determining that the bullet had gone straight through, the man bound up Jonathan's side wound.

"Looks like you took a hit on your temple, too, but that seems to already be crusted over. Now, about that arrow..."

"Pull it out!" Jonathan said through clenched teeth, trying to obliterate the pain that throbbed like a blast furnace.

"You sure of that, Friend? Don't you want to wait for the surgeon? They are coming from the camp with Dunbar. The General sent back for wagons for the wounded and medical supplies. They should be here soon. That arrow should be cut out."

Jonathan shook his head. "No..." he breathed hoarsely. "Pull it out!"

The Colonist put a hand on Jonathan's shoulder. "Friend, here, put this between your teeth."

He handed Jonathan a wooden stick, which the borderman clenched between his jaws, biting down hard, as the Colonist attempted to get a grip on the bloody arrow shaft. He pulled, and Jonathan groaned, but the elder man's hand slipped. Wiping his hands on his soiled pant leg, the Colonist again grasped the shaft, and with a mighty heave, the arrow came out of Jonathan's flesh. The borderman rolled his head back in agony, a scream caught in his throat, as the searing pain threatened to send him to oblivion.

"Did... you... get... it?" Jonathan panted, as shooting stars rang in his head.

"Well, Friend, the shaft came out, but I fear the arrowhead tip is still in your leg."

He lifted the shaft up so Jonathan could see, and there was no arrowhead at the tip end, only feathers at the hilt end of the straight arrow.

"Damn!" Jonathan uttered. "Just bind it up!"

"You sure, Friend?"

Jonathan nodded emphatically, and soon his throbbing thigh was tightly bound.

"Thanks," he said, his voice shaking from pain. "How did we get out of the ravine?"

"Well, Friend, those who could, carried out the wounded, but I fear we had no time to bury our dead. They are still back there."

In shock, Jonathan looked about. "Are these all that are left?"

The Colonist nodded. "I'm afraid so, Friend. Looks like we lost almost three quarters of our troops."

"Three quarters! My God!" Jonathan swore softly. "My brother was one of them, but I was able to hide his body under a log, for I fear the Indians will come back and take their trophies."

The Colonist nodded. "I fear so too, my Friend. There won't be much left of those poor devils," he muttered, looking back at the entrance to the ravine.

Jonathan shuddered at the thought, and was glad that Nathan's body would not be found, for he knew all too well how the Indians would take scalps, and mutilate the dead bodies by cutting off their privates, sometimes even cutting out their hearts.

After dark, all of the British soldiers who could walk fled the camp and disappeared into the night, like ghostly shadows fading into the trees. There were no campfires, for the General did not wish to make the straggling entourage an easy target. He feared the enemy was probably watching at the very moment, and would quickly regroup to finish the job.

General Braddock was weak with loss of blood, and was spitting up frothy pink in gasping coughing spells, as his lung had been fatally punctured. Though mortally wounded, he was painfully aware of the defeat of the brigade he had led. He was unable to rise, but tried to direct the army while he lay beneath a tree about half a mile from Turtle Creek.

"Has Washington returned yet with the supply wagons?" he croaked.

"No, General, he just left a few hours ago. He could not even be back to Little Meadow yet," was the reply.

"Damn the man! Doesn't he know we need help?" the General tried to shout, but ended in another coughing spell, spiting up blood that dribbled down the stubble that covered his chin.

"We must retreat! Pull out, men! Pull back! Take cover!" the General mumbled, now in delirium, thrashing in his make-shift bed.

The night wore on, and yet the moans could still be heard. Moonlight added a strange grotesqueness to the scene, and fireflies flitted in tiny flashes under the dark branches. Jonathan finally slept fitfully.

Chapter Thirty

W hen the relief wagons still had not arrived by dusk the following day, Braddock ordered the temporary camp to break and march. The walking wounded, of which Jonathan was one, although not a very mobile one, helped those who could not walk. They had salvaged a few wagons, to be pulled by such animals as they found that still could move. The sorry entourage was loaded onto the rumbling conveyances, and they slowly snaked their way down the roadway.

Jonathan was able to hobble with the help of a branch that he used as a crutch. Onward they marched, and staggered into the darkness of the night, with just enough moonlight to see the roadway that had been cut so recently by all the men who now lay dead in the ravine behind them. The going was slow, and Jonathan gritted his teeth with every painful step, his leg by now a fiery throb. He felt certain it was bleeding, as was the wound in his side, and realized that if there was much more loss of blood, he would not be able to continue.

On and on the battered remnants of the army staggered, hobbled, and crawled, putting whatever distance they could muster between themselves and the ill-fated Turtle Creek ravine, looking like a ghost army in the ethereal light of a partial moon. At ten that night they halted, unable to proceed any farther. The General, riding in one of the wagons, had weakened remarkably, and was not removed when they halted, but remained in his bed.

Jonathan threw himself upon the ground with a wrenching cry, exhausted. His heart was pounding in his ears with an alarmingly rapid tha-dud... tha-dud. His great chest heaved, straining to fill lungs that cried for life-giving blood, which was slowly dripping away from the wound in his side, and where the arrow was still imbedded in his thigh.

Can't think now, he thought to himself. *Must get some rest... must sleep... will have more strength tomorrow.* He drifted into merciful slumber. Even then, his breathing was labored, and his mighty heart still raced, for by now Jonathan had developed a fever. His body shook with chills sending spasms through his limbs.

The borderman awakened before dawn to the sounds of jingling harnesses and wagon wheels rolling on the dirt road. Subdued men's voices were urgently giving orders in calm, quiet ways. The convoy from Dunbar had finally reached the pitiful survivors of the massacre. Quickly and unceremoniously, the wounded were loaded into the hospital wagons, or lifted onto horseback, if they were able to cling to the animals' backs. In no time, the convoy turned around, and was moving rapidly back down the road toward Little Meadow, with Jonathan clinging to the back of a black horse. Every jarring step the animal made shattered Jonathan's senses, for the pain seared into his brain like sheets of lightning.

The mercy convoy arrived at Little Meadow camp in the early afternoon of July 11th, forty-eight hours after the disaster in the ravine at Turtle Creek. When the soldiers and regulars who had remained at Little Meadow heard of the rout from the survivors, and saw the extent of the devastation to their comrades, pandemonium broke out, and, stopping just long enough to grab their rifles, hundreds of men deserted and fled in panic.

At this point, Braddock, who lay white and listless on a cot, ordered the remaining officers to take what provisions would be needed for a flying march back to the fort, and to destroy all the rest, for he feared the French would follow and capture any supplies that remained. "We shall better know how to deal with them another time," the General said, and fell back, dead.

Swiftly, the remaining officers organized the flying march, sending the column at double time down the road. Just a few men stayed back to destroy the provisions. One officer had a deep hole dug into the roadway, and gently wrapped the General's body into a blanket, before lowering him to be laid to rest beneath the very roadway that would one day bear his name. Wagons rolled over the grave, obliterating the burial site, just as the officer had hoped, for the body needed to be hidden for fear it would be found by the hostiles and mutilated.

The last of the supplies were burned, and the remaining army galloped away down the trail to Fort Cumberland. Jonathan found himself mounted upon the very horse that Braddock had so proudly ridden when he first arrived at the fort several months ago. The black was swift, and Jonathan soon eased into the rhythm of the horse, as they loped along the trail, passing men and wagons. Soon, they were far ahead of the defeated army. Onward they galloped into the night, stopping only when they came to a small river. Painfully, Jonathan slid from the saddle, and after watering the horse and putting a hobble on the animal's front legs, he lay down on the moss beneath the spreading branches of a mighty oak, and slept.

Only the moan of the wind through the trees disturbed the night air. The soft snort of the black stallion could be heard as he grazed close to the river's edge, occasionally swishing his long black tail, and raising his fine head to cock an ear, as he munched on the tall lush grass. Jonathan slept the dreamless sleep of total exhaustion. Still, the fever burned his body, sapping what little strength was left.

In the faint light just before dawn, Jonathan rose gingerly, aching in every bone, and went to the river's edge. He knew by his swirling head that fever gripped his body, and the wounds still bled. After slaking his thirst, he lowered himself into the cool stream, allowing the water to flow over his limbs, cleansing the wounds with refreshing wetness. Jonathan would gladly have remained in the cold stream forever, for it would have been easy just to close his eyes and let his head drop under the water. Just let the water circle his head, let it invade his lungs. Just let go, let the life of him bubble out, and he could rest forever. Just float into nothingness. But he jerked himself back to reality.

Thus revived, even for a little while, he found the black stallion had not wandered far, and was happy, for he did not have the strength to go looking for his mount. Drawing the horse beside a rock onto which he could climb, the wounded man was able to swing his now stiffening leg over the saddle. Slumping over the horse's neck, Jonathan guided him back onto the trail, and once again they loped eastward, in a mind-numbing monotony of trees and bushes, passing like a whirling blur.

The frontiersman locked his fingers into the black's mane, and slumped farther over the horse's neck, for now everything was whirling in Jonathan's mind, and he was close to unconsciousness. He was aware enough to know that should he slide off the horse, he would never have the strength to remount, so with every effort that could be mustered, the borderman held onto his seat in the saddle. The next thing he knew, friendly hands were helping him slide from the horse, and he was carried into the fort.

Thank God, he thought, and everything went black.

Chapter Thirty-one

B ack at Fort Cumberland, the sad remnants of Braddock's army of road builders had all straggled in. The wounded were cared for lovingly by those few women of the fort who were left. Some of the men died of their wounds, while others, like Jonathan, slowly recovered. But the devastation of the defeat was hard to overcome, and the mood at the fort was dark and heavy. The women, mostly widows, were devastated by the fate of their loved ones, and kept to their quarters, or made plans to leave the fort and return to England.

Jonathan remained ill for weeks. He floated in and out of delirium while infection wracked his body, sapping the strength from his great frame. When the fever finally broke for good, summer had waned and the dry, hot days of late September were upon the land. The Colonists were harvesting what few crops there were, and life was returning somewhat to normal for the somber community.

Jonathan slowly regained his mobility and strength by exercising regularly, and walking as much as possible. He would forevermore walk with a limp, for it had become necessary for the medical officer of the fort to remove the imbedded arrowhead. The resulting muscle damage never did heal properly, so the tall man could be seen often limping along on the path to the river, forcing his limbs to perform. He rejoiced at every little triumph that came his way.

This was the situation one day when Jonathan made his painful way to Elizabeth's quarters, to inquire after her. He knew he should offer sympathies to her for the deaths of her father and Nathan. He thought it somewhat strange, however, that she had not come to visit him while he had been recuperating. When he arrived at her door, he found there was no answer, so he quietly inquired of the officer in charge of the fort.

"Do you know of the whereabouts of Mistress Elizabeth Wood, the Captain's daughter? Did she return to England after the massacre?"

The officer shook his head. "No, as a matter of fact, she disappeared, they tell me, rather suddenly, several weeks before the Turtle Creek tragedy."

Jonathan was stunned. "What do you mean, 'disappeared'? How could she just disappear?" The officer shrugged. After all, it was not his job to keep track of the civilians who lived at or around the fort.

"Who knows about this?" Jonathan demanded.

"You might find out something from one of the officers' wives, but most of them have gone back to England, after their husbands were killed."

"Damn it, man! Tell me who to see!"

"I really don't know who can help you. Now, I have work to do." The officer dismissed him abruptly.

Jonathan strode out of the fort, as swiftly as his wounded leg would allow, and confronted the proprietor of the trading post outside the gate. Surely, this man must have some knowledge, for he heard everything that went on around the fort. The grizzled old man shook his head.

"Can't help much, Friend. All I know is that a few weeks ago, one of the orderlies brought over this box of Mistress Wood's things. Seems they cleared out the Captain's quarters, and this is all that's left. She disappeared back in late June, they say. Some say she drowned herself in the river. Despondent over the death of her mother, you know. They never did find her body, though."

The proprietor shoved a box toward Jonathan, who placed shaking hands upon the parcel.

"Go ahead, son, you might as well take it, for no one else here is going to claim it." Jonathan retreated to his quarters near the fort, where he had been residing while recuperating. Placing the box upon his bunk, the borderman sat beside it and gingerly opened the top. He felt as though he were intruding upon the most private of matters as his eyes lit upon the contents.

Folded neatly were a few of Elizabeth's dresses, a pair of well worn shoes, a hairbrush, and a small mirror, a shawl and some undergarments that made Jonathan flush with embarrassment. At the bottom of the box, underneath a dark cloak, Jonathan found the letter that Nathan had slipped beneath Elizabeth's door.

Jonathan's fingers caressed the page, as the sight of Nathan's familiar hand caused a tug at his heart. He could not help the lump that came to his throat as his eyes scanned the neat writing. For weeks, he had tried to push Nathan's death and the horror of that ravine to the back of his thoughts, but now the ripping pain of that fateful day came crashing back upon Jonathan's mind. Once more he heard the volleys of gunfire, the screams of the wounded, the ferocious war whoops of the Indians. Again, he smelled the gunpowder, saw the blood spattering, and wondered why his life had been spared. His emotions waged back and forth. He felt guilt, rage, helplessness, and finally, spent, he fell into utter resignation.

Now an urgency came upon the borderman, and he felt compelled to return to the cabin on the mountain-top at once. He gathered his few possessions, namely the flintlock rifle and powder horn, and went to seek out those most responsible for his care during those terrible days when he had returned to the fort, more dead than alive.

"I want to thank you, Eb," Jonathan said, gripping the hand of a man who was well into his fifties, with graying hair and a hearty pink-cheeked face. "I mean to return to my home on the mountain. I thank you for pulling me through. I know it was your determination that kept me from dying, but I still wonder why you bothered. You should have just let me go."

"Nonsense!" the man retorted. "Ye were too stubborn to die. I had little to do with the whole matter. Sorry yer leg is going to be bummed up, but I guess it's better than losin' it all together."

Jonathan gave a special squeeze to the man's hand, and turned to go.

"Say there, Jonathan, my friend. I can't see ye tryin' to climb that mountain with yer leg that-a-way. Come, take that horse over yonder."

"Eb, I can't do that. I have no way of paying for such a mount."

"Jonathan, ye have already paid this army plenty, with the loss of yer twin brother, and the wounds ye received. This is little enough to give ye in return, for we can never repay ye fer yer services."

Jonathan felt humbled, and clasped the man in a bear hug, unable to speak. And so it was that Jonathan, astride the black stallion that had once belonged to General Braddock himself, returned to the mountain with the box of Elizabeth's belongings tied behind the saddle.

Chapter Thirty-two

All that fall, Jonathan struggled to build a corral and shelter for the horse. Swinging the ax built up his strength, but the leg wound still gave him problems. However, he overcame every obstacle with ingenuity and resolve, and before the snow flew, a snug shelter had been erected inside a split rail fence. He made one more trip back to the trading post that season to lay in a supply of grain to feed the horse during the long winter.

Jonathan hunted on foot, as was his custom, although the going was not as swift as before because of the old wound. He found those long treks rekindled his endurance, and by the time spring came to the mountain, his physical prowess had returned almost to normal. The leg ached only during certain times when the temperature dropped to its coldest and the winds howled outside, blowing snow up to the window top. The frontiersman would always have that reminder of one July day at Turtle Creek, in 1755, when a bone-jarring ache invaded his leg, and there was nothing the man could do to relieve the pain. He could only endure.

Fashioning a stone into the shape of a plow, Jonathan fastened it behind the black horse, and was able to turn the fertile dark loam into a field for planting, and soon had a garden growing. For all the years he had been in this new country, he could hardly imagine he was turning into a farmer. He had hunted and fished, and killed redskins when needed to protect the border. Now he was growing his own food. This was new for him, and he was excited as the plants grew and matured.

❧

Well over a year had gone by since the infamous day of Braddock's Defeat, as it had come to be known. Jonathan was off on one of his hunts, the final hunt of the fall, before the snow would fly again. He meant to lay in a goodly supply of meat for the winter. He had almost run short last season, and wanted plenty of dried venison for this year. Following deer tracks across the brow of the mountain, he found himself at a familiar spot.

It was the glen by an overhanging rock, from which he and Nathan had watched General Braddock enter the fort over a year and a half ago. It seemed like a lifetime ago now, in another world. Jonathan wandered back to the dark, cool pool of water, and lay flat on his belly to sip from the sweet spring. Water still trickled down the face of the rocky incline above the pool, just as it had done the first time he had entered the area. Ferns still guarded the quiet glen, gently swaying in the afternoon breeze. Curious, he followed the rocky abutment and found the entrance to the hidden cave that he had discovered so long ago.

It took his eyes a moment to adjust to the darkened interior, but suddenly, Jonathan stiffened, for on the floor of the cave, he found chippings from arrowheads, and a few broken points that seemed to have been tossed aside. He was positive that when he and Nathan had first entered this opening that time before, there had been no sign of any human habitation. Then the hair on Jonathan's neck stood up, and a chill coursed through his body. Upon further investigation, he found a broken arrow shaft. Surely Indians had used this area to flake their arrowheads, and make their arrows. There were even a few discarded feathers in the dust on the floor, left over from being fastened to the arrows themselves.

He stepped carefully, and could still see imprints from Indian moccasins in the fine dirt of the cave floor. Now using all his finely honed woodsman's skills, Jonathan emerged from the cave and searched for other clues. This was old, he thought; certainly nothing very recent had occurred here. He searched around the entrance to the cave, and moved away the overhanging bushes in the area, revealing matted leaves from last year's drop. A little further on, he discovered a piece of rawhide thong, obviously weathered.

Cautiously picking up the piece of leather in his fingers, Jonathan determined that it had been cut with a knife. There was no doubt about who had been here. Then, Jonathan froze in his tracks, and a sinking feeling descended upon the borderman. Almost buried beneath the wet leaves, he spied a piece of cloth. He almost overlooked it, for it had obviously been there for a long time. Carefully, almost gingerly, he pulled a once-white piece of lace from beneath the matted leaves. It was hardly recognizable, for the lace was tinged with mud, and stained from leaves and moisture.

Elizabeth! This was Elizabeth's bonnet! Jonathan's insides turned to ice as he recognized the tiny lace cap with the colored ribbons attached, now so covered with dirt and wet from the first frosts of winter. He had seen the girl wear that cap on several occasions, perched upon her golden hair. Now, the puzzle clicked in his head, and he knew what had transpired. She most likely had been kidnapped by the savages. Elizabeth Wood had not drowned in the river, as some had thought. She had been abducted by the Delaware Indians!

Once more, Jonathan searched the ground carefully, not wanting to overlook any other clue. He knew that almost a year and a half had gone by since the abduction, and held out little hope that he might find any more evidence. However, in a sheltered spot, he barely made out the imprint of a square heel in the soil. A sickening dread filled his every fiber, for he dared not contemplate the possible fate of the poor English girl.

Quickly, Jonathan returned to the cabin to determine his next move. He could hardly think straight, for he was trembling with rage. Why had no one at the fort even given any thought to the girl's fate? Why had they not initiated any kind of search? Jonathan was numb with outrage.

"Elizabeth! Elizabeth, dear girl! I will find you. For Nathan, I will find you! I must! For Nathan! ... For Nathan!" Jonathan groaned out loud, anguish in every word that he uttered.

He paced the confines of the cabin, his mind whirling with this newfound knowledge.

"Elizabeth! Oh, you poor unfortunate girl! Where did they take you? What have they done to you? Oh, God! If only I had known sooner. It may be too late!"

He walked out into the cold blast of the early winter afternoon, and watched scudding gray clouds move swiftly across the sky. He could smell snow in the air. The sudden cold of the day matched the cold despair he felt in his heart. Gripping his fists until his nails bit into the palms of his hands, Jonathan threw back his head and a scream rose from the depths of his throat to echo across the mountain.

"ELIZABETH!"

Chapter Thirty-three

I n the Delaware village, it was time to celebrate the Green Corn Festival once more, and was the second of such festivals that Elizabeth had witnessed. "So, it has been well over a year since I was captured," she thought. The angle of the sun had shifted, and she knew that fall was approaching by the deep blue skies overhead, and saw the vast expanse festooned with flat bottomed fluffs, drifting placidly above, like a huge armada at full sail.

Great orators proclaimed gratitude for all the spirit forces of the earth during the solemn festival. For crops, earth, water, grasses, trees, herbs, birds, wind, rain, the moon, stars, and to the Great Spirit. There were many dances, such as the Feather Dance, that were performed, and games were played during the four days of festivities.

For a few days during the Green Corn Festival, Elizabeth had been able to divert her mind from the constant and pathetic duty of caring for Stillwell, and was grateful for the short reprieve. Now, she must once again face the dismal task of trying to care for the crippled Englishman-turned-traitor. She retreated to her hut to take a bowl of venison stew to the man who remained paralyzed in their hut.

Stillwell had never regained the use of his body below the waist, and spent hours and days in raging fits of anger, directed at Elizabeth, the Indian Village, and the entire world. She cared for his everyday needs, feeling a sense of duty to the man, for reasons she could not fathom herself. She only knew she pitied herself and the plight of someone so stricken, and out of a sense of decency to another human being, took on the task of his care.

Te-tak-wa-o-ee had long since left the lodge, having set up another wigwam some distance away, once she realized that Stillwell could no longer be a man to her. The Indian girl had no tolerance for a cripple, especially one who thrashed and cursed, and bemoaned his fate as Stillwell did. In fact, it was not long after the man's injury that Te-Tak-wa-o-ee had taken a husband, a good-looking brave called Many Knives. Now, the slim Indian girl's belly swelled with his child, and she was due to give birth sometime before the Mid Winter Ceremonial, when the snows would fall.

So there was no one else to care for the injured white man except Elizabeth. Sometimes she was angry with herself because she had such a soft heart. She knew that Stillwell, the vile man that he was, got what he deserved, but could not bring herself to abandon the paralyzed man. It had taken Elizabeth months of mind-numbing pain to begin to start living again, after she found out about Braddock's Defeat, well over a year ago, on the darkest day of her life. Once Stillwell had blurted out the news of the massacre, he never spoke of the incident again, for which Elizabeth was most grateful. She had enough bad dreams and nightmares about the battle without further description from him.

At first, she had rejected his allegations about the massacre in the ravine, but gradually, after the agony of the initial shock wore off, the girl reluctantly accepted the fate, and resigned herself, for the moment, to life with the Delawares. Someday, she dreamed, she would find a way to return to Fort Cumberland and the white man's world. Somehow, she would escape.

On this night, at the end of the Green Corn Festival, Elizabeth entered the hut with a bowl of stew and approached Stillwell. He was in an extremely foul mood, for he cursed at her as she tried to offer the food. Elizabeth tried to ignore his tirade. Long ago, she had become used to his foul language, and no longer turned pink at his references to sex and banality. Though his cruel remarks still cut into her sensibilities, she chose not to react to his tirades, for she was determined not to let him upset her.

"I have brought you some stew," she said in a soft, steady voice.

"I don't want the stinking stuff!"

"You should eat something, Lieutenant."

"You think that will make my legs move again? Do you think that will cause me to stand up like a man again? To walk, and ride, and be a husband? To claim my wedding night rights?" By now, he was screaming in a red-faced rage, and knocked the bowl from Elizabeth's fingers.

Snatching her wrists, Stillwell twisted her arms so that Elizabeth dropped to her knees before him. He was still powerful in his upper body, and the girl winced as his fingers bit into her flesh. He jerked her close to his face, which was now covered with whiskers that had grown into a reddish beard, and looked at her with bloodshot eyes, from beneath puffy eyelids. His skin was coarse and grimy, his once-white teeth now dark and dingy, and his body reeked of old sweat and dried urine. For the past many months, the man had refused to allow Elizabeth to clean him, nor would he clean himself when she brought soap and water for his use.

"It's time for that wedding night, Mrs. Stillwell," he breathed, his breath hot upon her face.

"Lieutenant," she began, shaking her head. "You are just tired and upset again. Let me get you some water so you can bathe. It will make you feel better."

He twisted her arms again. "I've waited long enough! Tonight... now... here! You come to me... be my wife... tonight!"

"That... is not... possible," the frightened girl said faintly. "Why, you know that you can't...."

Stillwell grabbed Elizabeth's doeskin dress at the neck, and attempted to rip it from her body. Fortunately, the animal hide did not give way, and she was able to twist away from his reach. The scream that came from Stillwell's throat then was as unearthly a sound as Elizabeth had ever heard, and caused her hair to stand on end. It was a mournful scream of agony and death, of revenge, and rage.

Stillwell, still screaming, grabbed a long hunting knife. The blade flashed again and again into his groin and abdomen, slashing and ripping. With the power of both his hands on the handle, he plunged the knife to the hilt into his heart, as the last of a scream gurgled through his lips. Stillwell's eyes were already glazing as he turned his head toward her, and Elizabeth, with a scream frozen in her throat, could only watch in horror as the man slowly slumped sideways to the ground. A dark stream flowed out of his chest to soak the earth with his pulsing blood. A long, rattling sigh hissed slowly from his mouth, and he was still.

Chapter Thirty-four

An icy wind whipped around the hut, sculpting snow into drifts against the longhouses. Winter had spread its cold blanket upon the Delaware Village, the second such season that Elizabeth endured as a virtual prisoner in the Indian encampment. She had now been there for a year and a half, and the longing to return to Fort Cumberland grew stronger every day. Stillwell's death had spread a pall upon the village, and Elizabeth was left alone, for the Indians feared to even approach the hut where the white man had committed suicide. Many even suspected that Elizabeth had been the one who had wielded the knife. Some threatened to tear down the hut and throw Elizabeth out of the village, but Te-tak-wa-o-ee had come to her rescue and persuaded the elders to let the white girl remain.

A sad hunting accident that previous fall, before the winter snows had come, took Many Knives' life while he was off gathering meat for his new wife. He had slipped and fallen to his death from a cliff one cloudy, rainy day. Other hunters brought his body back to the village, and Te-tak-wa-o-ee's wails could be heard throughout the settlement. A disturbing gloom seemed to settle over the village that fall, while Elizabeth tried to console the young Indian woman, with little luck, and could only stand by and watch the girl grieve in silence.

As the early dusk approached, one winter day, Elizabeth was surprised when the bearskin flap of her hut was raised and Te-tak-wa-o-ee entered.

"It is time now. I go"

"Your baby?"

The dark skinned girl nodded, placing her hand to her swollen belly.

"Let me go with you," Elizabeth exclaimed, excitement suddenly surging in her voice.

Te-tak-wa-o-ee shook her head. "Indian woman go alone," and she disappeared out the doorway.

She trudged through the snow banks, leaning into the wind as icy pellets of snow bit into her skin. Like every Indian woman had done for eons before, the dusky young girl went away from the village to a private place in the woods to give birth to her child. The night was long and dark, and Te-tak-wa-o-ee found shelter beneath a grove of trees, near a rocky area. There, she grunted and moaned softly, squatting and spreading her knees. Hours went by, and still the girl labored, never letting a cry escape her lips. The wind continued to howl, and she drew the bearskin and turkey feather cape more closely around her body.

When the first light of dawn colored the sky, Te-tak-wa-o-ee pushed out a tiny, squirming little being that gave a lusty cry. She bit the cord in two, and washed the baby in the snow, then wrapped the tiny pink bundle in rabbit fur and offered her breast. Proudly, the young Indian woman returned to the village with her newborn daughter clutched in her arms. Elizabeth's hut was the one she entered.

"It is woman-child," Te-tak-wa-o-ee declared.

Elizabeth took the tiny bundle into her arms and marveled at the little miracle lying before her. In that instant, the young white girl wondered why there was strife between Indians and whites, and why men fought and killed each other. *We are all the same,* she thought. *All one... only the shade of our skin is different.*

❧

Te-tak-wa-o-ee stayed in Elizabeth's hut that winter, and so White Bird of Snow, the newborn infant, had two women to care for her. One of Te-tak-wa-o-ee's brothers supplied them with food, since Many Knives had not brought home the hunt. The Indian girl would have gone without food that winter, had it not been for the generosity of some of her family members.

Te-tak-wa-o-ee's baby was formally named White Bird of Snow at the Ceremonial of Midwinter. The Festival was always held on the last day of the old year, as calculated by the elders of the clan. All babies born between the Green Corn Festival and the Midwinter Ceremonial were part of the "Naming of the Babies" ritual.

The ashes in each lodge fire pit were stirred, symbolizing the scattering of the Old Year Fire, then a new fire was kindled, called the New Year Fire. Echoes of rhythmic dancing reverberated throughout the entire village, for this celebration was a major event in the village life. Many curative dances were held, and long hours were spent during which those who had dreamed during the year went from lodge to lodge to have the dream-guessing ceremony performed. It was known as the Great Riddle, for they went door to door, hinting at their dreams in forms of riddles. The listeners tried to describe the dreams, and those who guessed correctly were then obligated to satisfy that dream-desire, no matter how peculiar or extravagant the dream may have been. These Great Riddles were taken very seriously, for, not to grant the dreamer's wish would bring certain bad luck to the one who interpreted the dream correctly.

The whole Midwinter Ceremonial continued for six days, during which the Feather Dance, followed by the Thanksgiving Dance, were among the most popular dances performed. The last day was the Rite of Personal Chants, where each adult male sang his song. And so, the week-long festival of dream-searching, dancing, and games drew to a close.

With Te-tak-wa-o-ee's help, Elizabeth had related her own dream-riddle, and had entered into the dream-guessing ceremony. "Yellow Hair seeks the arrow which becomes an eagle," was her riddle. They went from lodge to lodge, and at each door, Te-tak-wa-o-ee repeated the riddle.

At the lodge of the fourth Indian, the one who had helped Elizabeth during her abduction, the answer came. The fourth Indian, whose name was Burning Tree, and who happened to be a brother of Many Knives, correctly answered the white girl's dream.

"Yellow Hair is a single gosling, separated from the Snow Goose flock. She seeks a seat upon an arrow, which turns into a sacred eagle, flying high above the mountaintops." A great deal of gesturing went along with Burning Tree's oration. "The eagle lands far away from here, where the gosling is carried to rejoin her flock. Yellow Hair seeks to return to her people."

With tears in her eyes, Elizabeth could only grasp Burning Tree's hand, and with a choked voice, said, "Yes, yes. That is my dream. To return to my people!"

Burning Tree contemplated for several minutes. One could see his mind churning as he mulled over the request. Finally, he said, "Burning Tree will grant Yellow Hair's dream." The Indian could do no other, for failing to grant the girl's dream, which the Delaware knew was a wish from the soul, would result in an extremely bad omen for the warrior. Such desires, unless fulfilled, would lead to misfortune for those who had correctly guessed the dream-presenter's wish. "When Father Sun drinks the snows of winter, and the Leaf Spirits return to the trees, Burning Tree will take the gosling to the Snow Goose Flock."

Chapter Thirty-five

J onathan spent the long winter in his cabin, virtually a prisoner of the snows that continually fell and drifted to record heights. He was uneasy and anxious the entire time, spending long days pacing the cabin, thinking of how much he would rather be on Elizabeth's trail than sitting in the confines of the log cabin. But the weather had closed in upon him before he had a chance to start out for the Delaware camp, and he was fully aware of the folly of trying to forge through the mountains during the bitter winter season. So he relegated himself to waiting until spring, but that did not stop the frustration he was feeling.

Every day he would look to the sky and check the snowdrift measure, watching for the first vestiges of warmer weather to come. In the soft glow of evening fires, while seated next to the hearth that he and Nathan had built, Jonathan lived and relived the battle and events of that fateful day in the ravine at Turtle Creek, a year and a half ago. Again and again, he experienced the wrenching of Nathan's death, and rubbed his hand against the thigh that bore the scar of the Indian arrow, aching now in response to the cold, damp winter.

When spring did arrive and the snows melted from the ground, a series of heavy rains blanketed the mountains, pouring torrents of water upon the melting snows, causing heavy flooding in streams and rivers. Once more, Jonathan was frustrated by the delay. He was sure he would burst if he could not start on the trail soon. It was so hard to be patient, so hard to wait, but experience of those border years told the man that he must pick the very best time for his journey, and rushing would only end in disaster. It would take all the cunning he could muster to go into Delaware country for the search and not get captured himself, for surely the Delaware still wanted his scalp.

Finally, when little leaves poked their way through the bursting buds on the tree limbs, Jonathan began his quest. Saddling up the black proved to be a task, he found out, since the horse had spent a restless winter cooped up in the lean-to barn. Now, the great beast wanted to run, and decided to be shy with the border-man.

"Come here, you lop-eared old nag." Jonathan cursed at the horse, trying to put the saddle on the stallion's back. Several times, he ended up sitting on his backside in the dirt, with the horse snorting and stomping above him. Again, Jonathan tried and eventually succeeded in saddling the black, who snorted and pawed the ground, as anxious to be on the trail as the man who mounted him. Together, they rode away like the wind, and Jonathan could feel the power of the horse between his legs. Like a tightly wound spring, the black uncoiled in gigantic strides, eating the ground with mind-boggling speed. They ran that way for almost an hour, the borderman allowing the mount to burn up pent-up energy before pulling him into a lope, then a trot, always heading northward.

They traveled thus most of the day, stopping twice to drink from mountain streams, as Jonathan munched on strips of dried meat while in the saddle, not bothering to stop at mid day. The horse was like a tireless machine, putting miles behind them, so when darkness approached, Jonathan figured they had covered some twenty-five miles, up and down tree-clad mountains. At this rate, he would reach the Delaware village in two days.

There was much to contemplate as he hobbled the stallion and prepared a bed for the night. He felt safe in lighting a fire, and cooked his meal, while the black contentedly grazed close by. When he had finished his meager meal, the borderman sat, a lonely figure, by the light of the campfire, and stared into the flames for a long time. He thought of Nathan, and remembered the hours the two used to spend smoking their long stemmed pipes together while they sat around just such a campfire. The twinge of loneliness he felt was more acute this time, and Jonathan grew restless. Solitude had never bothered the tall man before, but now, he yearned for companionship.

No longer was it enough to be in the wilderness, to spend the days tracking game and following the lonely trail. Evenings spent by the light of an open campfire no longer gave Jonathan peace. He gazed into the blackness of the quiet forest that surrounded his campsite and wondered why he no longer felt fulfilled. The night sounds no longer were a source of contentment, and the thrill of the chase and hunt no longer gave him the satisfaction it once had. Stars overhead blinking in the vast ocean of a black night sky no longer made him feel at ease in the familiar soft light, no longer beckoned him to a life in the wilderness.

Jonathan threw another stick on the fire, and disgustedly rose to stroll away into the darkness. Slowly, he circled the campsite, pacing mindlessly, wandering among the trees, fighting to pull his thoughts together. But it was of no use. He could not concentrate on his mission, for visions of Nathan invaded his thoughts. Nathan and Elizabeth... Elizabeth... the girl with the long golden hair. Would he find her alive? The chances were slim, but a faint twinge of hope still pushed him forward. He pulled out Elizabeth's little bonnet from beneath his fringed shirt, and let his finger trace the delicate lace. The memory of the girl's softness and beauty invaded Jonathan's mind then. No wonder Nathan had fallen in love with her. The borderman wistfully recalled her kindness and compassion, her gentle ways. He remembered the evening that he had sat with his arm around her, back at Fort Cumberland, when he had attempted to tell her of Nathan's love for her.

Even now, recalling the feeling of her small form pressing against his side on that night sent a surge of warmth through Jonathan's body. A strange mixture of emotions began to form in his mind, and he frowned, trying to shake those new thoughts away. Without knowing why, he put the lace cap up to his cheek and felt a strangling, churning inside. He pressed his lips to the cloth. "Elizabeth! I will find you alive! I must! I shall!"

A faint light began to appear on the eastern horizon when Jonathan finally fell asleep. Overhead, the stars twinkled and one by one were snuffed out by the oncoming dawn. He did not awaken until a shaft of sunlight streamed through the branches of an overhead tree, striking him in the face. Then, startled, he jumped up and hastily saddled and mounted the stallion, cursing the late start.

Turning northward again, Jonathan pushed the mount forward over yet another ridge of mountains, ignoring the hazy mist that clung to the valleys. His mind was so focused on the task ahead, that he did not take note of the grand scene before him. He was oblivious to the purple and blue ridges fading in folds as far as the eye could see. Nor did he see the mists curling between the mountains, like giant rivers of cotton, winding in a neverending maze. On he pushed, urging the horse over fallen trees, around boulders, and across streams.

Closer and closer to the Delaware village they went, passing the spot where years before, Blue Water had met her untimely death. Once, that would have brought searing memories back to him, but now Jonathan barely gave the rocky area a second thought. It was Elizabeth who now captured all of his attention. Elizabeth, with her golden hair glinting in the sun, her hazel eyes smiling... Elizabeth!

Chapter Thirty-six

Elizabeth strolled beside the river at twilight on the last evening she would ever spend in the Delaware Village. Tomorrow, she would begin her journey back to Fort Cumberland, accompanied by Burning Tree and two other braves. This was the last night to stay with her captives, the ones who had changed the course of her life. Tomorrow, she would be on her way to total liberation, with safe passage guaranteed by the Delaware tribe. Could this really be happening?

The girl's heart was soaring with the thought of home... of being able to rejoin her father, and hopefully, regain the relationship with Nathan. Long ago, she had rejected the gloomy news that Stillwell had tried to relay regarding the battle with Braddock's men, dismissing it as his way of using a scare tactic to frighten her. Home! To be able to speak English again with her own people made Elizabeth as excited as a school girl.

With a twinge of feeling, in a strange way she regretted leaving the village, for she had grown to appreciate the Delaware people. In many ways they were so much like her own people, wanting to live in peace, to be able to love, laugh, and raise their families. Elizabeth was impressed by the devotion all the Indians had for one another. She would always remember the rituals and ceremonies she had witnessed and taken part in during the almost two years of her captivity.

She had tried to bury the thoughts of those long months that she had spent with Lieutenant Stillwell, for every time she brought back the memories of the stricken man, a darkness invaded her mind. She had trouble shaking the morbid scene of his last months, and his violent death. Sometimes she shivered at the very thought of the man whose cruel and frightening ways were so disgusting and terrifying. It was strange that at first, it had been the Indians whom Elizabeth feared, and as it turned out, they ultimately had become her friends. It was Stillwell who had evoked the most terror and fright for the girl.

Now, Elizabeth watched the rosy twilight of the fading sunset being reflected in the waters of the river, as the colors changed to magenta, and then to purple.

The ripples in the water caught glints of the evening hues, and mesmerized the girl, as her thoughts reverted to a twilight many months ago that she shared with Nathan. A great longing surged through Elizabeth's very body then, as at last she could finally allow herself to dream of the future. For far too long, she had suppressed the thoughts and desires of any chance of returning to the white man's world. It had been too painful to even hope there could be a possibility months ago, and now Elizabeth dared to let the joy begin to creep into her very depths.

Nathan, for too long I have pushed every possible thought of you back into a far corner of my mind. I buried my love for you, for the pain was too great to bear. Now, at last, I can begin to let you come back into my life again, Elizabeth thought to herself. Nathan... she had tried to bring a picture of him into focus in her mind, but the image was fuzzy. A warm feeling started to envelope her when she recalled his tall form, and long black hair. A quiver of excitement wafted over the girl as she anticipated being reunited with the man who had stolen her heart.

A shock jarred the young girl when the sudden thought came to her mind that perhaps Nathan was not at the fort at all, but had returned to England. What if he were not there? What if the brothers had left the territory? Here-to-fore, Elizabeth had not given one moment's thought to that possibility. An unexpected chill coursed though her veins then at the mere idea that Nathan might not be there when she returned to Fort Cumberland. With that, Elizabeth's joy of the freedom to come turned to one of worry and concern.

As she turned to go away from the river, Te-tak-wa-o-ee appeared at her side, greeting Elizabeth with a silent outstretched hand, palm up. White Bird of Snow was wrapped snugly into the papoose board suspended on her mother's back, her tiny face peeping over the edge of the cradle board.

"E-liz-o-beth returns to her people when the dawn comes across the sky."

It was a simple statement, yet Elizabeth could sense a catch in the Indian girl's voice. The English girl nodded, and the two walked slowly side by side in the deepening twilight.

"I shall miss you, Te-tak-wa-o-ee," Elizabeth started, finding a tightening in her throat. "You have become a good friend. You were very kind to me, and embraced me into your lodge. You taught me the Delaware ways."

The Indian girl nodded, walking quietly along, staring straight ahead. Elizabeth could see the girl's profile, even in the fading light, and noted her rounded high cheekbones, and the slope of the girl's nose rising above full lips.

Te-tak-wa-o-ee's slender neck curved gracefully to disappear under the soft folds of her fringed doeskin dress. She was yet of such a tender age, Elizabeth thought, to be a mother and a widow. She had not reached sixteen winters.

"Te-tak-wa-o-ee cannot go where Yellow Hair goes."

"I know," Elizabeth replied. "You must stay with your people and raise little White Bird of Snow with her clan. White man's ways would not be good for the Delaware woman."

Elizabeth felt envy for the easy way the Delawares related to one another, showing love openly, and giving affection generously. If only the Colonists and the English could experience the warmth and love that she had witnessed while being detained in this place. There was so much laughter and love displayed by the Indians, totally without shame or embarrassment. *The English have much to learn*, Elizabeth decided.

The two returned in silence to their lodge, where Te-tak-wa-o-ee removed White Bird of Snow from the cradleboard and began to nurse the infant. The baby's chubby fingers clutched at the fringe of her mother's dress, and she suckled hungrily from the girl's brown breast. Elizabeth noted how much the Indian girl had filled out since the first time she had seen her, almost two years ago, when she had been with Stillwell. She was no longer the nubile slip of a girl that Elizabeth had first known, for now she was a woman in full bloom.

"Will you take a husband, Te-tak-wa-o-ee?"

"Dream Spirit told Te-tak-wa-o-ee one great hunter will come. Te-tak-wa-o-ee waits for the moon of the Green Corn Festival."

When White Bird of Snow had finished nursing, the Delaware girl handed the baby to Elizabeth, who held the infant to her shoulder and cuddled the girl-child to her cheek. She had grown to love the baby almost as if it were her own.

"I will miss you and White Bird of Snow."

"Yellow Hair happy to go to her people?"

"Oh, yes, I am extremely happy, but I will miss your friendship. You have been a good friend, Te-tak-wa-o-ee, and I owe you much for saving me from those who wanted my death."

"Stillwell wished for you to be his woman?"

"The poor man was crazed, and thought I was his wife. I never cared for him except that he was a human being, horribly wounded, and out of decency, I took care of him."

The two women sat quietly watching the small flames of the perpetual fire in the middle of the lodge lick and sputter into the darkening night. Te-tak-wa-o-ee then removed a small leather pouch that had hung from her neck, and placed it over Elizabeth's head. The pouch was decorated with dyed porcupine quills, fashioned into an intricate geometric design, and contained a sacred carved stone.

"For to remember Te-tak-wa-o-ee," The Indian girl said seriously, in her best English. Elizabeth fingered the pouch gently, and an unexpected lump rose in her throat. She knew how important the amulet was to the Delaware girl, for it contained the sacred stone given to the girl by the Spirit Woman of the tribe, when she had passed into puberty.

"I cannot take your sacred stone from you," Elizabeth said, her voice trembling with emotion.

"Sacred stone now belongs Yellow Hair. Will keep Yellow Hair safe always, forever."

Elizabeth's eyes were misty as she tried to express her gratitude, knowing that the giving of such a gift was a sacrifice of great proportion for Te-tak-wa-o-ee. The sacred stone encased in the small leather pouch was the most sought after honor that could be bestowed upon a Delaware girl when she came of age, and was given to only one girl each season, chosen from all those who were eligible in the tribe.

"Thank you," Elizabeth breathed, humbled by such a magnanimous gesture. She placed the baby upon a blanket near the fire, and disappeared deep into the shadows in the farthest corner of the lodge. Shortly, Elizabeth returned to the light of the fire, and handed the Indian girl her long, blond braid, which she had bound with a leather thong. Elizabeth had cut off her braided locks, the only possession she had that could be given as a gift, the single sacrifice that she could make to honor her Delaware friend. Te-tak-wa-o-ee took the braid with both hands, and lifted it up toward the roof of the lodge in a sacred gesture, then fastened the braid into her own hair, letting the blond tress fall over her shoulder.

"We are now sister," she declared.

"Sisters," Elizabeth echoed, and embraced the girl in a moment of emotion.

Chapter Thirty-seven

Elizabeth scarcely slept that night, and rose when the light of dawn paled outside the lodge. The village was stirring awake, as smoke from cook fires soon blanketed the area with aromas of burning wood and roasting meat drifting from the longhouses. A dog barked in the distance, and Elizabeth could hear children's voices coming from behind the longhouse walls.

Quickly bathing in the cold river, Elizabeth returned to the lodge and changed into a new doeskin dress. She ruffled her short curls near the fire to let the warmth dry her hair, which was now closely cropped. How strange it felt to be without her long tresses. She felt much lighter, and somehow, smaller. She was not worried, for she knew that her hair would grow back soon enough.

Burning Tree appeared in front of Elizabeth's doorway with two braves at his side. Now, the time had come to take leave of the village. Gathering her few possessions, Elizabeth turned to hug White Bird of Snow in one last embrace before stooping to go out the door. Once outside, she stood in front of Te-tak-wa-o-ee, and noticed her own blond braid coiled between the Indian girl's raven locks.

"May the Spirits walk with E-liz-o-beth," Te-tak-wa-o-ee said, carefully enunciating the words.

"And with you," Elizabeth whispered, unable to say more.

The two clasped each other's hands for a long moment, and gazed into each other's eyes. Then Te-tak-wa-o-ee turned and disappeared into the lodge. Elizabeth took a deep breath, nodded to Burning Tree, and the party left the village. There was no ceremony. In fact, few even noticed that the English girl was taking her leave. It was of no consequence to the villagers, for they went about their daily tasks without raising an eye to the departing foursome.

On the rise of a hill, Elizabeth took a final look back at the Delaware Village to imprint the image forever on her mind. She saw longhouses scattered in a loose pattern as if thrown from a giant hand, to land where they would. Smaller huts and a few teepees were interspersed at various intervals. Smoke and haze drifted in a lazy dance over the village, and women and children scurried about, performing their various daily rituals. Elizabeth stood for a long moment, then turned and continued walking behind the bronze trio.

Soon, they were out of sight of the village and deep into the wilderness. Elizabeth could see tiny wildflowers poking from beneath fallen leaves under the spreading branches of giant trees which were now leafing into spring. She breathed a great sigh of freedom as they trudged deeper and deeper into the forest, and a renewed vigor quickened her step.

By the second day, the party quit the trail and headed cross-country, traversing ravines and skirting large canyons. The mountain ranges undulated on as Elizabeth grew weary, and her legs became rubbery with fatigue. Burning Tree stopped early that evening to give the girl a rest, and they made camp in an area of rocks and ferns, next to a stream. Very little conversation took place, as Burning Tree only knew a few words of English, and his braves knew none at all.

What a difference from her captive march of nearly two years ago. Now the pace was easier, and Elizabeth felt no fear of the Indian guides. When the going became rugged, Burning Tree often helped Elizabeth to traverse the rough terrain by offering a strong hand or arm, which she did not hesitate to grasp. As the weary but elated girl rested beside the stream, gazing with unseeing eyes into the small crackling campfire, she barely heard the low mumblings of the Delaware conversation. Elizabeth's daydreams were all-consuming, and she paid little attention to her immediate surroundings.

The primary visions racing before Elizabeth's mind were of the reunion she would have in two more days with her father and the people of the fort. Two more days, and maybe one more night to be spent in the wilderness. The party was taking a more leisurely trek now than the forced march of two years ago, so perhaps it would require one additional night on the trail. In any case, Elizabeth could not contain the exuberance she felt from the knowledge that she was free, and would never again have to return to life in the Delaware village.

In her two years of captivity, except for the first few months, while she was physically restrained, Elizabeth could honestly say she had not been harmed by the savages. Her worst abuse, ironically, had come from one of her own, Lt. George Stillwell. The disgusting thought of him turning against his own regiment, his own country, and his vile actions toward her, turned Elizabeth's stomach even now. "May he rot in Hell forever," she uttered, surprised that she was capable of speaking about one so harshly, even to herself. It was also ironic that the Indian girl, Te-tak-wa-o-ee, who had so blatantly been Stillwell's sexual toy, had ultimately become Elizabeth's only friend in the Delaware Village. She warmed at the thought of the dusky young Indian woman, and the picture of her cradling tiny White Bird of Snow was vivid in Elizabeth's mind. She touched the curls that remained of her crowning glory, and did not regret for a moment that she had cut off her long braid as a gift to her friend.

Her hand went to the porcupine-quill-decorated pouch that hung from her neck, and took out the sacred stone. Holding the amulet up to the light of the campfire, the girl wondered what the strange carvings meant. At the same time, she felt a warmth go through her hand, and it gave her a start.

Elizabeth was restless, and rose from the fire to get a drink of water from the stream, a few paces away. The night was growing dark, with hardly a star visible between the overhanging branches, as she knelt at the water's edge. For some reason, she felt a shiver go through her, and a small jab of fear enveloped her at that moment. Quickly, she looked around into the velvet blackness under the trees, as if somewhere out there, danger lurked. Glancing back at the three Delawares clustered near the campfire, she could detect no noticeable change in their behavior, and dismissed the momentary feeling without another thought.

Rolling into her blanket, which lay upon a soft bed of moss, Elizabeth tried to close her eyes, but sleep would not come immediately. Try as hard as she might, there were too many thoughts tumbling in her mind, and she could not sort them out in any logical sense of order. The low droning voices of her companions seemed to eventually lull the girl into a fitful slumber. Once, during the night, she awoke from a formless dream to find herself covered from head to foot in chilling goose flesh. The sensation was not from the night air, for she was warm beneath her blanket, but came from a strange foreboding feeling in a half dream-like sleep.

Once more, Elizabeth finally drifted back into a deep sleep, and did not rouse again until the crack of a rifle startled her wide awake, and bloodcurdling screams sent terrifying waves of fear through her body.

Chapter Thirty-eight

J onathan hobbled the black horse in a meadow
where there was plenty of tender grass, near a small
pond. He was a few miles from the Delaware
Village, but preferred to advance on foot from this
point on, for he was aware that the Indians would have
lookouts posted a long way from the encampment. He
approached cautiously and quietly, glad that he was on
foot so he could avoid snapping twigs or rustling
leaves, which might have occurred, had he still been on
horseback.

He carried his flintlock rifle slung over his back, and
a powderhorn and bullets were at his belt. Two long
knives were thrust into leather cases, within easy reach.
He stealthily advanced, and the closer he drew to the

village, the more furtive became his movements. He glided from tree to tree, pausing each time to listen with a sharp ear, and watch with eyes like an eagle.

At one large tree trunk, Jonathan caught the glimpse of movement from the corner of his eye, and froze where he was. In a moment, a deer stepped slowly forward, nibbling at the tender new shoots of a sapling. He slowly let out the breath he was holding, and when the deer moved out of sight, continued to advance from the protection of the trees to the scrub bushes ahead. He had crossed two narrow trails which he recognized were used by the Indians, and knew he was closing in on the village.

From the cover of the underbrush, Jonathan crawled ahead on his belly until he could look over the brow of an embankment. Spread before him across the river was the Delaware Village. He saw familiar longhouses, and watched while the women of the village moved about, tending to their cooking fires. A group of women were scraping flesh from newly skinned deer hides, while others came down to the river to fill bladders with water. He saw Indian women bring their little ones to the river to bathe. One by one, the toddlers were immersed into the cool water, and were quickly washed and dried by their mothers. He could even hear the delighted squeals of the infants as they splashed happily in the shallow water.

Straining his eyes, Jonathan searched the whole village area, attempting to spot a white woman among the villagers. By now, of course, if Elizabeth were alive, she would be clothed in deerskin like all the other women, for surely her regular clothing would have been worn to shreds. All day, Jonathan kept his vigil at the river bank, well hidden. Life at the village seemed serene and normal.

By late afternoon, the borderman was growing stiff from remaining in one position for such a long time. His leg wound began to ache, and he felt it stiffening. Suddenly alert, Jonathan observed the slight form of a young girl approach the river. There was something odd about the girl's costume, and he looked more closely at a light streak that fell from the right side of her head. It could be a piece of deerskin, but that puzzled Jonathan, for he had never seen such an ornament in all his days at the village. He watched intently as the girl lifted an infant from the cradleboard, and bathed the little one in the river water. When she was finished, the Indian girl returned to a small lodge at the edge of the village, and he noted the location in his mind.

❧

Under darkness of night, Jonathan crossed the river downstream, and took up new surveillance from a closer vantage point. When the villagers first stirred at the new day's dawn, he was again alert to the comings and goings of all the tribal members. He recognized several of the warriors from his own captivity several years before, and mentally counted the probable number in his mind. "There's old Turtle Head," he mumbled under his breath, as he observed the shuffling form of an old male, now hunched and bowed with age. The Delaware's face was wrinkled beyond imagination, as if a giant hand had chiseled a wooden carving out of a tree trunk.

It would be sheer folly to enter the compound alone. No, the only way to determine if Elizabeth was still a captive here would be to have patience and watch, for sooner or later, Jonathan would surely catch sight of the girl.

At midmorning he watched the same slim Indian girl he had seen yesterday emerge from her small lodge with the cradleboard on her back. Clearly, she was headed into the forest; in fact, she was heading almost directly toward the hidden borderman. Jonathan was secreted beside a trail, well hidden by dense underbrush. He held his breath as the girl grew nearer, and pressed himself against the earth. A shock struck him like a blow when the Indian girl came close enough for him to recognize what the light streak in her hair actually was. It was a long blond braid of human hair... Elizabeth's!

Jonathan's heart sank as the enormity of the discovery descended upon him, and found his heart was pounding in his ears. He pressed his face into the earth to slowly allow his breath to release from his bursting lungs. The braid of her hair meant only one thing: Elizabeth was probably dead. Raising his head up slowly, until just his eyes peeped over the mossy rise, he watched as the girl went beyond him, carrying a basket on her hip. He allowed her to go fifty paces before he slowly, silently rose to follow. He took every step as stealthily as a cougar, and shadowed the girl as she went deeper into the forest.

Jonathan's movements were as calculated and lithe as if he were stalking the deadliest of beasts. His brown eyes scanned every inch of the forest about him for signs that other villagers or warriors had followed. Nothing moved, and when Jonathan was satisfied that they were quite alone, he advanced upon the Indian girl, closing the distance with remarkable speed. Choosing his moment, he jumped at her, and clamped a hand across the dusky girl's mouth, while holding her from behind in a vise like grip before she could take one step.

Tc-tak-wa o cc struggled like a captured doe caught in a snare, ferociously twisting and biting Jonathan's hand until he winced. He tightened his grip, and whispered harshly through his teeth, "Be still! I will not harm you."

The Indian girl suddenly stopped her struggling and became quiet in Jonathan's arms. Wary that she was using Delaware cunning to try to escape, he loosened his hold just enough to turn the girl around to face him, while still holding her mouth shut. The girl's terrified eyes suddenly widened even further, as if in recognition. She had been but a young girl when Jonathan had been held captive in the village but remembered the tall white man who had married her cousin, Blue Water.

As Jonathan looked closely at the young woman, a flicker of something familiar triggered from the back of his memory. However, he could not recall who the girl was. It had been six years since he had last set foot in Delaware territory. If he had seen the maiden at all, she would have been a child at the time he was there.

Now he looked sternly into her eyes and whispered again, "I will not harm you. Do not fight me. Do not scream." He could feel the tension relax in the girl's body, but still kept a hand clamped on her mouth. "Do you understand?"

Te-tak-wa-o-ee slowly nodded her head, her snapping brown eyes still wide. Cautiously Jonathan relaxed his grip ever so slightly, ready to clamp her mouth shut if even the slightest whimper came from her lips.

"Where did you get that blond braid?" he demanded, and pointed to the lock as it cascaded from her right temple. Te-tak-wa-o-ee only stared with puzzled eyes directly into Jonathan's. "Where did you get this?" he demanded, picking up the end of the braid between his finger tips to show the girl. She nodded her head with recognition in her eyes, and Jonathan loosened the grip on her mouth further.

With her enormous dark eyes shining, Te-tak-wa-o-ee uttered, "You... Herr-ing-ton."

Jonathan was shocked. "How do you know my name?"

"Many winters... Blue Water." Here she made the sign for marriage, but he did not recall what the sign meant.

"You remember when Blue Water was my wife?"

The Indian maiden nodded.

The borderman was stunned. "Where did you get this hair?" he repeated.

Te-tak-wa-o-ee explicitly said one word, "E... liz... o... beth."

The blood chilled in Jonathan's veins, and he turned pale. "Elizabeth Wood! Where is she? Is she dead?" His words came in a rush.

"E-liz-o-beth go away from village," The Indian girl said, pointing in a southerly direction.

"Is she alive?" Jonathan fairly shouted in his anxiety.

Te-tak-wa-o-ee nodded. "Yes... E-liz-o-beth lives. She lives dream-wish. Two days... she go... that way."

Again she pointed toward the mountains. "Burning Tree... two braves, they take E-liz-o-beth."

Chapter Thirty-nine

Jonathan dared not risk leaving Te-tak-wa-o-ee so close to the village for fear she would sound the alarm to the Delaware warriors, and they would soon be in hot pursuit. So he again clamped his hand around her mouth, and forced her to trot at his side as they left the village behind. She struggled, not understanding, and he found he had to half carry the unwilling girl into the dark forest.

When he came to within a half mile of where he had left his horse, Jonathan turned the girl loose. By now, White Bird of Snow was whimpering in her cradleboard, so Te-tak-wa-o-ee removed her infant to offer her breast. The last picture Jonathan saw of the dusky Indian girl, she was seated upon a fallen log, nursing her infant daughter, throwing dagger looks his way for having forced her to come so far away from her village.

Te-tak-wa-o-ee was silent as the borderman disappeared into the trees. Jonathan knew it would take the girl the remainder of the day to return to the village and turn in the alarm. By that time, he would be miles down the trail. Also knowing how cunning the Indian girl might be, Jonathan took pains to cover his tracks, even before he reached the spot where he had left the horse. The black nickered a soft greeting to him as he emerged from the forest into the small clearing. Sunlight filtered almost straight down through the trees, casting dappled shadows across the forest floor at mid day, and he knew that before the sun sank that evening, he would be well on Elizabeth's trail.

He swung into the saddle and turned the horse in the direction the Indian girl had motioned, picking the way carefully so his tracks would be hard to find. Jonathan's mind was racing with the news that Elizabeth was alive. His heart quickened at the thought, and a renewal of exuberance filled his body as he pushed ahead. It was not long before he detected some footprints on a trail he had come across.

Dismounting, he studied the ground closely, and could make out three distinct large moccasin prints, and one small print which had to be Elizabeth's. Again, he thrilled at the thought that she was alive, and had traveled this way so very recently. Assured that he had found the trail, Jonathan followed swiftly.

Where were these savages taking the girl? Quite possibly they were taking her to another village to trade as a slave. The Indians often kept white captives as slaves, and would use them for barter from village to village. A chill went through the borderman as he pictured Elizabeth's fate. He must reach her quickly, and effect a rescue before more harm could come to her.

On he pushed, letting his thoughts wander until he suddenly realized that he had lost the trail, so intense his daydream had become. The borderman had to back-track a ways until he found where the party had left the trail, and took off over the mountain ridge. Jonathan had to use all his tracking skills to follow their trail. He watched for soft depressions in the earth, a broken branch, a bent fern, or leaves and rocks that had been overturned on the ground.

"M-m-m," he mused, as he discovered the cold ashes of a campfire. "Must have camped here less than twenty-four hours ago." He sifted the ashes through his fingers. He glanced skyward and noted the sun had not yet reached the mid-afternoon point. There were several hours of daylight left, so perhaps he just might be able to catch up to the party by nightfall. Knowing how close he now must be getting, the excitement spurred Jonathan on even more. Quickly watering the horse, and quenching his own thirst, he picked up the tracks again, and followed their direction, covering the ground swiftly on horseback.

While he rode, Jonathan wondered how he would find Elizabeth's condition. Would the long months of captivity have so ravaged the girl that only a shell of the person remained? So many times on this wild border the settlers had rescued a loved one only to have them return so mentally and physically harmed that the person had become insane, or died of their tortured wounds. Tales of savage tortures chilled the bones of the frontier people, terrifying young and old alike.

❦

Horse and man continued on the trail of the four pairs of footprints, climbing steep sides of ravines, over rocks and rugged terrain. More than once, Jonathan had to dismount to study the ground before him, to find the smallest clue that someone had passed that way. An overturned rock, or small displacement of soil assured him that he was still in pursuit

Hours passed, and Jonathan grew excited when he found very fresh footprints in a grassy area. The bent blades had not even had time to spring fully back to their upright position when he discovered the fresh trail. Taking every precaution, the borderman decided he should approach the rest of the way on foot, so he hobbled the black, and went silently ahead, moving from tree to tree. Gliding stealthily forward, Jonathan took long moments to advance a foot or two.

The sun had now set, and twilight's gray gloom deepened into night before the borderman finally located the party. A tingle went up his spine when he caught a whiff of wood smoke which came from their campfire. Edging ever closer, taking every care not to snap a twig or rustle a leaf, Jonathan inched his way toward the faint orange glow that could be seen beneath the dark trees.

From across the stream, he made out three figures hunched around a smoldering camp fire. He surmised that it was Burning Tree and the two braves. But where was the girl? His eyes darted about in the dim light, then rested upon a slight form rolled in a blanket upon the ground, a few paces from the campfire. A thrill shot through Jonathan's body as he looked at the quiet figure beneath the blanket. At one point, the figure moved and rolled over, and the borderman thrilled again, assured that it was Elizabeth, and that she lived.

He watched for a long time, while the three Delawares sat murmuring beside the fire, and Jonathan tried to calm his excitement. A soft laugh escaped into the night sky, and he noted how relaxed the redskins seemed to be. Clearly, the Indians acted as if they expected no danger. This gave Jonathan enough encouragement to creep even closer to the encampment. Very quietly, he forded the small stream and crept in silence to the other side of the party. Again he lay on his belly, and inched forward pressing his body close to the earth as he moved.

It took twenty minutes to traverse just a few feet. Then he froze as he saw one of the braves rise and turn in his direction. Jonathan pressed himself even more closely to the ground, becoming one with the earth, and held his breath as the brave came into the woods, moving to within just a few paces of his hiding place. As the brave relieved himself in the underbrush, Jonathan could have reached out and grabbed the Indian's ankle, but continued to hold still, hoping the brave could not hear the thudding of his heart.

When the brave returned to the fire, Jonathan could hear their low guttural voices drone on into the night. He positioned himself even closer as the fire dwindled and the three Delawares ultimately rolled into their blankets. He noted that they did not post a guard, but wished that one of them had put a new log on the fire, for the dying embers gave precious little light, and the scene became too dim to make out any of the sleeping forms. Have to wait until dawn, he determined. The fact that at present he was within a stone's throw of Elizabeth both thrilled him and caused him excruciating anxiety. He wanted to strike immediately; however, to rush into the sleeping camp without being able to clearly see just where each one slept would not be wise. He dare not chance hurting the girl, who still lay quietly sleeping. For a few moments, Jonathan allowed himself to drift into slumber, since he had not slept for two days, but he slept lightly, and could still hear the soft snoring of the three Delawares.

Jackie Gould

Chapter Forty

Would the long night never end? Jonathan wondered when he fully awoke an hour later. He must plan carefully for the attack, making sure to plot his moves just so, to assure a swift but successful rescue. By this time, the fire had smoldered to gray ashes, with only the tiniest of embers still visible. There was no way, at that moment, that Jonathan could distinguish any of the sleeping forms, lumped, as they were, under their covers. He searched for a light in the sky, but it still remained as black as velvet. Only a few faint twinkling stars could be seen between the leafy branches. The hoot of a distant owl and the rustle of night creatures were the only sounds he could hear.

Wave after wave of excitement coursed through the borderman as he impatiently waited for the dawn. *On with it,* he thought, trying to still the anxious feelings that washed over his body. *I must remain calm. There can be no slip-ups, for surely they will kill Elizabeth if I do not get to them first. I know the Delaware, they are fierce fighters, and will fight to the death,* he said to himself, and a chill ran over him then, as he thought of the enormity of what he was about to attempt.

At last, the first promise of dawn crept into the early morning sky, and Jonathan was able to see the four shapes, still wrapped in their blankets. Long ago, he had primed his flintlock, in preparation for what he hoped would be a surprise attack, and now he raised himself without a sound, to silently crouch behind the low branch of a bush. Three blankets were grouped at one side of the ashes, and one small form could be seen off to the other side. Jonathan tried to gauge how many paces he would have to run before he could engage the savages.

Before he could fully formulate his plan, one of the Indians coughed and stirred, and started to rise from his blanket. Jonathan dared not wait, but sprang from his hiding place, and with a bloodcurdling scream, raced toward the three with his rifle at his shoulder. He fired at the one who was partially out of his blanket, hitting the brave squarely in the chest, sending the red man hurtling backward, dead before he hit the ground. There, his body twisted in a final death throe.

The two other Indians, now startled wide awake, scrambled out of their blankets, screaming menacing whoops of their own. One got partly twisted in his blanket just long enough for Jonathan to bash him in the head with the butt of his flintlock, sending the brave sprawling on the ground, blood oozing from a deep cut to his temple. Burning Tree had jumped to his feet, and in a flash, leaped over the ashes of the fire to where Elizabeth was just struggling to sit up in her blanket. With horror in the pit of his stomach, Jonathan saw Burning Tree raise his arm high above the girl, and bring his arm down, swinging hard, striking the girl to the ground, ending a scream she had caught in her throat.

Simultaneously, Jonathan leaped over the cold embers and lunged at Burning Tree with his long knife, slicing at the savage while the two grappled to earth, rolling in a deadly mass of flailing arms and legs. Jonathan's knife struck the Delaware more than once, but the Indian continued to struggle with superhuman strength. The borderman twisted out of the Indian's grasp and scrambled to his feet, cursing the pain that his old leg wound now gave, and lunged again at Burning Tree. The Delaware's face was fierce as he grasped Jonathan by the neck, knocking away the borderman's knife. The Indian had lost his own knife, and now was fighting with his bare hands.

Luckily, Jonathan had one more knife still encased at his belt, but could not reach it while trying to pry the Red man's hands from his throat. The two muscular men strained and grunted, twisting and turning on the ground. The pressure of the Indian's fingers grew hard against Jonathan's windpipe, and the latter's vision began to turn red. With one great burst of energy, Jonathan was able to get his feet under Burning Tree, and heaved with all his might, sending the Delaware crashing to the ground a few feet away. In a flash, Jonathan sprang on top of Burning Tree, and with the second knife in his hand, plunged it deep into the Indian's ribs. The warrior stared back into Jonathan's eyes with a startled expression of disbelief, and as the Delaware's grip loosened on Jonathan's arm, the borderman watched while a film came over the savage's gaze, and he, too, fell back dead.

Jonathan turned and saw the wounded brave, with blood flowing from his temple, stagger toward him. He had his tomahawk raised, and a crazed look appeared on the redskin's face. In one bound, Jonathan jumped forward, and drove the knife to the hilt into the remaining Indian's abdomen, pulling the knife viciously upward in one horrific motion, slicing him open before the brave could even lower his tomahawk. He watched as the Indian slumped to his knees, his hands holding his middle, and pitched forward, bathing the earth dark with his blood.

For a moment, the borderman stood, his chest heaving, limbs trembling, and surveyed the dim scene. He shuddered at the sight of the slaughter. Even he had never slain so many at one time in all the years of border life, except for the ambush of Braddock's Defeat.

With a sinking heart, Jonathan staggered to the girl's silent body, which was slumped frightfully quiet beneath her blanket. There, he knelt, afraid of what he might find, and with trembling hands, uncovered the girl and rolled her over gently so he could see her face. It was Elizabeth, all right, but with such short cropped golden hair, he scarcely recognized her. Her face was ghostly white, and Jonathan now feared the worst. Putting his ear to her chest, he found his own heart was pounding so wildly that he could hardly hear hers as he listened for a heartbeat.

Had she fainted, or had Burning Tree's knife found its mark? Jonathan, trying to control the tremor in his fingers, felt Elizabeth's neck, and was overjoyed to find a faint pulse. In his blind haste, he almost failed to see a dark stain on the girl's doeskin clad shoulder. He lifted her up to see if there were any other wounds which could be seen, and in so doing, her head fell back across his arm. A tingle went through his strong body, and he could not help but gather the unfortunate girl's limp form to his breast, where he held her and cradled her in his arms for a long moment.

"Elizabeth, Elizabeth! Thank God I have found you!" he said, his voice hoarse with emotion. He continued to hold her, and rock her gently back and forth. His cheek was against hers in his embrace, and he whispered her name over and over into her ear. He hardly could imagine that it had been months and months that he had waited to search for her, and now, she was here, safe in his arms. "I'll never let you go," he breathed.

He gently laid the girl back upon the ground, and using his knife, cut away the doeskin garment to expose the girl's shoulder. There, he found an ugly knife wound that oozed dark blood. It appeared Burning Tree's knife had struck only once, but that one time had been devastating. Jonathan felt a stab of embarrassment when he gazed upon the swell of Elizabeth's breast rising under the wound, and tried to cover her as best he could.

With water from the stream, the borderman cleansed her wounds, and he bound the shoulder with wet leaves of a healing plant he gathered from the forest floor. Thanks to the time he had spent at the Delaware Village, he had long ago learned the lore of Indian medicines and herbs. Elizabeth moaned softly as he bound her wound, and Jonathan felt that was a good sign, though she had not yet regained consciousness.

He hoped the knife had not nicked her lung, but since he found no pink tinge at her mouth, nor heard any gurgling when he listened to her chest, he felt confident that, except for loss of blood, the girl had been spared a mortal blow.

While the wounded girl remained under the trees, Jonathan dug graves for the three Delaware Indians, and buried their bodies in the glen. He carefully removed any signs of the struggle for fear that the young Indian girl had surely sent out a search party from the village by now. When satisfied that he had removed all clues from the spot, Jonathan retrieved his horse and brought him to the glen. There, gathering Elizabeth's light body into his arms, he mounted and headed in the direction of Fort Cumberland.

Jackie Gould

Chapter Forty-one

J onathan guided the black stallion, slowly picking the way cautiously so as to leave little trace of their passage. Instead of heading in a direct line to the fort, he chose to circle to the west, again trying to throw off those who would follow. The Delawares probably would make a beeline for the fort, knowing where he would be heading. Perhaps, he could out-circle them before they realized he had not gone there directly, before they could pick up his trail.

Almost without question, by now the search party was heading out of the Delaware camp, alerted by the young Indian girl, who certainly, by sunset the night before, had returned to the village and sounded the alarm. Jonathan figured to be at least two days ahead, and barring any untimely delay, would be able to reach the fort by circling around, to approach by way of Braddock's Road.

Holding Elizabeth's limp body in his arms, Jonathan continued to guide the horse carefully, trying not to jar the girl any more than necessary; however, he found that the going was slow, and could not help having a feeling of anxiety creep into his thoughts. More than once he gazed down at the young girl's ashen face, and a new feeling stirred within his breast, one that he thought had been buried years ago. He tried to dismiss the feeling as total lunacy, and chucked it away in his mind, hoping never to unbury thoughts about a woman again. Any love he ever had for a woman died when Blue Water was killed, years before, or so he thought.

By noon, Jonathan became aware that Elizabeth's wound was bleeding again, and that forced them to stop near a trickling stream. Very softly, he lowered the unconscious girl to mossy ground next to the water, and with a tenderness that belied his masculinity, Jonathan cleansed and repacked her wound. He gently bathed her face and squeezed a bit of water between her colorless lips. Ever so slightly, Elizabeth moved her head, and Jonathan once more splashed water on her face.

"Elizabeth! Elizabeth! Wake up!" he cried, as he patted her cheek.

Jonathan could see her eyes move beneath the closed lids, and was heartened when her lashes fluttered, and Elizabeth finally opened them. At first, those eyes seemed glazed and unseeing, staring off beyond his shoulder. Jonathan had not remembered how beautiful her hazel eyes were, and how they changed from gray to green in an instant. Now he saw the pain and blankness in their depths.

"Elizabeth, you are all right. You are safe now."

With some difficulty, she blinked, and with great effort, focused on Jonathan's face. Her eyes grew huge as recognition slowly flickered in their depths, and in a voice so low that Jonathan had to strain to hear, Elizabeth whispered, "Nathan! Oh, Nathan!" and once more slipped into unconsciousness. *No, dear girl,* Jonathan thought. *I am Jonathan, not Nathan.* Then a jabbing pain wrenched him as he realized that Elizabeth could not possibly have known about Nathan's death. She could not have known anything about the disaster of Braddock's Defeat in that tragic ravine almost two years ago. A sinking feeling jolted him with that realization.

Once more, Jonathan mounted the black, and cradled Elizabeth's unconscious body to him as they forged ahead. There was more color in the girl's face, for which the borderman rejoiced. All afternoon the two rode on, weaving between trees, and scaling steep slopes, often traveling down the middle of small rivers to hide their tracks. At least, Jonathan thought, the Indians would lose much time searching for his trail.

As the sun slanted far to the west, sending golden shafts of light dancing through the trees, Jonathan found a perfect spot to camp. Well hidden by a craggy boulder, with music of rippling water ending in a deep pool nearby, he fashioned a lean-to for shelter. It did not take Jonathan long to swiftly snare a rabbit, which he roasted over a quickly-built fire.

Turning to tend to Elizabeth's needs, Jonathan was dismayed to find her skin very hot and dry. When he inspected the wound, he found there was swelling and a deep colored redness around the puncture, and at once he became alarmed. Infection was setting in, and the girl was burning up with fever. Again, Jonathan treated the wound and bathed Elizabeth's face, forcing some water between her teeth. Now, he could tell that her pulse was racing, and her body was shaking with chills.

Twilight deepened dark into the night, and stars blinked on, one by one, when Jonathan found he had to hold Elizabeth close to keep her warm. Stretching out under the overhang, the borderman drew Elizabeth into his arms, and enfolded her to the contour of his body, putting a long leg over her limbs to let the warmth of him seep into her. Even as desperately ill as she was, Jonathan could not help the feeling that surged through him while he held her. He was painfully aware of every curve of her body, and could feel every breath that she took. He found his heart was surging at the thought of her touch, and trying to still her shaking body, held her even more tightly to his own.

In the middle of the night, a sputtering drizzle fell and continued on without let up. Jonathan was glad, for it would help erase some of their tracks. Elizabeth moved and moaned, and Jonathan rearranged the blanket covering them. Once more he pulled her close, careful not to disturb her shoulder wound. This time, he could feel the burning of her flesh through their doeskin clothing, even as she continued to shake with chills. Her teeth rattled, and she was trembling in great spasms. He put his hand to her cheek and knew that the girl was burning up with fever. He became alarmed, and his mind raced with the fear that perhaps he might lose her yet.

He pressed her curly head to his chest, trying to keep the shaking of her body from opening the wound again. Jonathan's hand caressed Elizabeth's short locks running his fingers over and through the girl's curls. His heart filled with emotion, and he fairly burst with the growing realization that he was in love with this girl, now knowing that he had been in love with her for months. But this was sheer lunacy! This was the first time that he allowed those thoughts to creep forward, having so carefully locked them away in the secret recesses of his mind. Could he possibly dare to love this girl? Would the fact that he had fallen in love with her defile Nathan's memory?

"Elizabeth, my Elizabeth. Hang on, dear one... don't leave me now. Not now, Elizabeth, for I... I love you!"

Jonathan's strangled voice shook with emotion, and he felt his eyes grow moist with the very thought that she might not pull through. If he could will her back to health, he would strain with the very effort. His thoughts went back to his own serious battle wounds, and the months that he had not cared whether he lived or died. How long and slow the recovery had been. Had it not been for the persistence of the grizzled old Colonist, Eb, and his wife, Molly, Jonathan knew that he would never have recovered.

Now, panic threatened to overtake him, and Jonathan knew that drastic measures must be taken if he were to keep Elizabeth from expiring from the fever right before his eyes. In the cover of utter darkness, he quickly stripped off his buckskins, and reaching for Elizabeth in the blackness, removed her doeskin dress and moccasins. Lifting the shaking nude girl into his arms, Jonathan gingerly felt his way to the pool with his bare feet, and was only a few feet from the lean-to when he found the edge of the pool. Carefully he lowered himself into the coolness of the water, while cradling Elizabeth, and the two submerged up to their chins.

He could not help the goose bumps that rose on his skin in the cold water, but he let the misty rain drench their heads, and hoped beyond hope that this would draw the girl's fever from her tortured body. It took all of Jonathan's willpower to force his mind away from the fact that he held the naked girl next to his own flesh. He certainly was thankful that the night was so black, for he feared he would not be able to withstand the desire now raging within him if he so much as caught a glimpse of Elizabeth's white flesh.

Long moments went by, and Jonathan's limbs had become stiff when he finally rose and lifted his precious load out of the water, and back to the lean-to. As he gently laid Elizabeth down upon the mossy ground, he felt her arm clasp around his neck, and his body shuddered as he realized she was awake. Even in the darkness, he was embarrassed, and quickly drew their clothes back on.

"Nathan, is that you?" Elizabeth's faint voice came from the black night. "Oh, how I have dreamed of you. How many months I dreamed that you would come and rescue me. Is it true? Are you here, Nathan, or am I dreaming?"

Jonathan swallowed hard, almost unable to speak, and the hair rose at the back of his neck.

"Nathan, are you here?" Elizabeth called in a pitifully weak voice.

"Yes, Lass, I am here," Jonathan lied. "You are not dreaming. Sh-hh, rest now, for you have a grievous wound."

Elizabeth's trembling hand reached out in the darkness and found Jonathan's. She grasped his hand, entwining her fingers in his, and he was happy to feel her skin to be more normal temperature. Surely the cold soaking in the pool had broken the fever. Even as dawn broke later to a misty drizzle, Jonathan sat beside the sleeping girl, his hand still entwined in hers, and his heart was filled with love for her as he gazed upon her peaceful face in the gray light of day.

Chapter Forty-two

Elizabeth slept until almost noon that morning. Jonathan had not attempted to awaken her, for he knew how much she needed the rest to help her regain her strength. At the same time, the frightening thought that the Delawares were probably at this very moment closing in on them gave him worry. He tried to remain calm as he warmed the rest of the rabbit meat for the girl's breakfast. Her eyes fluttered open, and Elizabeth gazed at Jonathan's back while he hunkered beside a small fire.

"Nathan," her voice still weak, "Nathan, I cannot believe it is you! I must still be dreaming."

Jonathan rose from the fire and knelt beside the girl, who was still wrapped in the warmth of a blanket. He smiled at her, but his insides knotted at the thought of deceiving her. However, at this moment, with Elizabeth in yet such a delicate state of heath, the borderman had no choice but to continue letting her believe he was Nathan.

His gaze softened as he looked into her hazel eyes, and he simply said, "Here I am."

"Oh-h..." Elizabeth said, as she painfully tried to sit up, just now aware of the stabbing ache in her shoulder. "What... what happened? Where are we?"

"I fear you were badly wounded during the skirmish," Jonathan ventured.

Elizabeth attempted to shake the cobwebs from her mind as Jonathan helped prop her into a sitting position.

"Oh, I... I seem to remember some screams and yelling, but... I fear little else." The pale girl gazed intently at Jonathan. "Nathan, oh, Nathan! I thought I would never see you again. How did you get here? Where are we? What happened?" Her voice quavered with weakness.

Jonathan was silent, unsure of how much to relate to her.

Suddenly, Elizabeth grabbed his arm in a grip that surprised him in its strength. "Where are my Indian guides?" she uttered in an alarmed tone.

Jonathan swallowed hard, a stab of fear beginning to rise in his chest. "Guides? What do you mean, guides? Where were they taking you?"

"I mean Burning Tree and his two friends. They were escorting me to Fort Cumberland," Elizabeth said, with alarm rising in her tone.

"Fort Cumberland?"

"Yes, they were fulfilling my dream-wish, and were returning me to the Fort."

Jonathan was silent for a long moment, trying to dispel the sickening feeling arising in the pit of his stomach.

"Where are they, Nathan?"

Jonathan turned to Elizabeth, and taking her hand in his, looked down, studying her slim fingers, as he stroked them with his own powerful hand. He cleared his throat. "Elizabeth... Lass... I..." He halted.

"What happened, Nathan?" Her voice was faint, as an unnamed fear invaded her being.

"They... they all lie dead in a clearing, miles back there," Jonathan said in a choking voice.

She slumped visibly. "Dead! Burning Tree and his braves are dead?"

"Lass, I had no way of knowing that the savages were bringing you back to the Fort. I only knew that I began searching for you as soon as I figured out that you had been captured by the Indians. I tracked you and the Indians to that campsite the night before last. I watched all night, and in the first light of dawn, I planned to sneak you out of the camp, but the savages woke up just as I entered the campsite."

He paused with his head lowered, trying not to meet her painful gaze. "I had to shoot one of them, and knocked another in the head. By that time, the third Indian leaped to where you were lying in your blanket, and slashed you on the shoulder with his knife. He meant to kill you, Lass."

Elizabeth was stunned, and gingerly put her hand up to her wounded shoulder as he spoke

"I had no choice, Lass. I am sorry. I confess. I killed them all... to save your life. To save both of our lives."

She was visibly shaken. How could she tell Nathan that those same savages had been her friends and protectors? Her head swam, and she felt a nauseating faintness creep over her then, and she slowly lay back down, with her eyes tightly shut.

Jonathan rose and walked away, trying to calm the disturbing feeling that filled his chest. His head reeled with this unexpected turn of events. So the savages had actually been taking Elizabeth home! They were not taking her to another village, a slave, as he had surmised. How was he to know they were friendly? Worse yet, now Elizabeth believed that he was Nathan. How could he tell her the truth? How could he break it to her that both Nathan and her father had been killed in Braddock's Defeat? He strode angrily into the forest, unable to get control of the conflicting emotions which began to rage within him. The delight he should be feeling, now that he had found Elizabeth, and she was safe, escaped him. In its place was a feeling of apprehension and doubt. How could Elizabeth have any feelings for him now, the killer of her friends and protectors? Jonathan shoved his fist into the trunk of a large oak tree in an angry gesture of frustration, ignoring the sharp pain that jarred his knuckles.

It was not until he glanced at the sky and recognized how late the hour was getting that Jonathan was jolted back to reality. They must quickly be on their way to the fort. Most certainly, a Delaware party was fast upon their trail at this very moment, perhaps closer than the borderman even suspected.

With deft fingers, Jonathan saddled the black and brought the horse close to the overhanging rock shelter. Silently, he scattered all traces of the lean-to and campfire, and without a word, helped Elizabeth onto the horse. She clutched him with her good arm, as he headed the horse westward. He could feel Elizabeth sag against his back, and noted that the arm she had around him was none too strong. He should have repacked the shoulder before they mounted, but now did not dare to take the time.

When the afternoon grew late, and they had traveled a good long distance, Jonathan could feel Elizabeth grow weaker, as her head bobbed against his back. He halted the horse, and slipped swiftly to the ground, reaching up to catch the slumping girl as she fell into his arms. Elizabeth seemed light as a feather, as he carried her and gently deposited her on the forest floor. To his utter dismay, he found that her wound was bleeding again, and she was once more unconscious.

Blast the luck, he thought and quickly washed and dressed the wound. He was satisfied that though the wound had reopened it looked good, without a sign of infection. Jonathan decided to make camp, for the hour was late, and Elizabeth was not strong enough to continue on today. He wondered how close the Delaware warrior party might be, and despite himself, a chill went up his spine.

Chapter Forty-three

Elizabeth roused in the middle of the night, blinking into the blackness that surrounded her. For a long moment, she lay trying to figure out where she was. Sounds of screams and a struggle echoed in her ears, and the sensation of a rocking motion jumbled in her mind. Mists of half-consciousness drifted before her, and she struggled to untangle her thoughts. What had happened? Where was she? Was she back in the Delaware Village? Was her dream-wish trip back to the fort only that, a dream? Where was the fire pit that should be in the middle of the lodge?

She felt for her eyelids, to make sure they were open, for the blackness was so intense, she wondered if she were dreaming. Perhaps she had been in an accident that left her blind. With a start, she sat up boldly, and instantly felt the stabbing pain in her shoulder. Then it all came back to her in a flooding rush. She had been wounded, but where was she now?

"Nathan?" Her voice quavered. "Nathan?"

"I am here, Lass," Jonathan answered in a low, strong voice, instantly awake.

She gave a sigh of relief, and reached out in the darkness to touch his arm. "I thought I had a terrible dream and was back in the Delaware Village... but it really is you!"

"Aye, Lass."

She pulled him close. "Is it night? I cannot see."

"Yes, Lass, I did not build a fire." He did not tell her the reason was because he feared discovery by the Indians.

"Nathan!" Elizabeth breathed, and reached up with her fingers to feel for his face. She put her arm around his neck, and shamefully drew him closer. She felt his arms go around her, and in the darkness, her lips searched for his mouth in a wild moment of passion. His heart suddenly surging, Jonathan gathered Elizabeth into his arms and found her mouth, trembling and eager. He could no longer deny his desires, and with a soft moan, opened his mouth to cover hers with a kiss so strong that it left Elizabeth tingling all over her body. She let a tear slide down her cheek, and with a rush of emotion, began to sob.

"Oh, Nathan! I love you!"

Again, she reached up with her lips to accept his kiss, and Jonathan could taste her salty tears as he kissed her in long, hungry spasms, hardly taking a breath. His body strained over hers, and they both lay back upon the ground with their lips still locked together. His long forgotten hunger came crashing to life, and Jonathan found he could not get enough of this delightful sweetness that he held in his arms.

"I love you, Nathan," Elizabeth gasped between sobs. "I missed you so! I thought I would never see you again."

"Elizabeth, my sweet," Jonathan said in a strangled voice, emotion filling his breast until he felt he would burst. Finally, he was able to admit to himself forever that he loved this girl with all his heart. "I love you!" his husky voice trembled.

Again, Elizabeth sobbed, emotion choking her throat, and dissolved into tears in Jonathan's arms. All the months of captivity, of longing, of hoping, of not knowing, of wishing, were released in her tears.

"There, there, Lass, everything is all right now. Don't cry, I am here, and you are safe."

He gathered her close and once more found her hungry lips, answering with a hunger of his own, straining, his mouth open to taste her softness. A burst of passion almost blinded him as he kissed her, and kissed her.

"Elizabeth, my sweet love," he groaned, trying to still the raging in his flesh.

"Nathan," Elizabeth breathed, "I have dreamed of this for months, and almost gave up any hope. Tell me this is real... tell me I am not dreaming."

"No, Lass, you are not dreaming," Jonathan said, his mouth against her ear, as he held her tightly to him.

They stayed locked in each other's arms the remainder of the night. Jonathan almost dreaded the thought of dawn, for he did not want this delicious moment to end. From time to time, the two exchanged soft kisses, and melted into one another even more. Elizabeth relaxed to relish the feeling of what she thought was Nathan's warm body pressed against hers, thrilling at each kiss with renewed passion. Tingling sensations roused from deep within her, and she fell wildly, more deeply in love.

❧

When the first tinge of dawn appeared beyond the trees, Jonathan found he was still holding Elizabeth in his arms, and reluctantly watched the light spread upon the land. She was sleeping peacefully, and as he gazed down at her soft face, a warmth spread through him anew.

Thoughts of how to tell this sweet girl the truth began to whirl in Jonathan's mind. How could he tell her about the massacre of Braddock's Defeat? How could he explain that he saw her father take a bullet between his eyes? How could he possibly tell her that he had buried Nathan beneath the fallen trunk of a giant oak tree? He certainly did not want to deceive this sweet, innocent girl, but how much could she take right now in her weakened condition?

Elizabeth stirred in his arms, and her eyes sleepily opened to gaze at Jonathan's face. The look of love that he saw in her eyes melted his heart once more, and he reached down to kiss her gently.

"Good morning, sweet Elizabeth."

"Good morning, my love," she replied, as she smiled at him, thrilling at the smoldering affection she saw in his gaze.

She found she was very weak when she attempted to rise from the ground, and Jonathan had to support her as they walked a few paces. Suddenly, she sat back down, her rubbery legs giving out in trembling weakness, and a whirling buzzing starting in her head.

"Oh," she breathed, "I fear I am not as strong as I thought."

Jonathan assured her that she would be all right, and he brought the horse close to the encampment. While Elizabeth remained seated on the ground, Jonathan squatted next to her, tracing a circle in the dirt with a twig. "Elizabeth," he started, with a sudden serious tone. "We shall reach the Fort in a short morning ride. Before we get there, there is something you should know. I do not want you to hear it from any of the settlers. I want you to hear it from me."

She looked up at him, and could see how distressed he seemed to be. "What is it, Nathan?" A slight frown creased her forehead.

Jonathan took Elizabeth's hand in his, but could not look into her inquisitive eyes. This was the moment of dread, the time he had wished would never come. How to tell her? How?

"Lass," here he cleared his throat. "I have some bad news." There was a long pause as he gathered himself. "Your father is not at the Fort." He concentrated his gaze on her fingers, which lay in his large palm, and stroked them with his thumb. Gathering courage, with a huge heave of his breast, Jonathan looked her squarely in her lovely hazel eyes. "Your father was killed in Braddock's Defeat, when the road building brigade was ambushed by the French and Indian renegades, almost two years ago."

"Oh!" Elizabeth shrank back as if she had been struck by a blow.

"I am so sorry I had to tell you such bad news, my dear, for I did not want you to be told by strangers, after we reach the Fort." There was a huskiness in his voice that he could not overcome.

She nodded, as tears welled in her eyes. "Father...." she said, her voice trailing as the news began to sink in.

Her eyes shot up to Jonathan in alarm. "And your twin brother, Jonathan? Where is he?"

Jonathan lowered his eyes, unable to match her gaze, unable to look into her pathetic face, and a great lump rose in his throat. This was the question he feared the most, the moment he dreaded above all. How could he answer?

"My.... brother.... is... dead. He died in battle, also," he said in a hoarse whisper.

"Oh, Nathan!" Elizabeth placed her small hand on his sleeve. "How horrible! Father and Jonathan... both gone!"

Tears slipped down her cheeks, and a sob escaped her lips. She lowered her head and wept. He could say no more, but held her in his arms as he consoled her.

Silently, with no further conversation, the two mounted the black and swiftly wove through the forest. Elizabeth rode behind Jonathan, gripping him about the waist, and leaned her head against his back, tears still flowing down her cheeks. She was lost in memories of her father and Jonathan. The news of their deaths had shocked her, and now she remembered the chilling words of George Stillwell, when he had returned from that very battle. She could still hear his voice, mocking her, telling her that everyone in the brigade had died. She had refused to believe him at the time, but now, with dread and sadness in her heart, she had to admit that Stillwell must have told her the truth.

At mid-morning, Jonathan pulled the horse to a halt and dismounted, letting the animal drink from a rushing stream. Warily, he looked about, and could not rid himself of the feeling that the savages were just beyond each tree. He looked up at Elizabeth as she sat in the saddle, while he offered her a drink. Out of the corner of his eye, he thought he perceived a movement high up on the ridge behind them. In one more moment, he saw one, two... no, four horses threading their way down the mountainside. In one flash, Jonathan leaped onto the horse behind Elizabeth and dug his heels into the black's flanks

"Hang on!" he yelled into Elizabeth's ear. "Indians!"

Her eyes were wide with fright as she bounced in the wild ride, desperately trying to maintain her seat in the saddle. Jonathan held her tightly with one arm as he used the other to direct the horse in their mad dash, leaping fallen logs, and skirting dangerous rocks and boulders. He felt a surge of relief twenty minutes later when they burst into the open, and found Braddock's Road at a spot he judged to be about five miles from the Fort. The smooth, wide dirt highway flashed under them as Jonathan urged the black into a dead gallop. He glanced back over his shoulder, and saw the four savages on their ponies, just gaining the roadway, and figured them to be at least a half mile behind.

Keep those feet under you, he thought, referring to the mount. *No stumbling, no falling now. Run, Black, run!* The horse flicked his ears back toward Jonathan, as if he were listening to the borderman's thoughts. On they flew, horse and two riders, flat out in a dead run. Jonathan lifted up a thankful prayer that it was he who was seated behind Elizabeth, so that his body would be the one to take the Indian arrows, should the savages get close enough to shoot. Minutes ticked by, and Jonathan could see the Indians in hot pursuit, but their ponies were no match for the black. Even then he could hear the yipping and yelling above the pounding of the horse's hooves as they slashed the road below. They were moving so swiftly, Jonathan wondered if the horse's feet touched earth at all. A few more minutes elapsed, when coming around a curve in the road, they saw the river ahead, and beyond that loomed the safety of the Fort.

Without breaking stride, Jonathan galloped the horse headlong into the water, where the beast swam with powerful strokes, coming up on the opposite bank, his flanks heaving, and nostrils flaring. As Jonathan urged the horse up the hill toward the open gate of the fort, the animal snorted, and carried them on trembling legs to safety.

Looking back, he saw the Indians halt on the other side of the river, and for a long moment stare in his direction. Finally, in disgust, they turned their ponies and disappeared into the forest.

Chapter Forty-four

All through the summer, Elizabeth recuperated from her ordeal at the home of Molly and Ebenezer Payne, the kindly settlers who had nursed Jonathan back to health following the injuries he suffered in Braddock's Defeat. Privately, Jonathan had explained to the two how Elizabeth had mistaken him for Nathan, and being the trusting kind that they were, the pair never let on his true identity to Elizabeth nor anyone else in the fort. With the loving care that Molly gave to Elizabeth, in no time the color returned to the girl's cheeks, and she was well on her way to complete recovery.

Jonathan had withdrawn to his mountain cabin, assured in his mind that he had done the right thing by leaving Elizabeth in the care of his two friends. It never would have done to have taken the young girl to his cabin without the benefit of marriage, so Jonathan figured it best for her to remain close to the fort with those whom he trusted while she recovered.

In the weeks that followed her return to Fort Cumberland, Elizabeth grew steadily stronger. Her wound healed nicely, and time was all that was needed to bring the rose back to her cheeks, and strength back to her body. She counted the days and looked forward to the one whom she believed to be Nathan make many visits, for he came as often as his duties would allow. Molly and Eb had long since related to Elizabeth the extent of how badly wounded the borderman had been as a result of the massacre, never letting on to her his real identity. Elizabeth was surprised to know that Nathan carried so many scars from the battle. They had never talked of Braddock's Defeat since the one time he had told her of the deaths of her father and Jonathan.

Elizabeth rallied visibly each time the borderman paid a visit, and soon was able to stroll with him arm and arm beneath the canopy of trees whose spreading branches arched above the pathway in a gigantic umbrella of dappled shade. The tall, dark-haired borderman of the Colonial Frontier, and the slim, blond-tressed young woman were now totally absorbed in each other, matching steps in a leisurely stroll, oblivious of their surroundings. God Himself could have come down from Heaven, and the two would never have taken their eyes off one another.

"You look very well, my Sweet," Jonathan said, smiling, as he gazed at the girl beside him, and squeezed her arm, which he held against his side.

"I feel completely well. In fact, I feel better than I can ever remember, especially now that you are here, Nathan," Elizabeth replied, throwing back her head to let a spot of sunshine cascade upon her face, relishing the warmth that peeked between the branches. She looked shyly up at the rugged borderman's square-jawed face, and noticed the shock of dark hair that fell across his forehead, loving the casual way that stray lock always caressed his brow. She knew at this moment she could not be happier, and a tickle of excitement flowed through her very being. She was totally, irrevocably, forever in love.

Jonathan stopped, and pulled her close to enfold her in his arms. He felt every soft curve of her body, and never wanted to let her go. His heart swelled with love and longing, and he could not believe the events that had led to this wonderful moment. Indian captures... battles... bloodshed... wounds... deaths... rescues... now were all things of the past, memories that he wanted to wipe from his mind. How could God favor him so much as to lead him to this moment, with this girl, at this time?

Jonathan slowly bent down and reached for Elizabeth's lips with his mouth, and softly kissed her, as the love he felt for her burst like a rocket within him. He felt her slide her arms around his neck and tiptoe up to return his kiss, pulling them both down upon a large boulder. Jonathan leaned back upon one elbow, clasped her fingers in his, and gazed with smoldering love into Elizabeth's eyes, as if he could not get enough of her. It amazed him that she could stir the deep emotions within him that he so carefully had locked away so many years before. No longer did he have to squash those feelings, bury them deep, deny that he could ever love again. No... he was in love... so much in love that the world tumbled around him, and he knew joy once more!

"Marry me, Elizabeth... Elizabeth Wood... be my wife! I love you!"

Those words momentarily made the young woman's head swirl, and she could only look into the bronze face of the man she adored, and smile into his warm brown eyes.

"I love you, my Sweet Elizabeth! Be my wife?" he repeated, not sure at first if she grasped the full rich meaning of his bequest.

There was no hesitation, but Elizabeth's small voice quavered slightly as she answered. "Yes, oh, yes, Nathan! I shall marry you... and I love you too, with all my heart!"

Jonathan leaped up and swept the girl off the rock, to swing her around in joyous abandon, delighting at every squeal that came from her pink lips. They both fell to the ground on their knees, laughing, and it was Jonathan who grew silent first.

His expression turned somber, and quietly, with a tenderness that Elizabeth had never seen coming from him before, Jonathan uttered in an almost strangled voice, "Would that I could bring back you father, God rest his soul, so I could properly ask for your hand in marriage."

Solemnly he pulled Elizabeth to her feet.

"Perhaps he can see us from heaven," she whispered.

"Perhaps he can."

With that, Jonathan removed his fur cap and dropped to one knee in front of the girl, who stood motionless before him. With his eyes tightly shut, and turning his face skyward, Jonathan stretched out his arms, beseeching the heavens in his quest.

"Captain Wood, whose soul now rests with the ages, I beseech thee, dear Sir, to ask for your daughter's hand in marriage. I ask that you look down favorably from on high into my heart so you can know that I cherish your daughter, and will worship her until the day I die. I ask you to grant your blessing, Sir, that even from heaven, you will approve of this match."

There came a soft rustling of breeze through the trees, as if someone had brushed past, and Elizabeth felt a shiver. It was as if a hand had caressed her cheek. In a branch close by, a thrush trilled a warbling whistle, and other than that, the forest was silent. Jonathan, still kneeling before her, lifted Elizabeth's fingers to his lips.

"Dear, Sweet Elizabeth, I ask for your hand in marriage. I feel strongly that your father would have happily given his permission. I give you my heart, my very soul. I love you with every depth of my being!"

With tears welling in her eyes, Elizabeth placed both of her trembling hands upon the borderman's face, and leaned forward to kiss his lips. "Yes, Nathan, I shall marry you. I love you, too. Oh, my heart is bursting with love for you!"

Jonathan could taste a salty tear as he slowly rose, embracing his bride-to-be. She laid her head against his chest, and could hear the comforting thump-thump of his heartbeat.

Dear, Sweet Elizabeth, forgive me, my love! Jonathan thought, his mind agonizing over his true identity. *Forgive me for allowing you to think I am Nathan!* Jonathan felt the old hurt return, and once more found his dead twin's presence fill him. He and his identical twin had been so close in life, sharing every twist and turn together, like two souls traveling on a parallel journey. A special bond locked them together that not even death could tear apart.

That cruel twist of fate which had wrenched his brother from him one hot July day two years ago, in that fateful massacre known as Braddock's Defeat, had failed to end the strong love they held for each other. And even now, Jonathan knew that Nathan's spirit hovered close by, often feeling his dead brother's presence so strongly that sometimes he gazed around, expecting to see Nathan's smiling face at any instant. *Forgive me, Nathan, and forgive me, dear, sweet girl, but I cannot tell you who I really am. Not now, not yet.*

❧

Molly Payne clapped her hands together in joy, then poked her husband Eb in the ribs. "Ah, a weddin' we'll be havin' soon! Imagine that! Do ye hear that, Eb? A weddin' right here at Fort Cumberland!"

A few weeks later as the magnificent foliage on the surrounding mountains changed to crimson and orange, and the crisp air held the promise of one last fling of warmth before winter; Nathan (really Jonathan) Herrington and Elizabeth Wood were united in marriage on a late October day of 1757. Everyone knew the story of Elizabeth's rescue from the Delaware Indians, and felt a warm kinship for the heroics of the quiet borderman who had brought her back to civilization. The fact that love had sprung from that incident sent romantic shock waves through the small community, and all the women, young and old alike, were fascinated by the events, secretly fantasizing about such an adventure in their own quiet lives.

Elizabeth appeared in a dazzling emerald green dress which Molly had fashioned from goods stored deep in her own belongings. Jonathan fairly sucked in his breath in amazement when he first caught a glimpse of his bride that day. She was heart-breakingly lovely, and her great hazel eyes were bright with excitement.

Jonathan looked splendid himself, appearing in a new, soft, fringed buckskin hunting shirt, and tight leggings tucked into high topped moccasins. His long black hair was fastened at the nape of his neck by a leather thong wrapped around his locks. A long knife was thrust in its usual place in his belt, and he was never far from the flintlock rifle which accompanied him everywhere, and now rested nearby against the wall of the chapel. He stood tall and proud at Elizabeth's side as an Elder from the Episcopal Church, newly arrived from England, said the words. The vows were repeated, prayers offered, and he then pronounced them duly joined in matrimony in the eyes of the church.

Soon sounds of fiddles and fifes echoed through the golden fall afternoon, and the parade ground within the fort turned into a festive dance area. Every chance for a celebration in the early colonial times was gleefully anticipated by the settlers of that frontier era. Life was hard, and often bleak, so when an occasion such as a wedding came along, the revelers joyfully entered into the festivities, grateful for a few hours of release from their tedious lives.

This particular day, the guests feasted on roast partridge, venison, squash, cabbage and beans. Pot pies of chicken and vegetables were devoured along with tankards of ale and an occasional bottle of wine. Freshly pressed apple cider, cakes and sweets adorned the wedding table.

Elizabeth was radiant as she happily danced with each man in turn, whirling in breathless circles in time with the fiddler's tunes. Jonathan was shy, and although not as adept at dancing as he was tramping through the woods on a hunt, now gamely tried his best to take his turn with all the ladies. After a few tankards of ale, he whirled the ladies around with so much vigor, he left them shrieking with delight.

Toward the end of the afternoon, as the sun was casting long streaks of gold across the scene, amid laughter and revelry, the men of the settlement playfully surrounded Elizabeth, elbowing Jonathan to the outside of the circle, not allowing him to claim his bride. The women and girls grabbed Jonathan, blindfolded him, and spun him round and round, before linking their hands with his, and formed a circle around the men. Jonathan stumbled as he was first pulled one direction, then the other... to the right, then to the left.

Hilarious laughter and screams from the young girls and women almost drowned out the raucous gruff shouts of the men.

Jonathan heard Elizabeth scream in mock terror as she was repeatedly tossed into the air from a blanket the men were holding taut. Each time they threw her higher and higher, until the bride's screams of delight became weaker as she collapsed in so much laughter, she could hardly utter any more sound. Jonathan, too, was laughing, groping his way toward the sound of his new wife's voice. Slowly, the crowd parted, allowing the groom, still blindfolded, to make his way to his beloved. Elizabeth giggled, trying to stifle the sound, and watched breathlessly as her new husband advanced toward her, his arms reaching out in front of him.

By now the guests had formed a complete ring around the couple, and were clapping their hands in a rhythmic cadence, shouting "You are getting hotter... no... now you are getting colder..." giving the sightless groom directions as he stumbled his way along.

Elizabeth would soundlessly slip aside when Jonathan neared, playing the game of hide and seek with delight. Suddenly, the groom would hear her lilting laughter behind him, and he would whirl to the sound, flailing his arms, trying to touch his bride. Shouts of encouragement came from all sides, and he burst into laughter once more, calling Elizabeth to identify herself. The game ended as his hand brushed her shoulder when Elizabeth was too slow to dodge out of his way. The breathless bride shrieked with laughter as the groom, his face flushed a ruddy bronze, swept her up in his arms, jerking the blindfold from his head at the same instant. Emboldened by the game, and the ale he had consumed, the borderman claimed his bride with a big kiss on the blushing young woman's lips.

Everyone applauded as Jonathan carried his bride to set her upon the broad back of his big black stallion. Someone had festooned the great horse with late blooming flowers braided into the animal's mane and tail. Jonathan easily swung into the saddle behind his young bride, and put his arm around her waist as she leaned her head affectionately back against his shoulder.

The newlyweds waved to the crowd as the horse reared slightly, responding to the pressure of Jonathan's heels. The great steed shook his massive head, causing the flowers to dance and jangle as the two departed the fort, then stepped proud and high, just as he used to when he had carried General Braddock in parades several years ago.

"Hip, hip, hooray! Hip, hip, hooray! To Nathan and Elizabeth! Hip, hip, hooray!" the settlers shouted after the departing couple, and watched until they were out of sight.

Chapter Forty-five

Elizabeth and Jonathan's first baby decided to be born in the middle of the night during one of the coldest winters they had yet encountered. Snow piled high up on the cabin, and Jonathan was hard pressed to have enough firewood chopped to burn in the hearth. All that day, Elizabeth had experienced labor pains, pacing the small quarters for hours. Jonathan attempted to give his wife what support he could, silently cursing the snow drifts that had prevented him from taking her down to the fort where she could have had female companionship during her confinement.

Peering out the window, Jonathan could make out snowflakes flying almost at a horizontal pitch, while mounds of the white stuff seemed to encase the whole cabin. The wind howled mercilessly, sending drafts through every tiny opening in the chinks and under the door, no matter how hard they tried to stuff makeshift stoppers in areas they discovered. The dim gray light that came through the window barely illuminated the cabin interior, and darkness came early that day. Elizabeth continued to pace, putting her hands at the small of her back to ease the dull pain.

She allowed Jonathan to make her a cup of hot tea. He sweetened it with a bit of honey from the honeycomb he had fetched home on a previous hunt.

"I am sorry we could not get you to the fort," Jonathan said as he laid a big hand softly onto Elizabeth's arm.

She smiled bravely at him. "It is all right, Nathan, my Love. I shall be fine. As long as I have you with me, we will do just fine." Her eyes belied the words, however, and he detected a worried look that crossed her face.

"I wish..." she started, wistfully.

"Wish what, Sweet?"

"I wish that mother and father were alive to greet their first grandchild."

Jonathan nodded, his mind a long way off. As another, more powerful spasm consumed her, Elizabeth clutched at the edges of the table. She breathed harder, letting her breath out in a slow sigh, and gazed at her husband's face, seeing the worried concern in his eyes. Hoping to distract him, she changed the subject.

"You miss him very much, don't you?

"Who, Love?" Jonathan asked, startled from his reverie.

"Jonathan, of course. Your brother, Jonathan."

Jonathan gave a start. They had not discussed the death of his twin ever since he first told her of the loss.

"You miss Jonathan very much, don't you, Nathan?"

At that moment, Jonathan could not meet her eyes, but stared at the floor as he silently nodded his head.

"He must have been such a great part of your life. I cannot imagine what it would be like to have such a close tie with another person. Especially one who had shared every moment of life from before birth, and one who looked identical. It must have been like looking into a mirror, every time you two looked at each other."

Jonathan waited a long time before replying. "Yes, I miss... Jonathan... very much," he muttered in a low voice, his head still hanging low, eyes on the floor.

With great effort, Elizabeth rose from the chair and came around behind Jonathan to place her arms about him. She leaned close to his ear, and kissed his cheek. "Then, we shall name the baby Jonathan," she said softly into his ear.

Jonathan jerked with a start, and pulled her gently onto his lap, hoping she could not see the flush that colored his bronzed face.

"Is that what you want, Sweet?" he asked, kissing her gently on the lips.

She nodded. "Yes, we should name him after the dear brother that you lost. And if it is a girl, we shall name her Johanna."

Jonathan nodded in agreement, and could say no more for fear of giving away his secret.

"Come, now, Nathan, help me into bed, for I fear the pains are becoming very strong now."

She gasped and bent over as a long spasm eclipsed any of the previous pains she had so far experienced.

Jonathan helped her shed her skirt and top and pulled a long nightdress over her head. For long hours, the labor increased, and the young woman clung to Jonathan as she bore down. He winced at her every pain, and wished that he could bear some of the suffering himself. He rose from their bed only long enough to add other logs to the fire. Outside, the wind continued to howl, blowing sleet and snow against the cabin walls.

Toward the wee hours of a new day, January 1st 1759, Elizabeth delivered a healthy baby boy. Jonathan quickly dried the infant and cut the cord, somehow knowing instinctively the things to do. A lusty cry came from the babe's mouth, and Jonathan, overcome momentarily by the experience, placed the swaddled baby in Elizabeth's arms. He smoothed back the hair from her moist brow, and kissed her ever so gently upon her lips.

"Here is our son, my Love," he said softly into her ear.

With shining eyes, Elizabeth gazed at the tiny being that lay in the crook of her arm. "Jonathan," she whispered. "Little Jonathan Herrington, welcome."

Jonathan beamed, and held the infant's tiny fingers in his own. "You were wonderful, my Sweet. You were like a strong Delaware woman, not even allowing a scream to escape your lips."

Elizabeth lay back, resting from the exertion. "Nothing... to scream... about," she panted, still out of breath. "Only the... hard... effort."

"I'm so proud of you." Jonathan kissed her once more. "Rest now, Love. You did a long night's work."

Little Jonathan squirmed in his mother's arms, and gave a small squealing cry, screwing up his puckered little pink face to show toothless gums. Elizabeth smiled faintly, and struggled to open her gown. Awkwardly, she gave the infant her breast, and immediately the little one suckled strongly.

Elizabeth looked up at Jonathan with love in her eyes. "Just like his father," she laughed.

Jackie Gould

Chapter Forty-six

When the snows had melted and the first signs of spring appeared on the mountaintop, Jonathan, Elizabeth and Little Jonathan were about to set off for the fort. It would be the first time that Elizabeth had been away from the cabin in months, and certainly the young woman relished the idea of having a visit with some of the women settlers at Fort Cumberland.

Elizabeth was brushing her hair with the brush that Jonathan had retrieved along with her other belongings in the wooden box he had fetched from the fort. The young woman's hair had re-grown to well past her shoulders, and she gathered it, pinning it up under a lace cap. Now that she was a mother, Elizabeth felt that it was no longer proper to let her hair hang loose, even though Nathan preferred to run his fingers through the full length of her locks, especially when they made love in the warmth of their bed.

Jonathan approached behind Elizabeth's chair as she put the finishing touches to her coiffure, gazing into a small piece of looking glass while she pondered her looks. He put his arms around her, and placed his cheek next to hers.

"You are lovelier than ever, Sweet," he murmured, his lips close to her ear.

Elizabeth glowed at his compliment, and turned her head so her lips could meet his. They exchanged a long kiss.

"Thank you, Nathan. I feel almost back to normal since Little Jonathan's birth."

It was true, Elizabeth could once more fit into her tight-waisted dresses, and except for the fact that her bosom had enlarged with the nursing of the infant, she was the same girl that Jonathan had married, only now more rounded and exciting.

"Are you anxious to go back to the fort?" Jonathan inquired, helping lift Elizabeth onto the black horse's back. He reached up and handed her the baby, who was bundled in a blanket and rested in his mother's arms.

"Oh, yes, I cannot wait to show the baby to Molly Payne. She is such a sweet woman." Jonathan nodded in agreement and swung up behind his wife, guiding the horse onto the faint trail. Their cabin was still fairly isolated, although some settlers had built a dwelling about three miles from them, and were now their closest neighbors.

A fifteen minute ride brought them to the brow of the mountain, and Jonathan turned the black into the glen where the secret cave was hidden.

"Oh, Nathan! I remember this place! When the Indians abducted me, we stopped here. Oh..." Elizabeth's voice trailed off, with a noticeable edge of distress.

Jonathan slipped off the horse and reached up, lifting Elizabeth and baby to the ground. They sat upon a fallen log, next to the deep pool at the base of the trickling waterfall.

"You know," Jonathan began, "no one at the fort knew what had happened to you."

Elizabeth's eyes were big with contemplation. "I never gave it a thought, I guess. Who could have known that I was missing? Just some of the girls. You and father and Jonathan were off on General Braddock's mission."

"How did you get captured?"

"I was... I was down at the river where I went frequently to watch the road. I was sure that you would return any day, Nathan, and I wanted to rush to greet you."

For a moment, Jonathan was silent.

"One day, as I was daydreaming about you, an Indian sneaked up and grabbed me, and put a gag in my mouth and carried me off. There were three Indians who carried me, kicking and squirming, trying to get free. When we reached this spot, they removed my gag, and we rested for a while. Suddenly, a fourth Indian... I know now that it was Burning Tree, appeared out of that wall, and we left on the march to the Delaware Village."

Jonathan was almost afraid to ask the next question... the question that had burned in his mind for all these many years since he rescued her. Now, he cleared his throat and timidly inquired, "Were you... were you... harmed in any way, Elizabeth?" Such a sharp seriousness shown in his eyes, that Elizabeth was sure she could see stark fear there. She shook her head. "No, Love, I was never touched... that way. In fact, it was Burning Tree who protected me from some of the others."

Jonathan let out a deep breath, trying to disguise the fact he was breathing such a sigh of relief. "Well, it was months later, when I had recovered from the wounds inflicted by that infamous battle, that I first inquired after you. They had it at the fort that you had drowned yourself in the river. No one heard or knew about your whereabouts. I was devastated by the news, and retreated to my cabin."

"Oh, Nathan! You thought I was dead?" Jonathan nodded his head.

"Oh, Love, how horrible! And all the while I was wishing beyond hope that you would come and find me."

Jonathan continued, "It was not until late that fall, just before the snows flew, that I came upon this place again. Nath ... Jonathan and I had known of this quiet glen and the secret cave from a previous time. It was here, under those branches, that I discovered your lace cap, half buried beneath mud and leaves. I knew instantly that it belonged to you."

Elizabeth apparently did not hear the near slip of his tongue.

"Then, it all became clear to me. You had not died. You had been taken by the Delaware Indians. It was not until the snows melted that next spring that I could follow you to the Delaware Village and look for you. You know the rest."

Elizabeth sat still, holding Little Jonathan in her arms, and a tear slipped down her cheek. "Oh, Nathan! I am so glad you finally told me how you discovered that I was missing. For all those long months, I had almost given up hope. I thought I was abandoned and I would have to spend the rest of my life with the Indians."

"How were you treated at the Village?"

Elizabeth paused, unsure of how much to tell the man she loved of her captivity. "At first, I was restrained in a lodge that I later found out was occupied by an Englishman, a traitor. He deserted the English Army and joined the French. His name was George Stillwell. Do you remember him?"

Jonathan searched his memory and vaguely recalled the man.

"As it turned out, it was Stillwell who had engineered my abduction. He wanted me for himself."

Jonathan's heart sank at the very thought, and his deepest fears again rose from his very depths.

Elizabeth continued, "Before he could force me to be his wife, he went off with the French to fight Braddock's brigade, where you and Jonathan and Father were marching. He came back horribly wounded... crippled forever... unable to walk." Here, Elizabeth stopped momentarily lost in thought.

Jonathan ached to ask the question uppermost in his mind, but kept quiet, and let Elizabeth continue.

"Stillwell eventually killed himself before my very eyes. I tried to help the man, but he became despondent at his fate, and turned into a crazed, raging beast. After his death, Te-tak-wa-o-ee was my only friend. She prevented any of the villagers from doing me harm."

For a long time, Jonathan contemplated Elizabeth's revelation. Finally, he asked, "How was it that you were returning from the village to the fort?"

Elizabeth related the dream-wish that Burning Tree had guessed, and told how the Indians were escorting her back to the safety of the English fort. "Before he died, Stillwell had told me that all of Braddock's men had been slaughtered. I did not believe him. I still thought that you were alive. But I became puzzled when so many months went by, and no one tried to rescue me. I thought I had been forgotten. I thought perhaps that I had treated you so badly the last time we had been together, that you had wiped me out of your thoughts."

"You know different now, my Love. I thought you were dead. It was not until I found your cap here in this place that I knew you were still alive. At least I hoped that you were alive. And then I found you!" Jonathan leaned close and kissed Elizabeth's mouth in a tender, yet yearning way.

She put her arms around his neck and clung to him for a long moment.

"Thank you, my Love, for never giving up on me. I dreamed of you every day. Now that we are together, I can scarcely believe how lucky I am."

Chapter Forty-seven

"A h... let me see the wee one!" Molly cried as she held out her arms when Jonathan and Elizabeth reached the Payne cabin. "What a big one ye are! 'Tis it a boy child or a girl child?" she asked, taking the bundle from Elizabeth's arms.

"A boy. His name is Jonathan," Elizabeth breathlessly answered, beaming.

Molly cast a quick, nervous glance at her husband Eb, who very slightly shook his head to warn her not to say more. He moved to his wife's side to gaze into the blankets at the infant.

"Jonathan. My, what a strong little feller he be!" Eb said, scratching his whiskered chin as he grinned an almost toothless grin.

"Aye, ain't he a sweet one?" Molly cooed, fairly hugging the little one to death.

Ebenezer Payne clapped his hand upon Jonathan's shoulder. "Good work, son! Ye sired a strong young'un there. Ye must be bustin' with pride."

Jonathan grinned and allowed Eb to lead him off to the barn where they could have a good man-talk. Meanwhile, the women retreated into the cozy cabin where Molly poured mugs of hot tea.

"Ye birthed a fine youngster, Elizabeth Herrington!" Molly smiled, as she continued to fawn over the infant who now lay asleep in a basket that the older woman had provided.

Elizabeth smiled, her eyes bright with pride. "Yes, I never knew being a mother was so rewarding. We both love him so very much. He has brought so much joy to our lives."

"And ye did it all by yourself!" Molly was amazed.

"Nathan was there... he helped. I don't know what I would have done without him."

Molly raised her eyebrows. "He was there? Helpin' with the birthin' of this young'un? Now, don't that beat all? Eb never wanted to be near me 'til ours was weaned!" Molly laughed.

"Molly, I don't believe you. But it is true. Nathan was right there, cutting the cord and everything."

Molly shook her head. "Too bad the little tyke came in the dead of winter, else I would have been there durin' yer confinement."

The women continued to visit with each other, and Elizabeth was especially anxious to know of news from all the other settlers. She found out that many of those whom she had known either had returned to England, or had moved back to Baltimore Town. The frontier was too harsh for them.

Out at the corral near the barn, Jonathan and Eb puffed on their pipes and discussed crops and animals.

"I aim to get us a milk cow," Jonathan said between puffs on his long-stemmed pipe.

Eb nodded. "Ye be needin' one now fer the youngster. I got an extra... there, that brown and white standin' over there. See how big her milk bag is? She would do you dandy. I'll give her to ye for a right fair price. She's a good milker, that one. Ye won't go wrong."

Jonathan strode over and gave a good close look at the animal, running his hand over her flanks, and reaching under her belly to feel the fullness of the cow's udder. He nodded approval.

"Yup. Looks like she would do just fine for me. How much, Eb? I don't have much in the way of cash."

"Well, we'll work out a deal. Say, ye hear anythin' about them redskins?"

"No," Jonathan replied, shaking his head. "What's up?"

"Well," Eb said as he rose and knocked the ashes from his pipe, then slowly re-packed the bowl with a fresh bit of tobacco. He took a long time to light the pipe and pull a few puffs of smoke before he continued. "Seems as though them Indians is gettin' pesky, hangin' around the tradin' post and gettin' some quarrelsome. Some of the settlers livin' out a ways is gettin' their cattle an' horses stole."

Jonathan related an experience from last fall's hunt of running across a party of hunters much closer than ever to his place. "Seems like the Delaware Village had been moved closer to the fort. What do you make of that, Eb?"

The grizzled old man scratched his balding head. "I don't like the looks of it, Jonathan."

"Nathan to you, Eb. Remember? I am supposed to be Nathan."

"Ye still haven't told yer wife?"

"That's right. I am still Nathan to her. She wanted to name the boy after my dead brother, and so the little one is named Jonathan."

"I suspected so," Eb said as he blew a puff of smoke away. "Well, my friend, I'll keep my lips shut an' hope in my old age not to fergit."

Jonathan heaved a sigh of relief and continued, "Do you suspect the French are pushing the Indians to mischief, or are they doing this on their own?"

"I heerd they was some ugly uprisin's in other areas. Some killin' took place at a fort up north. Indians massacreed some of the settlers along the frontier. I fear we got us some anxious times ahead, friend."

"I fear you may be right, Eb." Jonathan drew a long puff on his pipe and fell into silence, contemplating what the future might hold.

Changing the subject, Eb asked, "How's thet bum leg of yers?"

"It's still bothersome, Eb. Can't run like I used to, and it pains some when the weather changes."

"Yer lucky ye got yer whole leg. Why, we thought it would have to come off. Ye took a real nasty arrow that time, friend."

"That seems like a lifetime ago, now, Eb. What's it been, three, four years?"

Eb frowned, trying to recall. "Let's see. That was '55 and now we are in the Lord's year of 1759. Yup, four years come this summer."

Molly called from the front stoop of the cabin to tell the men to come in to eat. She had prepared some meat and freshly baked bread for the noon meal, and bustled about in her good natured way. It tickled Elizabeth to see how the older woman fussed over the baby, and the afternoon flew by before she realized how fast the time had gone. When it came time to depart, Molly was reluctant to hand the baby over to Elizabeth.

"Now ye take good care o' this young'un, hear?" Molly said in a voice that was tightening in spite of herself. "Don't be so long in comin' back."

While Elizabeth rode, Jonathan followed, leading the milk cow, and they turned up the trail toward their mountain cabin. She flashed a broad smile and waved to the couple who stood in front of the little log dwelling.

"Right handsome family, there ..." Eb said as he stood with his arm draped over Molly's shoulder.

"Aye, that be the truth, Eb." Molly replied, and reached her hand up to place it on top of her husband's rough and gnarled fingers. They entered the cabin doorway together.

"Seems empty now, don't it, Eb?"

Eb nodded and patted Molly's hip. "Sure wisht our young'uns could hev lived to hev growed up."

Molly wiped a tear from the corner of her eye and turned to tend the fire.

Chapter Forty-eight

How many times during Little Jonathan's first year had Elizabeth wished for a cradle board just like Te-tak-wa-o-ee used to have for White Bird of Snow? It seemed the young woman was forever running after her small son to keep his little fingers away from the hot fireplace, or out of mischief of some kind. The Indian women had it right, Elizabeth determined, to keep the toddlers from harm while freeing up their own hands for the daily tasks. Little Jonathan's first birthday had come and gone, and now, with the approach of yet another summer, the baby was walking and forever curious. His hair was dark and curly, and he had his father's brown eyes, set deep in his cherubic face.

Now pregnant with her second child, Elizabeth placed Little Jonathan upon the ground outside the cabin door while she attempted to wash clothes. The toddler decided to chase a chicken around the yard, and laughed heartily as his chubby legs propelled him in jerky movements about the area. He fell twice, getting his feet tangled up, and pushing himself upright once more, pursued the clucking hen with glee.

Elizabeth laughed in spite of herself, as she watched the baby's futile attempts to pet the chicken. *Oh, well,* she thought, as she scrubbed the laundry upon a wooden scrub board. *At least he is amusing himself, and out of trouble for a little while.*

She and the baby were alone today, for the borderman had once more gone off on a hunt. Elizabeth was anxious to be able to grow their own animals for butchering so Nathan would not have to be away so much. She did not like his long hunting trips, and could hardly wait for his return each time, even though he brought them wonderful provisions. As she soaped and scrubbed the clothes her thoughts drifted to how happy she had become as a wife and a mother.

She was daydreaming when out of the corner of her eye, she caught a movement, and raised up from the scrub board, her hands dripping wet, scanning the area of the barn and corral. Seeing nothing, she returned to her task, noting that her back was beginning to ache from leaning over the tub for so long.

Moments later, she heard the bawling of their milk cow, and was horrified to see the animal being led out of the corral by a half-naked Indian. The savage's head was shaven except for a top knot along the crest of his shining skull. Hideous paintings adorned his face, and the Indian brazenly looked Elizabeth's way. For a moment she stood transfixed, then a cold fright turned her stomach to jelly, and her heart flipped in erratic beats.

Stifling a scream, Elizabeth ran to snatch Little Jonathan up from the ground and raced with him into the cabin, slamming the door shut. Quickly she sent the wooden bolt through its lock, and threw the tumbler in place before running to the window. The baby sat on the floor in the middle of the room, crying, not under-standing why he had been snatched away so quickly from the fun he was having chasing chickens. Trembling, scarcely daring to breathe, Elizabeth watched out the window as the Indian walked over to the wash tub, and angrily tipped it over. He brandished a tomahawk in her direction.

Elizabeth was shaking as she peered out at the frightening scene. Her breath was coming in gulps while she watched the Indian pick up the rope around the cow's neck and pull the animal behind the barn, to disappear into the forest. She watched the spot where the savage had vanished, and stood transfixed, fearing he would reappear at any moment. Her heart was pounding so hard, she wondered if it would leap out of her chest.

Minutes ticked frantically by, and finally Elizabeth slid down on shaky legs until she was sitting on the floor where she dissolved into tears. With trembling arms she gathered Little Jonathan to her breast and comforted him, burying her face into his neck. She clutched him until he finally wiggled to be free, then sat with her hands to her face and could not stop weeping. She realized that Nathan had tried not to worry her with talk of Indian raids, but she had known for a long time that the savages were getting more brazen. When she had journeyed to the fort, the talk was prevalent from those at the trading post.

She wished she could have discussed her worries with her friend Molly, but the poor woman had died the previous winter. Pneumonia, they said, had claimed the woman. Elizabeth had heard tales of atrocities which had taken place involving some of the hapless settlers. Abduction, murder, rape, and torture stories became more frequent, and had at present set the Colonists in the area on edge. Now, Elizabeth became filled with terror at the thought that an Indian had actually invaded their land and stolen one of their animals.

❧

When he returned that evening from his hunt, Jonathan found the door still bolted, and the first alarm shot through his body as he called out, "Elizabeth, open the door." From inside, he could hear his son babbling in the baby talk that the borderman had grown to love. "Elizabeth, Sweet, open up!"

The door flung open and Elizabeth flew into Jonathan's arms. "Oh, Nathan! Thank God you have returned!"

Jonathan felt the trembling in his wife's body as he held her close. "What is it, Love? What is the matter?"

"Nathan, Oh, I was so frightened..." her voice quivered, and she tried to speak. "He stole our cow! He just snuck in here and stole our cow!"

"Calm down, Love. Who stole our cow?" Jonathan was now completely alarmed, and fear struck him like a sword.

"An Indian! Oh, he was fierce looking, his face all painted and his head shaven."

Gently Jonathan steered his near-hysterical wife to a chair and helped her sit down, all the while trying to calm the fears that rose in his own heart. He knelt in front of Elizabeth, holding her hands, while Little Jonathan tried to climb on his father's back, happily chirping "Da-da."

"Be calm, my Sweet, tell me," Jonathan soothed, attempting to show outward control.

Elizabeth gulped air and tried to stop her trembling. She clutched wildly at Jonathan's hands and looked at him, her eyes great with fear.

"I was out front... washing clothes in the tub..." she paused and gulped another breath. "I saw... I saw an Indian with a shaven head, and his face was painted in a horrible design...." Here, she shivered, and Jonathan put his arms around her. "He had a rope around the cow's neck, and stared at me and Little Jonathan. He raised his tomahawk and shook it at us. Then he disappeared into the woods."

"So, they are getting very bold coming this far toward the fort, Jonathan mused, more to himself than addressing Elizabeth. "I shall not leave you alone anymore, my Love." he said, his lips against her hair. *God!* he thought, *I would die if anything happened to Elizabeth or Little Jonathan now!* Feeling the tenseness leave his wife's body, Jonathan cupped Elizabeth's face between his big hands and kissed her gently on the sweet curve of her mouth.

"I am here now, Love. You are safe. I shall not let anything happen to you or Little Jonathan."

"I am sorry I got so upset; I thought I was stronger than that. Thought I could face anything," she almost sobbed.

"You had a right to be frightened. Fortunately, it seems all they wanted was the cow."

Jonathan did not tell his wife of the worried concerns that were battering his mind. He deliberately did not relate any of the stories that he had heard about from old Eb at the fort. Indeed he did not dare tell her of the smoking ruins he had discovered that very afternoon at their nearest neighbor's place, a scant three miles away.

There was no need to terrorize Elizabeth with more stories of brutal murders and burnings of cabins. Not now, in her condition, for in three more months she would give birth to their second child. Softly, Jonathan stroked her hair, and continued to hold her close, while unthinkable thoughts raced unchecked through his mind.

Later that night in the darkness of their bed, while Jonathan wrapped his long body around Elizabeth in the comfortable position they had become used to, he received the shock of his life.

"I know your secret," Elizabeth's faint voice came out of the darkness to send a sudden chill up Jonathan's spine.

Chapter Forty-nine

"You aren't really Nathan, are you?" Elizabeth asked, her voice barely audible, as they lay in the blackness, her cheek resting on the borderman's chest.

Like a bolt of lightening, the words sent a shock wave through Jonathan's entire body, and his heart began to pound. Surely Elizabeth could feel it thudding under his ribs below her cheek. Pretending that he had not heard, he mumbled, "Hm-m? What, Love?"

Elizabeth raised herself up on an elbow until she could look down at her husband's face. Faint light from a half-moon shown though the window, and she could just barely make out Jonathan's features in the blackness of the cabin interior.

"You have kept a terrible secret, haven't you?"

"I do not know what you are talking about, Elizabeth." Jonathan said, struggling to sit up in bed.

"Jonathan," she said his name, and it was like a cannon shot to him, even though her voice was but a low whisper. "You have kept this awful secret all these years. You are really Jonathan, not Nathan, aren't you?"

There was a long silence in the room, and the only sound came from the rhythmic breathing of Little Jonathan as he slept peacefully in the cradle that his father had made. Jonathan reached for Elizabeth's shoulders and held her at arm's length.

"What are you saying?" he gasped, his words rasping in a strangled choke.

"I think you have kept an awful truth from me." Elizabeth's voice cracked slightly, as she attempted to keep her tone even, trying not to show the deep anxiety as she spoke.

Jonathan's mind raced, searching frantically for the words he could say at this moment, to the one person in all the world most dear to him. "What makes you think that, Sweet?"

"I have known for a long time that you are really Jonathan, not Nathan."

Jonathan shook his head. "But what in the world would cause you to believe that? Has someone said something to you?" he uttered, still trying to maintain his innocence.

"No... no one had to tell me what I figured out for myself," Elizabeth said in a pitifully small voice, and Jonathan could hear the hurt in her tone, and realized that nothing could ever again be the same between them from that moment on.

"I repeat, why do you think I am Jonathan?"

Elizabeth reached her hands up to place them on each side of his rugged face. Her thumbs gently traced the lines at each side of Jonathan's mouth that creased into deep dimples when he smiled. She then moved her right hand slowly down under Jonathan's left ear, and her fingers felt for the long indentation along his neck.

"Nathan once told me long ago how to tell the two of you apart. He told me of your capture by the Indians, and the scar that you carried from a arrow under your left ear. The next time I saw you, I looked for that scar, and he was right."

Jonathan remained silent, a thousand thoughts churning inside his head. "Oh, God!" he grimaced to himself.

"I just want to know why you never told me the truth," Elizabeth said gently, with a slight catch in her throat.

Jonathan grasped both her hands in his, took a deep breath, and turning her palms up, kissed each one in turn, anguish battering every cell of his body. "I never meant to deceive you, Elizabeth. Please know that."

Jonathan struggled, his throat tightening, and it was hard for him to get the words out.

"I wanted to tell you many times, but when I first rescued you, and you were so very ill from your wound, you woke up and thought I was Nathan. The look in your eyes then, and the fact that you were so overjoyed that Nathan had returned... I just did not have the heart to tell you otherwise. I could not tell you that our dear Nathan had perished in Braddock's Defeat. I felt your health was too tenuous at that point. One thing led to another... you were so ecstatically happy at the thought that Nathan had come back into your life, that I could not dampen your dream by telling you who I really was." He shuddered in nervous anxiety.

Elizabeth drew her arms around Jonathan's neck and pulled him back down upon the bed, where he cautiously enfolded her in his brawny arms, leaning his brow into the curve of her neck. "I have suspected for a long time that you were not Nathan," Elizabeth said in a hoarse whisper.

"Do you forgive me?" Jonathan managed to say, though he was filled with dread.

"Yes, my Love, I forgive you. I do remember how thrilled I was thinking that you were Nathan, when I awoke from my knife wound. I guess I never gave you a chance to tell me otherwise."

"I could just never bring myself to destroy the love and gratefulness you held for Nathan. I have gone through my own kind of hell all this time, for keeping the truth from you."

"Did you love me then?" Elizabeth asked timidly, and her heart skipped a beat. What would be his answer?

Jonathan turned her head with his fingers so his lips could reach hers, and the kiss he gave her was worth all the words he could ever utter. His lips were warm and moist, and engulfed her whole mouth in the gentlest, most erotic kiss he had ever given her. He was desperately attempting to convey his devotion in the only way he knew how.

"Elizabeth, my Sweet, I fell in love with you before I rescued you. My love was and is sincere. I am not playing out a role by pretending to be my brother, believe me. I loved you then, and have fallen even deeper in love with you every day since."

Elizabeth's eyes grew misty, and she clung to him in desperate joy, thinking she could never be any happier than now.

"How long have you known that I was not Nathan?" Jonathan asked, stroking the hair back from her face.

"It was the day Little Jonathan was born. I put my arms around you from behind, while you were sitting down, and I whispered something in your ear. It was then that I saw and remembered the scar on your neck."

"Are you angry with me?"

Elizabeth shook her head, and reached up with her lips, searching for his mouth. "No, Jonathan, I am not angry with you."

They held each other for a long time in the darkness, and Jonathan's hands roamed over her body as if to assure himself that all had not been lost in the revelation of his true identity

"How did he die, Jonathan?"

Elizabeth's question was another tomahawk blow to his heart. "Oh, my Sweet Love, you really do not want to know," Jonathan replied in an anguished voice.

Elizabeth shifted slightly in his arms. "Yes," she insisted, her mouth against the curve of his neck. He could feel her warm breath against his skin.

Slowly, gently, Jonathan related the moments of the battle that led to Nathan's death. He told of burying his brother's body beneath the fall oak log. "It was like burying a part of me. We had been so close... insepara-ble. I could barely continue on. I wanted to die, too."

Elizabeth's eyes were moist. "It must have been horrible for you," she whispered.

"That was a long time ago. And now I live for him... and love for him...and for myself, too."

They lay quietly in each other's arms for a long time in the darkness of the Appalachian forest night. Eventually, Jonathan rose from the bed and stood looking out the window, lost in thought. Elizabeth could make out his silhouette against the pale square of the cabin window, and her heart ached for the torment she knew he must have gone through those many long years while he kept the truth of his identity to himself.

"Jonathan," she called softly. He turned and looked in her direction "Jonathan... I love you!"

Groping his way back to the bed in the dark, he found her arms, and allowed himself to sink into her embrace. He buried his head into her breast. "Oh, God! How I love you, Elizabeth!"

Carefully, gently, Jonathan made desperate love to her that night, again and again, and ecstasy shot through them both, exploding in a new and more pure passion than they had ever known.

It was the first time that Jonathan had felt fully free since Braddock's Defeat... since Nathan's death. Free of the haunting feeling that Nathan's presence forever seemed to hang on his shoulders. Tonight that feeling was finally gone. Tonight, Jonathan Herrington could truly be himself.

Chapter Fifty

There was little if any sleep that night for the frontiersman and his wife. The two of them talked and made love throughout the short night, and before either one realized, the gray light of a new day was creeping in the window. Jonathan reluctantly crawled from beneath the blanket, stooped to kiss Elizabeth as she lay sleepy-eyed in the warmth of their bed, and drew on his fringed shirt and leggings. He tried not to awaken Little Jonathan, who still slept in his cradle. Going quietly out the door, Jonathan carried his moccasins to the front stoop where he sat and pulled them on, and automatically strapped the hunting knife to his belt.

Inside, Elizabeth put on her lindsey skirt, and found she had to let it out another notch to accommodate the size of her enlarging belly, smiling at the thought of the new life within her. Quickly brushing her long hair, which now had grown nearly to its old length, she slipped her feet into the soft moccasins that Jonathan had fashioned for her. Immediately the young woman busied herself building a fire in the hearth while picking up Little Jonathan who by this time was awake and demanding to be fed.

Suddenly, the door burst open with a clatter, and Jonathan came in screaming, "Indians! Elizabeth, take the baby and run for the fort!" He grabbed the baby and thrust him into Elizabeth's arms, at the same time reaching for his flintlock rifle. "Run, Elizabeth! Run!"

With horror in her heart, Elizabeth grabbed the only thing within her grasp to use as a weapon; a wooden rolling pin that Jonathan had crudely fashioned for her long ago from the branch of a hard maple tree. Gripping the pin in one hand, she ran with Little Jonathan in her arms toward the brow of the mountain, where she knew there was a trail to the fort. With fear in her eyes, she looked back over her shoulder and saw smoke curling up from the barn area. Her heart sank, and terror clutched at her insides.

"Jonathan!" The bloodcurdling scream escaped her lips, and wafted back to Jonathan's ears as he futilely attempted to prevent the savages from burning the buildings. Two of the Indians had captured the black stallion, and were leading the great horse off into the woods. Chilling sounds of war whoops echoed through the early morning forest, as several painted savages were ransacking the barn. Fire had been set to the lean-to attached to the barn, and in the blink of an eye, the whole thing burst into flames. Jonathan's last hopes were dashed, and with a sinking heart, he knew there was no possibility of saving the cabin. With one last desperate look, he turned and took off after Elizabeth. Now he could hear the yips of the Indians behind him as he ran. God! They were in pursuit! Clutching the heavy rifle, he stopped, whirled, and pulled the trigger, striking one of the three Indians who followed, and saw the brave crumple to the ground.

The borderman sprinted into the forest, dodging trees, leaping over brush and fallen logs. He tried to draw the savages away from the direction that Elizabeth had taken. It was not long before the old wound in his leg let him know he no longer had the speed of old. Still, those legs pumped and propelled him pell-mell, crashing ahead into the heart of the forest. He could hear the two remaining Indians still pounding behind him, their cries echoing in his ears. He reloaded the flintlock on the run, jamming the ramrod home. Once more he halted, aimed and fired. This time he missed.

Now panic threatened to cloud his senses, and Jonathan knew he must try to remain calm. A large task, considering the circumstances he was now experiencing. He reloaded again as he ran, and dodged around trees and bushes. Thorn branches tore at his buckskins, impeding his progress.

A half mile away, Elizabeth ran awkwardly, carrying Little Jonathan in her arms. Already her lungs were bursting as the weight of her pregnancy, combined with the added weight of the child, was ripping every shred of energy she had. Her arms ached, and her muscles shrieked as she sped with her precious burden down the path toward the safety of the fort.

Little Jonathan was screaming hysterically at the jostling, his face screwed into a red mass of wrinkles. Tears and drool ran down his puckered chin. Around her neck, Elizabeth wore the porcupine-quilled amulet that Te-tak-wa-o-ee had given her years before. Inside, where the sacred stone had rested for so long, the pocket was now empty. Somehow, in her flight, the stone had fallen out... vanished. But in her blind haste, Elizabeth was not aware that the stone, which Indians believed would keep the bearer safe, had slipped out of its holding place and was lost forever on the forest floor.

By now, her legs shaking with fatigue, and her lungs on fire, Elizabeth spied the cool glen where she had been held captive five years before. Stumbling to a halt, the young mother sank to her knees beside the deep pool, and offered Little Jonathan a drink from her shaking, cupped hand. She tried to soothe the baby, cuddling him to her heaving breast, still gasping for air, while her heart thudded in wild gyrations beneath her ribs.

"Sh-h, little one, hush. Mother is here, and I will protect you," she uttered between gasps for breath. A small pang in her lower abdomen shot through her body, causing fear to strike anew. She threw splashes of water onto her face and head, trying to cool the heat that rose from her exhaustion. Elizabeth washed the tears from the baby's face, and tried to soothe his whimpers by offering her breast for comfort. He had stopped nursing months ago, and now refused his mother's frantic efforts. In a moment, her heart almost stopped beating altogether, as thudding footsteps crashed into the glen, and a figure in buckskin raced toward her. She screamed and hugged Little Jonathan lightly to her breast, bending her head protectively over his dark curly head.

"Elizabeth!" Jonathan panted, out of breath. "We must run... they know of this place!" He grabbed the baby from her grasp with one hand, and lifted her up with the other, pulling her on the run beside him. He clutched the rifle and Little Jonathan in one arm, while helping support Elizabeth with the other. She leaned against his side, her legs leaden, and could not move to keep stride with Jonathan. Incredibly she still held the rolling pin in her hand with a grip of steel.

Down the sloping mountainside, they ran, husband and wife... father and mother... stumbling... slipping... almost falling. They dodged rocks and trees, and sped past until all was a blur. Jonathan's lungs were bursting, his chest heaving, as he attempted to carry the baby and pull Elizabeth along. Their feet thudded with jarring steps on the trail, scattering twigs and leaves about.

"Jonathan! I... cannot... continue..." Elizabeth pleaded in a croaking voice, unable to catch her breath. Pains continued to increase, and she doubled over, as cramping spasms clamped all her muscles, sending her body into one giant agony. She gasped for breath, and thought her heart would gallop right out of her chest.

"Just a little farther, Love," Jonathan urged. "Try... try to run."

She leaned heavily against him, totally exhausted, her energy deflated like a balloon. Now, every muscle in Jonathan's body also was screaming. He limped badly on the wounded leg, but forced himself to trot on. His chest heaved in convulsive spasms, and a sudden, sharp pain grabbed inside his ribs, as if something had burst within him. Brilliant flashes of light seared into his brain, and was almost blinding in intensity.

Elizabeth collapsed completely, and Jonathan was forced to swing her and Little Jonathan up in his arms. The great borderman tried to stagger on with his precious load. Every inch of him now was one huge searing pain, and he dragged himself the last few hundred yards to the bank of the river. High above on the mountainside, he could hear the yells of the Indians as they descended upon their trail. Across the river lay the safety of the fort. If only he could signal someone for help! He knew he could never swim with his burden and make it across.

Sinking heavily to his knees, Jonathan's vision was beginning to cloud to a red haze. He desperately held on to Elizabeth's now limp body, and his heart sank as he noticed a bloody stain on her skirt. He gazed into her pale face, his chest heaving in great jerks. At the same time, Little Jonathan struggled to be free, and with what strength Jonathan had left, he tried to hold on to his son. Pains streaked through his chest and arms. "Dear Lord, have mercy!" he pleaded to the wind.

Across the river, he saw some settlers, and attempted to get their attention, but they did not look his way. He tried to yell, but a faint squeak barely came from his parched throat. So, raising the rifle with difficulty, he shot into the air, then half-collapsed on the ground.

Elizabeth hardly roused at the sound, and with glazed eyes that were already miles away, looked at her husband. Scenes darted through her mind... of walking hand in hand through the trees with Nathan. Of a wedding... of Te-tak-wa-o-ee and the Indian village... of her baby... of the cabin... of Little Jonathan's cherubic smile.

"Jonathan..." she breathed, and weakly reached her hand toward him. She saw him dimly, and her heart swelled with a love beyond comprehension. She thought she was smiling, but her mouth never moved, and a blackness drew over her like a silent, heavy curtain.

"No! Oh, God! No! Oh, my Sweet! Not my Sweet Love!" Jonathan cried, not really sure whether he cried out loud, or only deep inside his brain, as he realized that his beloved had slipped beyond him into her eternity. A stabbing pain once more wrenched at his chest, and with what strength he had left, he gathered her lifeless form into his arms, her long golden hair spilling across his arm.

"Elizabeth, my Darling, Sweet Elizabeth!" He threw back his head, screaming an agonizing, bone chilling "Aaagghh!" which reverberated up and down the river valley with a sound never heard before in the Appalachian Mountains. Little Jonathan tugged at his mother's dress, crying, "Mommy! Mommy!" as a boat pulled up from the opposite shore, and two Colonists leaped out, rushing to the doomed couple.

"Indians," Jonathan managed to mutter, as he gasped for breath... The Colonists tried to pry Elizabeth from his grasp, but Jonathan would not let her go, and hung on tightly, as yet another pain shot dizzily through him. He continued to cradle his wife's body, his fingers caressing her cooling cheek, brushing back her golden hair so he could see her lifeless eyes. He gently closed those hazel eyes for the last time, and bent to kiss her lips.

Oh, God! My love... my life... my Elizabeth! It was only a thought that crossed his mind now, for he felt himself slipping into a strange darkness.

"The boy," Jonathan whispered as the Colonists leaned closer. "Herrington... his name... is... Jon... Herrington." His voice trailed off, and a final blackness engulfed the frontiersman. Inside his chest, Jonathan's great heart struggled, jerking wildly, spasmodically. The heart that had carried him through the devastating saga of Braddock's Defeat. The same heart that was filled with an undying love for his twin brother, Nathan, and the very heart that he had lost forever to the golden-haired Elizabeth, now skipped, stuttered and lost its beat.

Epilog

"**A**wh! Sure now, we lost 'em both, poor devils," one of the men uttered, and slammed his fist into the palm of his other hand. "Damn the redskins and their marauding ways!"

The other shook his head sadly. "They must hev run a long way... an' savages chasin' 'em most of the way, too." He gently took Little Jonathan in his arms and turned away from the sad sight. "Come on, little tyke, ye are safe now. What ye be called again?"

"John Herrington. The daddy here said the little one's name is John Herrington."

Jonathan felt himself floating now, and somehow Elizabeth was at his side, smiling and holding his hand, her hair gleaming in the brightness. Together, they were moving effortlessly toward the bright light. Ahead seemed all brilliance, and in the distance they saw a familiar figure waiting in the whiteness. Elizabeth and Jonathan glanced back and smiled to see the two Colonists gently pick up Little Jonathan to take him to the safety of the fort, and watched as their own lifeless bodies were lifted into the settler's boat.

They looked at each other with such a love in their gaze that it would fairly open the gates of Heaven itself, and continued to float in the bright, misty fog, moving closer to the figure ahead. As they approached, there stood Nathan in the brilliance, waiting for them, and all three embraced. Then the power of love that descended upon the trio could not be measured by any terms known on earth, and the three disappeared into the radiance... beyond forever.

Author's Note

Though this tale is one of fiction, part of the known family history tells that when John Herrington reached manhood, after having served in the Revolutionary War, he lived to the advanced age of 103, his death being noted as May 18, 1862. It is told that in his 100th year, he walked three miles to Augusta, Ohio to cast his vote, and walked the three miles back. He homesteaded seven different farms in western Pennsylvania and eastern Ohio, three of them in Jefferson County, Ohio. John fathered eleven children, among which there was a set of twins.

To Elizabeth and Jonathan, (whoever you were,) thank you for your loving sacrifice, for if it had not been for your sheer determination to save the baby, there would not at this time be hundreds of Herrington descendants alive today.

To John Herrington, the Patriarch, you were a part of a strong generation of early settlers of this great country. Modest and unassuming, you lived out a life that perhaps you deemed mundane and uneventful, but in the course of history, was far from that. Your legacy is that you led a moral life, raised a large family, taught us all the importance of Love of God, fellow man, and hard work. To you, we your family members, are beholden.

J. G.

Also from the author of

Beyond Forever...

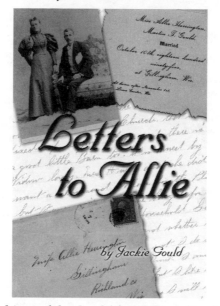

In the archives of the Gould family lie fading letters telling
a story of forbidden love. As Jackie Gould read these letters
from her Grandfather Martin to his future bride, Allie, their
story came vividly to life. The author quotes from Martin's
letters written in 1895 and fleshes out the lovers' tale from the
artfully imagined perspective of Allie to transport us to an era
of simplicity and strict social mores. One hundred years later,
their story is a testament of the sustaining quality of love.

ISBN 0-9762224-0-X; 178 pages; $10.95 + $2.50 s&h
To order, call Acacia Publishing toll-free: 866-265-4553.